Into Thin Air

DEBORAH ROGERS

Copyright Information

ISBN 978-0-473-52146-2
TITLE: Into Thin Air
First worldwide publication 2020

Published by Lawson Publishing (NZ).

For Rocky. Words cannot describe.

1

The first thing Dr. Julia Norris notices is how black the lung is. Black with tar and other impurities. Fifty years of smoking will do that. It's a miracle the patient can breathe at all. Julia leans closer and slips her fingers inside the patient's chest, cradling the lung in the palm of her hand. Center right, tucked behind the lung, the heart pulsates in a pool of liquid.

The lung belongs to Mrs. Tammy Keller, a seventy-two-year-old San Francisco native who presented three days ago with severe breathing difficulties. Julia's initial thoughts were pleurisy, but a chest X-ray showed a spontaneous pneumothorax, aka punctured lung. The likely cause was the rupture of a blister on diseased lung tissue, causing air to leak into the pleural space. Mrs. Keller had been traveling with her daughter in Asia, and Julia's calculated guess was that a blister had burst midair due to the pressurized cabin air.

With the tip of her gloved thumb, Julia feels the underside of Mrs. Keller's lung for the abnormality. Next to her, Paul Sweeny, the twenty-six-year-old resident who's on his surgical rotation, shifts uncomfortably on his feet. He's shivering. Julia feels bad. She'd forgotten to tell him to wear long sleeves. Theater is cold. The temperature is set at a strict sixty-six degrees Fahrenheit, mainly to inhibit blood loss in the patient, but also to keep the surgeons alert.

Paul lets out a breath, rubs his nose with his forefinger. Some people never get used to the smell of warm blood.

"Okay?" says Julia.

"Absolutely."

Julia nods, then hitches up her surgical mask, flicks on the electrocautery tool, and delicately cauterizes a membrane to separate the lung for a better vantage point.

"There," she says, thumbing the large blister. "You see that?"

Paul leans over. Julia smells garlic and onions even though he's wearing a mask.

"Yeah, I do."

"Now we staple and cut. The plan is the lung will seal and become fully functional again." She looks up at Sue, the scrub nurse. "May I have the 60mm endo-stapler with 4.8 staples and peristrips, please, Sue?"

"Yes, Jules, that I can surely do," says Sue, winking at Julia.

Julia smiles under her mask. Only Sue could get away with that. She is the oldest teenager Julia's ever met. A forty-two-year-old serial-dater and over-sharer, forever trying to lure Julia onto Plenty of Fish. You're only thirty-seven, Jules, she had said the last time they'd met for coffee, there are ninety-year-olds on Tinder having more fun than you.

Julia cuts and seals the lung with the endo-stapler then drops the dissected lump of tissue into a steel kidney dish for disposal. The entire procedure is over in less than ten seconds.

Julia looks at Paul. "You can go ahead and do the internal sutures if you like."

His eyes widen. "But I'm only meant to observe."

Julia smiles warmly. "You'll do fine, Paul. I'm here if you need me."

"I'm not sure I know how," he says, perspiration sprouting on his forehead.

Julia glances over her shoulder at Sue. "Suture kit, please, Sue, if you wouldn't mind." She turns back to Paul. "Deep dermal sutures, Paul, just like you would have been shown in med school."

He lets out a breath. "Okay. Deep dermal. I got it."

Sue passes Paul a pre-threaded surgical needle, shaped like a large C, which he nearly drops into the open cavity of Mrs. Keller's chest.

"You can do this, Paul," says Julia.

"Yes," he says, licking his lips. "Yes, I can."

He swallows deeply and goes in for the first stitch, hands trembling.

"You're doing great, Paul," she says. "Keep it neat. Even. That's it."

When he's finished, he stands back and holds up his hands.

"Terrific job," she says. And she means it. He's done extremely well.

His face lights up. "Thank you, Dr. Norris."

"You very welcome, Paul. We'll make a surgeon out of you yet."

2

Julia's bone tired. She always is after surgery. The responsibility of having someone else's life in your hands never gets easier. It doesn't help that she's had surgery nine days in a row. Two coronary artery bypasses. One bilobectomy. Two lobectomies. Repair of a congenital heart defect. Removal of a cyst. An excise of a tumor. There's a shortage of cardiothoracic surgeons in the bay area, and now with her colleague Rod Johnson out on paternity leave, it's probably only going to get worse.

On the way home, she calls into her neighborhood grocery store, because despite Sue's best endeavors to entice Julia out on a blind date with her brother's best friend, it's a night in for Julia. Opting for a fresh, ready-made quinoa salad for one and a generous-sized salmon steak, she's out of the store in less than ten minutes and angling her silver Toyota Prius in front of her apartment just before 7 p.m.

When she opens her front door, Bishop jumps down from the windowsill where he's been basking in the last rays of sun and pads over to greet her.

"Hey, cat," says Julia, bending to stroke him with her free hand.

He purrs loudly. "Oh, I know what you want," she says. "Come on, let's get you some dinner."

Julia heads for the kitchen, Bishop mewing and figure-eighting her calves as she goes.

"Boy, you're one pushy feline, aren't you?"

Setting the groceries down on the counter, she shakes some dry cat food into Bishop's bowl and watches him demolish the lot in less than a minute. She feels a pang, remembering the day she and Leo went to collect Bishop from the animal shelter. The poor thing had been dumped in a trash bag in a creek with eleven of its siblings. Only three had survived. Leo had wanted to take them all home but Julia had put her foot down: one pet to look after was plenty enough.

She shakes off the memory. Trips down memory lane never got anyone anywhere. She pours herself a glass of red wine and carries it over to the living room, where she takes a seat on the sofa facing the harbor. God, how she loves this view. It's particularly beautiful tonight, with the last of the light fading over the bay, the golden gate looming in the distance, Marin Headlands and Point Benita beyond that. Julia's eyes track to the right, where low-lying clouds shroud the northern end of the bridge, near Sausalito, the laid-back seaside enclave where Leo had proposed to her one sunny Sunday afternoon. He had put the ring in her meatball sub when she wasn't looking and she had nearly lost a tooth.

Which reminds her. Dentist. She needs to cancel her appointment for next week. With her current work schedule, her six-month check-up will just have to wait. She looks at her watch. It's after 7 p.m. Too late to call so an email will have to do.

She logs into her Inbox and frowns when she sees the message waiting for her. It's from someone she doesn't recognize. A person named Yasmin Jefferson. But that's not what bothers her. It's the headline that causes her heart to skip a beat. Three words in bold font. **Toni is Missing**.

3

Julia stares at the message, breathing. Toni is missing in Istanbul. From Yasmin. Please call me. Followed by a phone number. Julia puts the phone on the coffee table, shoves it away. Two years since they've last spoken. Now this. Another Toni drama. For Pete's sake.

She should email this Yasmin person back and tell her not to be sucked in, that Toni could do that to you, suck you in and before you knew it, you were drowning in the quicksand that was Toni's life.

Bishop yowls and leaps onto the coffee table. He wants to play.

"Not now, Bish."

Julia shoos him off and tries to think back to the last time she's heard from Toni. Two months ago? Three? Toni sends Julia emails from time to time, most of which Julia avoids opening, all of which she has never replied to. The emails detail "TONI'S BIG ADVENTURES." Look at me, I'm on the top of Mount Kilimanjaro, on a train in Siberia, swimming with the dolphins in the South Island of New Zealand. Toni still trying. Toni still wanting to connect. Toni and her crazy screwed up life.

But it is too late for that. Julia has given her chances, dozens of them, and Toni blew each one. Toni is old enough to look after herself. Toni is wherever she wants to be, pulling the wool over people's eyes, just like always. Well, as far as Julia is concerned, her immature, irresponsible, and self-absorbed sister can stay missing.

Julia simply does not want to know anymore.

She picks up her phone, finds the **Toni is Missing** email, and pushes delete.

*

Julia enters the elevator and hits the button to the fourteenth-floor recovery ward. She checks her phone for the third time that morning. No more emails from Yasmin Jefferson. She frowns, unsure whether she's glad or not.

She glimpses herself in the stainless-steel doors. Her ponytail has come loose. There are dark circles under her eyes. Last night had been a restless one and it definitely shows. She'd spent most of it seesawing between annoyance and worry. What if she'd been too hasty deleting the email? What if this time there was a genuine problem? But there have been false alarms before, haven't there? Not to mention the countless chances she's given Toni over the years, and all the disappointment Julia has suffered as a consequence. In the end the alarm had gone off and Julia had lain there staring at the ceiling, having achieved absolutely nothing at all except for a splitting headache.

The elevator doors ping and Julia exits, redoing her ponytail as she walks. No, she tells herself, I've done the right thing. I have to be strong. I am getting my life in order. Things are going well. I do not want to jeopardize that again.

Julia pushes through the swing doors into the cardiothoracic wing. The cleaner's just been in, leaving behind damp half circles on the linoleum and the strong scent of Lysol. She passes the nurses' station, a glassed off area midway down the corridor, and sees fresh-faced nurses mingling with tired ones as they conduct shift changeover. Julia doesn't stop to chat, carrying on until she locates the correct room, third from the end.

A perky Mrs. Keller is sitting up in bed spooning cornflakes and what looks like stewed plums into her mouth. *The Today Show* plays silently on a tiny television bracketed in the corner opposite the bed.

Mrs. Keller's face lights up when she sees Julia. "Hiya, sweetheart!"

"Good morning, Mrs. Keller. You're looking well."

The older lady beams. "I feel like a million bucks. All thanks to you."

Someone had brought in a multicolored afghan and spread it across Mrs. Keller's bed, giving the room a homey feel.

"Has everything been okay, Mrs. Keller? Any pain in the lung? Is the pain relief enough?"

The older lady touches the oxygen cannula inserted into her nostrils. "Can I take this off? It's hurting my nose."

Julia checks the chart. Mrs. Keller's oxygen levels were last taken at 4:07 a.m. The reading was for 75 mm Hg. Still a little on the low side.

"I'll make a note for the supplement oxygen to be removed as soon as you reach 90 mm Hg. All going well, you'll be out of here in a few days. You'll just need to clear the lung function test. Have you got someone to look after you when you get home?" Julia's phone rings. A number she doesn't recognize. "Excuse me, Mrs. Keller, I'd better take this."

"You go ahead, sweetheart. I'm not going anywhere."

Julia steps into the corridor and answers. "Dr. Norris speaking."

"Julia-Anne?"

Julia pauses. No one ever calls her that.

"Are you there, Julia-Anne?"

"Who's calling please?"

"I've been trying to get hold of you. My name is Yasmin Jefferson. I sent emails. About Toni. You are her sister, aren't you? I've got the right person, haven't I?"

Julia swallows. "Yes, I'm Toni's sister."

"I'm calling from Istanbul. Toni was meant to meet a group of us here at the hostel, but she never showed up."

"I wouldn't worry about Toni," says Julia.

"It's a code we've got."

"Code?"

"A traveler's thing—if you don't turn up, report it to family."

Julia's mouth goes dry.

"Are you there, Julia-Anne?" says Yasmin.

Julia licks her lips. "Julia. My name is Julia."

"Sorry—Julia."

Julia clears her throat. "Listen, Ms. Jefferson, thank you very much for your concern about my sister. But she does this from time to time. Gets in these little fixes and expects people to bail her out. I'm sure she's fine. She'll be out there somewhere enjoying herself. She's just irresponsible, that's all. But thank you again for contacting me. Sorry, I've really got to go now. Goodbye."

Julia disconnects. She hates hanging up, but she has to be firm. Toni is not going to ruin her life again.

That night Julia watches shadows argue on the bedroom ceiling. She lies there and thinks about Yasmin's call, a little ball of dread forming in the pit of her stomach. She'd been wrong to snap. This Yasmin person hadn't deserved that, she was just trying to look out for Toni. But that's what Toni does to Julia, turns her into a person she doesn't like, an abrupt, bad-tempered, butt-clenching person. Toni has always brought out the worst in her.

Julia had told Yasmin Toni was just being irresponsible, but what if she was wrong? What if this is serious and Julia does nothing? She would have to live with that for the rest of her life.

The sinking feeling gets worse. She flips over. Bishop's sleeping on the dresser. In the dark light, she can just make out his two fat white paws folded together in a perfect M.

Damn you, Toni. Damn you.

4

In the morning Julia heads for the police station. But when she gets there, they tell her they don't deal with missing abroad cases and give her a number to call instead. She finds a quiet corner in a Starbucks close to the hospital and dials. But when she's put through, she isn't sure what to say.

"It's my sister. A friend of hers says she never turned up at an agreed time and place in Istanbul. It's probably nothing."

The operator transfers her to an embassy advisory, John Miller. Julia relays the Yasmin conversation and John Miller advises her that the US Embassy in Turkey will make some inquiries.

"Try not to worry," he says. "Nine times out of ten they turn up."

Julia wants to say I'm not worried, I'm embarrassed. My sister's just being her usual careless self; she's going to turn up someplace, grinning on a stupid Facebook post, saying oops, guys, I didn't stop to think.

The conversation ends with John Miller promising to give Julia an update in a day or two.

Julia looks at her watch. Terrific. Now she's more than thirty minutes late for her monthly cardiothoracic team committee meeting. She hates being late. She prides herself on timeliness. It's part of her work ethic.

*

The committee chair, Petra Fields, a pediatric congenital heart defect specialist, peers over her cat-eye Tom Ford glasses as Julia hurries to take a seat next to Sue at the table. The nine other committee members are already present. Seven cardiothoracic surgeons that Julia knows in various degrees, and three specialist nurses, including Sue.

Petra returns to the agenda. Item number three. Changes in reimbursement.

"As I was saying..."

Sue reaches for the plate of glazed pastries, takes a pecan and maple Danish, offers one to Julia. Julia shakes her head and pours herself a glass of water instead.

Sue leans closer, chewing. "You okay?" she whispers.

Julia would rather keep things to herself but knows Sue will keep pushing.

"Family issue," Julia whispers back. "My sister."

Sue looks surprised. "I didn't know you had a sister."

Petra Fields shoots them a frown over her Tom Fords. Julia studies the agenda and tries to focus. But she can't concentrate. What was it that John Miller had said? Nine times out of ten they turn up. She's done the same thing as a doctor, rattled off statistics in an effort to reassure patients. But when it comes to the crunch, when it is you or one of your family members on the line, statistics mean nothing. Why hadn't she questioned him more thoroughly about the process? She should have asked him if there was anything else she should be doing. She never even offered to send him a photograph.

Petra turns to agenda item number four, Lawsuits Lessons, and switches on the projector for a PowerPoint presentation, throwing a vibrant shade of violet onto the blank screen.

Julia is struck by the sudden need to get away.

"Sorry," she says, pushing back her chair and getting to her feet. "I have to go."

"Go where?" says Petra, startled. "We're in the middle of a meeting."

Julia snatches up her handbag. "I know. I'm sorry."

She feels their eyes on her. Judging. Except for Sue, whose face is soft with concern.

"Sorry," Julia says again and walks out the door.

5

She drives to her old neighborhood. A hangdog, dirtbag of a place, skirting East Oakland. Julia's not sure why she's come here. What she hopes to achieve. There's nothing here except dead history. Her eyes track left and right, taking in the unchanged streets. Everything looks smaller, dirtier, like a childhood friend you encounter at a school reunion who has let herself go. The tiny postage stamp park on the corner of Dixon and Rem streets where the kids used to huff solvents. The corner store that charged desperate families credit at twenty-five percent interest. The elementary school where she learned that the best she could hope for was to become a shop girl or factory shift worker or housekeeper for one of the fancy San Fran hotels.

She drives deep into the neighborhood, amongst the derelict housing and treeless streets and bare-dirt front yards. Kids who should be in school wheel around on Frankenstein bikes. Contraptions made up of mismatched parts, salvaged (or most likely stolen) from different bicycles. A mountain bike frame mixed with a ten-speed's ram's horn handlebars. A small, low-slung BMX paired with the oversized wheels from an old-fashioned butcher's bike. Julia feels sorry for the kids. She remembers what it was like. The boredom, the hopelessness, scrounging around for loose change to buy a can of soda. Where a trip into the city over the Oakland Bay Bridge was an event you dressed up for.

She passes by Jimmy Levine's house. The kid who used to taunt Julia and Toni on their way to school.

"Didn't you hear what I said, white trash, your mama's a hooker and I bet you little bitches will do the same."

Even though his words stung, Julia knew Jimmy Levine was as poor as they were and that his mother was out on the corner of Northcote and Seawell every night of the week, so Julia never said a thing back.

Up ahead, at the end of the street, is her old house. The last one she lived in with Toni and her mother. Their mother was addicted to fresh starts so there had been many other houses before this one. But the rundown Craftsman bungalow was their longest spell in one place.

She angles her car into a parallel parking spot and sits at the wheel, looking. The white picket fence surrounding the front yard has half its pickets missing. The little gate is off its hinges and hangs askew. Tall grass left to grow wild is littered with junk. Car tires. A rusty tricycle. A sagging trampoline. The house itself hasn't changed much considering over twenty years has passed. The paint on the gables is still peeling. The shingles under the roof are still rotting. But the place looks different, diminished somehow, sadder, as if Julia had built it up in her mind to be something it wasn't.

One of the front windows is boarded up with cardboard, the room she had shared with Toni, and for a moment Julia wonders if the place has been abandoned. Then a burst of laughter followed by a cry carries from the house out on to the street.

Julia gets out of the car. Walks the cracked concrete path up to the porch, sidestepping two overflowing trash bags and a dirty diaper, spread open and buzzing with flies. She reaches the front door. Hesitates. What the heck is she doing? She turns around, ready to retreat, but changes her mind and knocks firmly. She waits there for a long time.

The door is finally wrenched open by a woman barely out of her teens, drugstore blonde, jumbo hoop earrings, sticky-faced toddler perched on her hip.

"Hi," says Julia.

The woman's eyes narrow. "You with the repo men? I told them on the phone that I just missed the one payment on the washing machine and I plan to make that up next week."

Julia shakes her head. "Oh, no. I'm not with any repossession agency. I used to live here."

The woman looks Julia up and down. "You?"

Julia nods. "With my mother and sister."

The child screeches and tugs on his mother's left earring. Somewhere in a back room a baby screams then goes silent.

Julia pauses. "I was wondering if I could come in and take a look around."

The woman's face darkens. "You're social services."

"What?" says Julia, startled. "No. I'm a doctor. In the city. I help people."

The toddler starts to cry. Tears run down his grubby little face.

The young woman thrusts out her chin. "Just because I'm young and poor doesn't mean I beat my kids, lady." She holds out the crying toddler. "He look beat up to you? See any black eyes on his face?"

Julia raises her hands in apology. "I'm sorry. I just wanted to take a look around. For old times' sake. I meant no harm."

A man appears behind the woman, dirty shirt to match the dirty stare, eating a sandwich. Fish.

"The baby needs fixing, Skye, if you can't hear it," he says.

"I know that," says the woman. "I got ears."

"Well, then," he says, staring at Julia. "Better get to it."

The woman steps back ready to close the door but Julia blocks it with her hand. The man stops chewing. The toddler goes silent. There's a flash of concern on the young woman's face. Julia looks back and forth between them. But she can't bring herself to say it. That it was there, next to the door, right where the young woman is standing with the child on her hip, that Julia's mother had died from a single shotgun blast right to the heart.

She lets her hand fall away.

"All the best for you and your family," she says.

Then she gets in her car and drives away.

That night Julia Googles Turkey. It borders countries like Syria and Iraq and Iran, but Istanbul is far from those war-torn places and situated in the northwest side of the country close to Europe. Julia hasn't done much traveling. She's been too busy studying and building a career. Besides, as Leo had reminded her many times before, "doing fun" isn't exactly her strong suit.

She logs on to her email and finds Toni's last message, sent from some place in South Korea six months ago. There's a selfie attached. Toni sitting atop a military tank in a park wearing flip-flops, a toe ring, and harem pants, most probably bought in some Southeast Asian market. Toni is grinning like an idiot. Korean locals stare up at her as they pass, this neo-punk chick with a septum piercing and crazy fuchsia hair, which she had, at that point in time, shaved along one side but left to grow long on the other.

Julia stares at the photograph and feels a lump in her throat. Toni, you idiot.

She hits reply to the ancient email and types, "People are worried. Let someone know where you are."

After that, Julia goes on YouTube and finds a clip about Cheap Eats in Istanbul and falls asleep watching it.

6

At 3:03 a.m. the phone rings. Bishop's claws dig through the covers into Julia's thigh. It's John Miller, the embassy advisor.

"She turned up, didn't she?" sighs Julia, switching on the bedside light. "I'm so sorry she wasted your time."

He pauses. "Do you have someone there with you?"

Her heart skips. "Why? What is it?"

Another pause. "We have some information."

Julia feels the sudden need to move. She casts aside her blankets, gets out of bed, heads for the living room.

"Are you still there, Dr. Norris?"

She tells herself to exhale. "Yes, I'm here. What's going on, Mr. Miller?"

"You sure you don't want to call someone first?"

"Just tell me," she says.

He lets out a breath. "They found your sister's backpack and passport discarded along the waterfront in a southern part of Istanbul. The US Embassy in Turkey has launched a missing person's investigation."

Julia stands immobile in the doorway, phone in one hand, hem of her nightshirt clutched in the other.

"It could be nothing," says John Miller.

"But it could be something."

A pause. "Yes. It's not a good sign."

Bishop looks at her, tail swaying. He knows something has changed, that the world isn't the same as before.

"She's in trouble."

"We don't know that yet. It could be a simple theft. We won't know until further investigation is carried out."

"I should go there."

"To Istanbul? Not a good idea, Dr. Norris. And totally unnecessary. You won't be able to do anything."

"You don't understand. It's just me and my sister. She doesn't have anyone else."

It could be nothing but it could be something. Kidnapping. Rape. Murder.

"Our recommendation is for families of loved ones missing in foreign territories to stay home."

Julia stares out at the glittering lights of the harbor. The last time she had seen Toni she'd screamed at her to get out of her house and to never come back.

"You'll be kept fully informed, I promise you," says John Miller.

After the call ends, Julia stands there for a long time, thinking.

7

She waits in her Prius in the parking lot of the diner. She's been sitting here for over fifteen minutes, hands locked on the steering wheel. She and Leo used to come here when they were first married. Brunch on a Saturday. Pancakes with syrup for Julia. Hash browns, eggs, and spicy sausage for Leo.

His dust-covered silver truck is parked over by the entrance. The same truck he'd had when they were married. Norris construction co. is printed in yellow along the side. The truck is loaded with supplies. Wooden planks. Metal sheeting. Poles of some sort.

Julia wasn't sure he would come. She looks at his truck now and thinks about starting her engine and driving away. She hates asking for help. But this time she needs it.

She takes a breath, forces herself to get out, and crosses the parking lot. She pushes through the cafe doors and is hit with the aroma of cooked bacon, fried butter, and hot rolls. Leo's waiting for her third booth from the back. When he sees her, he rises and kisses her cheek. No aftershave, just him. Sun and salt and timber.

"Good to see you, Julia."

He stands there a touch too long, looking at her, before jamming his hands in his pockets and sitting back down.

"Thanks for coming," she says, taking the seat opposite.

The lines on his face have grown deeper, his blond hair darker. But his observant blue eyes are exactly the same.

"Got a job on at Wilmont Avenue so I can't stay long," he says, glancing at his wristwatch. The Hager Julia had bought as an anniversary gift years ago. The once pristine glass face all scratched up now.

"This won't take long," she says.

The waitress comes over, pours coffee. Leo brings the rim of the mug to his lips and blows. The nail on his forefinger is black.

He sees her looking. "Occupational hazard."

"How many times is that now?" says Julia.

"Five, maybe. I'll be lucky if it grows back."

"Toni is missing," she says.

It's the first time Julia has said it out loud and it gives her a chill.

"Why didn't you tell me?" he says.

"I'm telling you now."

"All right."

"I need to go there," says Julia.

"Where?"

"Turkey."

He looks into his coffee, seems to relax, takes a swig. "You know Toni, she'll turn up."

Julia brushes the hair from her face. "I could kill her."

"They ask you to go? The police, whatever?"

"On the contrary. They don't want me there, said I would probably just get in the way."

He pauses. "Why are you then?"

"It's not like I have a choice. She's my sister, Leo."

He rakes his fingers across the stubble on his chin. "Everyone has choices, Julia."

"This time feels different. Serious."

"Whatever mess Toni has got herself into again, let her clean it up. It's the only way she's ever going to learn."

"I don't know how long I'll be," she says.

He looks at her. "You want me to congratulate you on being the better person, is that it?"

"Will you take Bish?"

"Julia, the martyr. The poor, downtrodden sister."

"I don't want to put him in a cattery, he might fret."

"You love it when she screws up, don't you?"

"Forget it," she says, looking out the window. "I'll ask someone else."

Leo gets to his feet. "You want me to say sorry again, but I won't. This has nothing to do with me."

"I never said that it did," she says.

His work boots shift on the faded green linoleum. He has that half-angry, half-concerned face.

"So will you take him?" she says.

He breathes out through his nose. "I'll take the damn cat."

"Thank you."

He pauses. "You want me to go with you?"

"No."

"Julia, come on."

"I said no, Leo."

"You can't go by yourself." He stands looking at her. "I'll get time off."

She puts down her cup. "I'll be fine."

He clenches his jaw. "Same old Julia. I don't need anyone. I can do it all by myself."

She looks away, out the window at his truck. She feels him standing there, fighting not to say something.

"Don't let me keep you," she says.

When she looks again, he's gone.

8

Traffic is hectic thanks to the rain and Julia misses the San Bruno Avenue exit to the long-stay parking lot and has to do the circuit all over again. Seeing Leo hasn't helped. In fact, contacting him had been a stupid mistake. It's shaken her up more than she likes to admit, and as she circles around the junction again, she finds herself imagining that he might have someone new. She feels a stab of jealousy. Hates herself for it. She's being ridiculous. He has every right to move on. Whatever they once had is well and truly gone. Besides, she has more important things to worry about, like making sure she doesn't miss her flight to Istanbul.

Julia turns left at the traffic signal, follows the signs to the parking area, and finds a space up on level two. Fifteen minutes later she's inside the brightly lit international terminal looking at the Departures and Arrival screen. Her heart sinks. Her flight's been delayed.

She starts walking, wheeling her suitcase behind her, searching for the United Airlines counter to find out what's going on. A few laps of the terminal later, she spots it. The line is enormous. All five counters are full with United Airlines staff processing queries from irate passengers.

"Oh boy."

She turns to see a man standing at her shoulder. Early forties. Clean-cut. Dark-haired. Handsome. Sue most definitely would approve. He drops his satchel to the floor.

"Looks like we're in for a long wait," he says.

"Do you know why there's a delay to Istanbul?" she says.

He laughs. "Delay? Haven't you heard? The flight's been cancelled. Ataturk Airport in Istanbul has been shut because of a possible terrorist threat."

Julia blinks. "What? But I need to get to Istanbul urgently."

He frowns at her, concerned. "Sounds serious."

"It could be," she says, swallowing.

Over at counter three, a senior citizen in a baseball cap is shouting at the United Airlines woman.

"This is getting ugly," says the man. He taps his pocket. "Tell you what, I'm a member of the airport lounge. Can I interest you in a drink? A bite to eat? We can rebook our flights up there."

She can hear Sue's voice urging her to go.

"That's very kind, but no."

The man stands there looking awkward. She feels bad but there's no point in leading him on.

She tilts her chin toward the counter. "Is there another way of getting to Istanbul? Maybe flying into another city and driving from there?"

He considers this for a moment. "As a matter of fact, there is. You could fly into Ankara, Turkey's capital. Istanbul's about a five-hour drive northeast from there. From memory, though, United doesn't fly to Ankara so you'll have to go with another carrier."

"Any idea what airline does?"

He shrugs. "Turkish Airlines probably."

"Thank you," she says, hurrying off. "You've been a great help."

"Don't mention it," he calls after her, "and if you change your mind about that drink…"

*

She strides the length of the terminal and finds the Turkish Airlines counter hidden in the second to last aisle. Her shoulders slump. The line's almost as big as the other one. Someone touches her arm. The airport lounge man, she thinks. But when she turns around, it isn't him at all.

"Leo."

Leo lowers his duffel bag to the floor. "Hey."

"What are you doing here?"

"What does it look like?"

Her spine stiffens. "I told you I don't need your help."

"I know what you said and I'm ignoring it."

He's changed from his work clothes to khaki chinos and a blue-checkered shirt. He'd worn the same thing on their final trip together. Hawaii. The disaster trip.

She crosses her arms. "I wasn't kidding. You can't come with me."

His blue eyes study her face. "I'm not letting you do this on your own, Julia."

She pauses. "Look, I appreciate the gesture but you're not my husband anymore."

He stares at her. "Jesus Christ, Julia."

She feels like a bitch. "I'm sorry, Leo, but it's true."

"Well, last time I checked," he says, "there wasn't any law forbidding ex-husbands from flying to the same country as their ex-wives so I guess I can come whether you like it or not."

Julia grabs the handle of her suitcase, starts wheeling. "I can't do this with you now. Please go."

He reaches for her arm. Julia has a flash of a happier time. Their first date all those years ago. A bad movie, even worse pizza.

"Listen," he says, gentler. "Think about it from a practical level for a minute, would you? Two heads are better than one, aren't they? It might actually help having me there, did you ever think of that? You never know when—" He stops midsentence and stares at something over her shoulder. "Who the hell is that?"

She turns. The airport lounge man is waving and half-jogging toward them.

"Hey!" he calls. "They've reopened Ataturk Airport." He reaches them, rests his hands on his knees to catch his breath. "False alarm apparently. United has opened more counters. If you hurry, you should be able to check in and make your original flight."

"Oh, that's good news," says Julia. "Thanks so much for letting me know."

The man notices Leo for the first time. He looks at Julia. "This guy bothering you?"

Julia feels awkward, shifts on her feet. "Oh no, everything's fine. Leo is—" she pauses, settles on, "a friend of the family."

Beside her, the anger is coming off Leo in waves.

"Well, if you're sure," says the man, not appearing entirely convinced. "By the way, I never caught your name?"

"Julia."

He extends his hand and they shake for a second time. "It was nice meeting you, Julia. I'm Tim. Best of luck with your situation. I hope it works out. And don't forget about that drink. Bye for now."

He flashes her a smile and turns to walk back in the direction he came from.

"Don't let me stop you," says Leo, after he's gone.

"Honestly, Leo. Sometimes you can be an infant."

They stand looking at each other, neither one speaking.

Finally, Julia lets out a breath. "What about Bishop?"

"Candy."

Candy, his sister. Type A personality. Allergic to everything.

"Are you insane? Candy won't cope," says Julia.

"It will help build up her immunity. Besides we're doing her a favor when you think about it."

She studies his face. "All right," she says, reluctantly. "You can come. But this is about Toni, not about you and me."

"I wouldn't want it any other way."

"Well, that's good, Leo, because there isn't any other way. Just so we're loud and clear on that."

"Oh, crystal," he says.

9

Whatever terrorist threat there had been, there's no sign of it when Julia and Leo step off the plane at Ataturk Airport. Julia's surprised by the state of the airport. Dusty and forlorn-looking. Chipped linoleum and walls in need of a fresh coat of paint. The place feels more like a railway station than an international airport. Functional, but that's about it. Julia had expected armed security, too, especially given the potential terrorist threat. But she's lucky to spot a luggage handler let alone an armed guard.

After passing through passport control, Julia and Leo follow the crowd to a squeaking luggage carousel and wait for their bags to emerge. It seems to take forever. Julia glances up and spots the trio of western backpackers watching the conveyer belt, bleary-eyed and ragged. They look exactly how she feels.

Looking around, Julia wonders how Toni did this all the time. Be so far from home, in strange places, all by herself. Not knowing how to speak the language or read the signs. Which plane, bus, or train to catch. There's a strange type of terror to it. But that's Toni to a T, isn't it?

Leo yawns and rubs his eyes. "I'd kill for a coffee right now."

Julia envies him. He'd slept for most of the flight. She, on the other hand, had not even managed five minutes. The brain chatter had been too loud. The checklists she had formed and reformed in her mind. The awful scenarios she had played out in all their gory and graphic detail. The sense of being totally and overwhelmingly out of her depth. Her sister is missing in a country of eighty million people. She does not have a single clue about where to begin. Open heart surgery is far less complicated.

Julia watches as the same motley collection of luggage travels around the conveyer belt for the third time and thinks that maybe, just maybe, this is all one giant mistake, and Toni will be waiting on the other side of the arrival gates with a simple explanation and contrite apology.

But after they collect their bags and walk through the arrival gates, there's no Toni, just a middle-aged man in a plain brown suit holding a sign with Julia's name on it.

"I'm Dr. Norris," Julia says, approaching him.

"Driver from the embassy. Follow. Please."

The man grabs their suitcases and strides off toward the exit.

"Wait a minute," she says, fast-walking to keep up. "Ms. Fletcher was supposed to meet us."

"Julia, I'm sure it's fine," says Leo.

"You don't know that, Leo."

The man gives no indication he's heard Julia and carries on through the sliding doors to a loading zone outside the terminal where a shiny black Lexus is parked. The man unlocks the trunk and dumps their suitcases inside.

"Sir, if you could just wait a moment while I make a call to find out what's going on."

Leo looks at her. "Maybe you made a mistake."

She glances at him dismissively, reaching into her bag for her phone. "I didn't make a mistake, Leo. When I gave John Miller the flight and accommodation details, he said an embassy representative named Christine Fletcher would be here to meet us."

The driver shrugs. "They tell me take doctor to hotel, so that's what I do."

"Hotel?" exclaims Julia. "What? No, there's been some sort of mistake. Please take us directly to the American embassy."

The driver opens the back door for them. "This I cannot do."

Julia's throat tightens. "You don't understand. My sister is missing."

Leo touches her arm. "Hey, we'll call from the hotel, find out what's going on."

The man plants himself in the driver's seat and turns on the ignition.

"We go now, okay," he says, staring out the windshield.

Julia stands on the sidewalk, shaking. She doesn't like this feeling. When things don't go according to plan, when things happen outside of her control.

Leo lowers his voice. "Like I said, it's probably just a misunderstanding. We'll sort it out."

Finally, she relents and gets in the car. It isn't as if she has much of a choice.

"Hot shower and something to eat, you'll be as good as new," says Leo, sliding in after her.

"I'm not a child, Leo," she says, facing the window.

But right about now that's exactly how she feels.

10

Julia isn't prepared for the beauty of it. But even in her current state of gnawing anxiety, she can see Istanbul for the marvel that it is. She's read about it, of course. In high school she'd studied the rise and fall of the Ottoman Empire, and how, unlike any other city in the world, Istanbul was split between two continents, Asia and Europe. But seeing it in person is a whole other matter.

As the Lexus races along the four-lane road, she tries to take in the splendor. To the right, the restless Bosporus Sea is in constant motion, all peaks and valleys, the color of the deepest blue. While out in the middle of the strait, the tankers and trawlers blow black smoke and drift back and forth across the channel. Beyond that, there's the modern side of Istanbul, the Asian side, with its concrete high rises and commercial center.

The Lexus rounds a corner, and the surrounding low-lying hills that make up the old quarter come into view. Exquisite mosques with gorgeous vaulted domes and slender minarets stud the crowded landscape, their exotic silhouettes prominent against the clear blue sky. Stone buildings of various heights, the color of sand and amber, cluster together in a strange blend of order and chaos.

Julia had once been to a cardiothoracic conference in Rome. The Istanbul vista reminds her of that. The soft earthy hues. The way the golden light falls between the dips and rises of the hills. The profound historic nature of it, so unlike anything back home. But Julia reminds herself that as beautiful as it is, it's also the place that has swallowed Toni whole.

The driver takes a sharp left and Julia and Leo slip along the leather seats until Leo's thigh pushes against hers. She can smell his scent. Flinty and raw.

"How are you doing?" he says, shifting back a respectable distance.

Small. Insignificant. Completely out of her depth. "I'm fine," she says. "You don't need to worry about me."

He glances out the window and she can tell he's hurt.

"It's just a lot to take in," she says.

"We'll call from the hotel. There'll be a simple explanation for why this Fletcher lady couldn't meet us at the airport."

She pushes the fringe from her eyes. "I just wish people would keep their word. This entire thing is bad enough as it is."

The driver's phone rings. He flips it open and starts barking Turkish. Driving with one hand on the steering wheel, he continues the conversation, zipping in and out of lanes at an uncomfortable speed. Julia gets nervous. Speed and cell phones are not a good mix. She had firsthand experience of this when she was on ER rotation as an intern.

She glances at Leo, but he's looking out the window at the flags lining the road; the red Turkish flag with its distinctive white star and crescent. There are political billboards, too. Faces of middle-aged men beam out. Clean-cut, respectable, trimmed moustaches, suits and ties. Julia wonders when the elections are and hopes to be well gone by then.

She's on the verge of saying something about the driver's speed when the traffic slows to a crawl. The driver ends his phone call and cranes his head out his window to take a look. He tuts impatiently and drums his fingers along the steering wheel.

A few minutes later, they see the reason for the holdup. A dirty white 1970s Vauxhall is blocking one of the lanes. Julia's heart skips a beat. She's thinking terrorism. A car bomb. An ambush lying in wait.

Holding her breath as they pass, she fixes her eyes on the Vauxhall. The rear wheel is propped up on a block. A flat tire. Julia exhales and winds down her window, letting the diesel-tinged air of the Bosporus blow on her face.

The Lexus takes a sharp left and veers uphill into a labyrinth of steep cobbled streets. A plaque fastened to a white rendered wall announces the area as Sultanahmet. Footpaths teem with foreigners snapping photos and ducking in and out of little shops overflowing with mosaic plates and wind chimes and Turkish rugs and hanging lamps. There are lots of Turkish men, too, standing in doorways, talking, smoking, and drinking tea from tiny glasses. It's a bustling, noisy atmosphere, tinged with an exoticness that Julia has never encountered before. Beside her, Leo seems just as enthralled, and for a brief moment she wishes they were married again and that this was a pleasure trip, a vacation, where the two of them could just enjoy exploring and discovering the delights of a new country together.

The driver heads down an incline toward a high red-brick wall bordering a railway. A small hotel comes into view, wedged between a pokey laundromat and restaurant. A sad, faded strip of red carpet trails up to a plain front door propped open with a gray brick. Sadder still is the old, weather-beaten maroon canopy above the entranceway, which has a torn section flapping listlessly in the wind. Next to the hotel entrance, a dark-haired man in a porter's uniform is leaning against a banister, texting.

The driver lurches to a stop and looks at Julia and Leo in the rearview.

"Here we arrive," he says.

11

Julia and Leo stand looking at the cheerless hotel.

"It seemed better online," says Julia.

In her rush to get to Istanbul, she hadn't bothered to check reviews and had just booked the first hotel that looked half-decent on Tripadvisor.

"They always do," says Leo.

His face drops suddenly. "Oh boy."

Julia looks at him. "What is it?"

"I never thought about booking a hotel for myself."

She feels a flash of irritation. Even when they were married, he had always left everything up to her.

She decides to let it go. "You should be okay. It doesn't exactly look like they're run off their feet."

The hotel attendant takes their luggage and they follow him up the scruffy carpet through the entrance. Unfortunately, the inside isn't any more inspiring than the outside. While the tired decor in the empty lobby hints at opulence, whatever splendor there might have once been is well and truly gone. The walnut parquet floor, for instance, is horrendously chipped and in bad need of repair. The maroon and cream curtains framing the large picture book window are sun-faded and fraying along the edges. Even the lone crystal chandelier hanging in the compact reception area, once clearly a glorious statement piece, is missing some of its pretty pear-shaped crystals. The only thing that looks fresh is the gold paint on the architraves accenting the alabaster ceiling.

Julia hears a cough, the hacking cough of a long-term smoker. It's coming from a plump, older woman in a small seating area. She's sitting at one of the two wingback chairs, hunched over an oval glass-topped coffee table with a deck of cards in her hand, utterly absorbed in a game of solitaire. Her choice of clothing is interesting to say the least. Blue sweater, gray skirt, knee-high sports socks, and aqua-colored Nikes.

"Cute," says Leo.

"Shush. She'll hear you."

Julia tings the desk bell at the unmanned reception. The woman in the seating area casts a look over her shoulder. Julia's about to apologize for disturbing her when the woman springs to her feet, hurries toward them, and slips in behind the counter.

"*Merhaba*, welcome to the Golden Horn Hotel," she says, breathlessly. "I am Ada. Pleased to make your acquaintance." She looks from Leo to Julia. "Honeymoon in Istanbul?"

"Honeymoon?" says Julia, momentarily confused. "Oh, God no. We're just traveling together. He needs his own room."

Ada looks crestfallen. "Oh."

Julia gives her the booking number. Ada taps on the computer keyboard and stares intently at the screen.

"I cannot find the booking," she says, frowning. Ada waves a hand. "But do not worry. I have many rooms. Passport, please."

As Ada runs their passports through a small photocopier to the left of the desk, Julia's phone vibrates. It's a text message: *Apologies for not meeting you at airport. Will pick you up from hotel this afternoon. CF.*

Julia shows Leo.

"See," he says. "I told you everything would be okay."

Julia isn't entirely convinced and thinks about calling Christine Fletcher back to get a firm time of arrival but decides against it. She doesn't want to become a pest and have the information flow shut down completely.

Her phone vibrates again. It's a text from the hospital. Mrs. Keller is getting discharged today. Julia feels a pang and wishes she could be there to wish her luck. It feels uncomfortable, being away from work. Julia doesn't like it at all. Rescheduling all her upcoming surgeries had been hard. People relied on her. Patients, colleagues, the community. She'd felt like she was deserting her already understaffed department in their hour of need.

"Everything all right?" says Leo.

"The hospital," says Julia, slipping her phone into her pocket.

"Tourist map?" says Ada, handing over the key cards.

Julia pauses, thinking.

"Actually, you might be able to help me with something."

Julia crouches down and unzips her suitcase. She reaches inside and finds her stack of flyers and puts one on the counter.

"My sister is missing. We're in Istanbul to look for her. Have you seen her?"

"Julia," says Leo, softly. "Istanbul's a big place."

Julia ignores him and pushes the flyer closer to Ada. "Her hair may be different now. Please look closely and see if you recognize her. Maybe she stayed here? Maybe you saw her when you were out on the street? Anything you can think of will be a great help."

Julia had used Toni's Facebook profile picture. The same selfie as the Korean one with the fuchsia hair. The photograph was at least six months old but it was the best that Julia could do.

Ada studies the flyer. She lifts her head and looks at Julia. "Sorry, I have not seen this young lady."

Julia feels a hit of disappointment.

"Perhaps you could put this up somewhere? Do you have a notice board where your staff and guests can see it?"

Ada's eyes drop to the flyer, hesitating.

"Please," says Julia.

"I will put in the business center, okay?" Ada says, jerking a thumb to the left, toward a room at the end of the narrow corridor.

"That's very kind. Thank you so much."

Ada looks down at the flyer again. "This is not good. Your sister being in trouble in Istanbul. Give me some more poster and I will give to my friend. He runs a shop. I will ask him to put some up for you."

Julia's touched. "Really? I can't tell you how much I would appreciate that."

Julia returns to her suitcase, gets a whole stack out, and gives them to Ada.

It feels good to finally be doing something.

12

The porter slips the key card into room 313 and ushers Julia inside. Hidden away at the end of a poorly lit hallway, the room is basic but impeccably clean. A pair of twin beds, made with military precision, take up most of the space. There's a small counter opposite, two drinking glasses in paper wrappers on top, minibar fridge wedged beneath. Completing the arrangement is a single, leather-look tub chair in the corner near the window.

Julia stifles a groan when she sees an adjoining doorway to the room next door. In her experience rooms with adjoining doors mean noise. The last time she'd been in one, she hadn't been able to sleep at all. In fact, she'd even been able to hear the occupants turn over in bed. To make matters worse, it dawns on her now that she's forgotten to pack her custom-made ear plugs, something she used even when sleeping alone at home. She considers asking for a different room but just doesn't have the energy.

Julia opens the ratty maroon curtains to let in some light. Any hope of a decent view crumbles when she sees the brick wall and trash-littered alleyway below.

She runs her tongue around her mouth. She needs water. The flight has left her dehydrated and she's at risk of getting a migraine. Crossing the floor, she crouches to check the mini-fridge for bottled water. But apart from an impressive build-up of ice around the tiny metal freezer box, the fridge is empty.

Exhausted, Julia drops to the end of the bed. Was it really less than forty-eight hours ago that she received the call from John Miller? Her mind swims with everything. The sense of foreboding that she's done so well to hold at bay suddenly overwhelms her. She reaches for her bag and takes out a flyer. She studies the photo of Toni. Toni, her thoughtless, cavalier, free-spirited sister. Julia gets to her feet and pins it to the wall.

*

Julia wakes with Leo standing over her, Ada at his shoulder.

Julia sits up, disorientated. "What is it?"

"I kept knocking but got no answer. Ada let me in," he says.

Julia follows Leo's gaze to the adjoining door, which is now wide open. She looks over her shoulder and sees the imprint of her body on the comforter.

"I must have fallen asleep."

Leo's frown grows deeper. "You don't look so good."

Julia tucks a lock of sweaty hair behind her ear. "I'm tired, Leo, not sick."

"When was the last time you had something to eat?"

Julia stands, feels shaky on her feet. "I'm fine, Leo. Please don't fuss."

"I go now, okay," says Ada, glancing at them both.

"Of course. Thank you for your help," says Julia.

Ada discreetly slips out the door.

Julia faces Leo. "Really, I'm okay. Go back to whatever you were doing."

"Wait there," he says.

Before she can argue, he ducks through the adjoining door and returns holding a candy bar.

He wiggles it back and forth in front of her face. "It's Paleo."

"Paleo?"

"I've been training for a marathon."

She stifles a laugh. "You've never run a mile in your life."

"People can change, Julia. I take care of myself now. Better than you apparently. When was the last time you saw the inside of a gym?"

"Leo, I'm on my feet all day in surgery."

"Spare me," he scoffs. He removes the wrapper and gives her the bar. "Eat it."

She takes it, chews, feels better almost immediately. He disappears into the bathroom, comes back with a glass of water, and holds it out.

She shakes her head. "No way. That's diarrhea in a glass."

He shrugs and drinks it in one go.

"For God's sake, Leo," cries Julia. "You'll get sick."

He pats his belly. "Constitution of an ox, Julia, you know that."

He looks at the flyer of Toni on the wall. She immediately feels stupid for putting it up there.

She turns away. "Like I said, I'm fine now, Leo. I don't need a guardian."

"I know you don't," he says, grabbing the TV remote.

He makes himself comfortable on the bed, hand behind his head, legs stretched out and crossed at the ankles. He flicks through the channels. CNN. Turkish News. *Home Alone 2.* Finds a sports game. Settles on that. South Africa vs. All Blacks. Rugby.

Julia hates sports but decides it's not worth the fight. Instead she takes a seat in the tub chair and checks her phone. "It's been hours, they should have come for us up by now."

But Leo's not listening. The player in the number fifteen jersey has just kicked a goal.

13

Light has all but faded by the time the knock on the door finally arrives. This time Leo's the one who's fallen asleep and Julia gives him a nudge as she crosses the floor.

"Hey, wake up. I think they're here."

The first thing she notices when she opens the door is the man's incredibly sad eyes. Dark pools of deep hazel that betray a lifetime of human grief. It's the way he holds himself too, shoulders rounded beneath his crumpled suit, the slight bend of his head. She's seen the same thing before with the surviving spouses of terminal patients. He's a larger build than Leo, with black hair streaked with silver. Early sixties or thereabouts, Julia guesses.

The man wipes a big hand on his trouser leg and offers it to Julia. "*Merhaba*, I am Emri Muhtar. I am Turkish police detective. Please, I am showing you this." He holds up a photo ID written in Turkish. "Okay? Like I say, police."

"Police?"

"Correct."

He steps inside the room and glances around.

Julia's puzzled. "We were expecting someone from the embassy. A Christine Fletcher."

He stops to look at the flyer of Toni on the wall. Without turning, he says, "I am taking you to the embassy now."

"Do you have news?" says Julia.

"We still search."

He turns to look at her, then Leo, then at the open door to the adjacent room.

"My apologies," says Julia. "This is Leo Fraser. My former husband."

Leo shakes his hand.

The detective blinks. "Okay, nice. All the family is here."

"Have you dealt with missing persons investigations before?" asks Julia.

The detective looks at his shoe. The lace is undone. He crouches to tie it.

"It is better that we speak at embassy," he says, standing. "We go now, okay?"

He shows them to his car, a navy Fiat in serious need of a clean. There's a huge dent in the driver's door and a crack along the corner of the back window. Leaning into the back seat, the detective sweeps aside food wrappers, crumpled coffee cups, and newspapers. There's a suit jacket and sweater, too. He snatches them up and tosses them in the front seat, then stands back and gestures for Julia and Leo to get in.

"Please."

Julia slides across and Leo follows. It stinks of stale smoke and French fries and Julia wishes she could wind down the window but doesn't want to appear rude.

"So far, so good," whispers Leo.

But Julia doesn't think it's funny. She gives Leo a look, then stares out the window, trying to quell her growing sense of concern.

They drive through the same area as before, up and down the narrow roads, past the shops and footpaths still busy with tourists. It's later now, though, so people are eating in the open-air restaurants, crouched on cushions around low tables, tearing chunks from pita bread and scooping them into bowls of hummus. It's dark out and there are lights, pretty ones, old-fashioned streetlamps radiating a warm glow across the stone cobbles, and clusters of stained-glass lanterns hanging from shop eaves, emitting a kaleidoscope of striking ruby, emerald, and sapphire colors. Julia wonders if Toni has seen any of this, whether she has eaten alfresco at one of the busy restaurants or walked beneath the streetlamps along the narrow footpaths searching for trinkets.

There's a shuffle from the front seat as Detective Muhtar digs inside his jacket pocket, pulls out a pack of cigarettes, and puts one in his mouth. He flicks the lighter, then pauses, eyes hitting the rearview.

"Okay to smoke?" he says, unlit cigarette dangling between his lips.

"Actually, I'm a doctor," says Julia.

He blinks at her and nods, takes the cigarette from his mouth.

"Yes. Dirty habit. I try to stop many times."

They carry on uphill, driving parallel with the overland commuter train. Quite suddenly, a haunting Arabic voice rings out above the building tops.

"The call to prayer," says Detective Muhtar, seeing their surprise. "It happens five times a day. All the prayers are in Arabic but Turks speak Turkish so we never know what the imam is saying. Not for my whole life do I know what he is saying."

He shakes his head as if he thinks the whole thing is ridiculous.

"Imam?" says Leo.

"The holy man. Like your priest or preacher in the West."

"But you're Muslim?"

"Sure."

"Don't you need to stop and pray?"

Detective Muhtar shrugs. "Religion is for the old people, really."

He looks out the window and signals to the office building on the left with his chin.

"We arrive at the embassy," he says.

"Here?" says Julia, looking at the nondescript office building.

Detective Muhtar nods. "There was a bombing last week at the main American embassy. They come here for temporary measure."

"A bombing?" says Julia, glancing at Leo. "I hope no one was hurt."

"Do not worry. You are safe here," Detective Muhtar says, getting out of the car.

Julia waits until he shuts the door before turning to Leo. "I don't have a good feeling about him, Leo," she whispers. "He doesn't exactly look like their best and brightest."

Leo stares at the building. "Let's hold off judgment until we speak to our guys first, find out what Christine Fletcher has to say."

Before Julia can reply, Detective Muhtar opens their door.

"Let us go. Ms. Fletcher is waiting."

14

He ushers them into the foyer and through security screening, where a uniformed guard X-rays the contents of Julia's satchel and Leo's pockets, and another guard conducts a pat-down and wand scan on each of their bodies. Once they're given the all clear, they take the elevator to the fifth floor and follow Detective Muhtar down a carpeted corridor to a doorway flanked by two heavily armed guards.

Detective Muhtar flips his ID and the guards admit them to a small holding area where Leo and Julia are required to pass through another metal detector and have their belongings X-rayed again. With that done, they are shown to a temporary reception area.

Julia looks around. Someone's done their best to make it look official. A large US flag is propped up on a standing pole in the corner. On the wall above a standard office desk there's the round United States of America embassy seal complete with bald eagle insignia.

It's not long before a red-headed woman emerges from a backroom. Mid-forties, sober face free of makeup. Black pants, white shirt. Competent, practical, personable. Julia likes her immediately.

The woman extends her hand. "*Merhaba*, Dr. Norris, I'm Christine Fletcher."

Julia shakes it, notes the wedding ring. "Nice to meet you, Christine. And please call me Julia. This is Leo Fraser, my former husband."

Christine shakes his hand. "*Merhaba*, Leo." She nods toward the door she emerged from. "Let's talk in my office."

They follow her through the doorway, up a flight of stairs, across an open plan area where a dozen or so workers are seated at laptops—American by the looks of them—and into a small, windowless room. The room is cramped with a plain pine wooden desk, four white plastic tub chairs, a cabinet to the left, three sealed cartons in the corner to the right. Even though the hurried, temporary nature of the office is obvious, Christine Fletcher has clearly taken the time to make the space orderly, her desk especially. A manila folder and large legal notepad sit side-by-side at the center, a jug of water and some mismatched glasses next to that. Her nameplate is positioned, facing out, in the upper righthand corner, while in the other corner, at a perfect right angle, there's a photograph in a simple black frame. A happy shot of Christine and a man. Husband probably. Taken years earlier, in front of the Taj Mahal.

The room smells faintly of mildew and Julia spies a smattering of mold in the corner of the ceiling above a rattling air conditioner.

"Not exactly ideal, I know," says Christine Fletcher, taking a seat behind the desk. "But there was an incident at our embassy last week."

"We heard," says Julia. "I hope everyone was okay."

Christine frowns. "One casualty, unfortunately."

"Oh, I'm sorry."

"I'm not going to lie, it's been rough. But we're not here to talk about that, you want to know what we're doing to find Toni," says Christine, resting her forearms on the desk and knitting her fingers together.

"I know they told me to stay away," says Julia, "but she's my sister. I had to come."

Christine waves a hand. "Absolutely. If it was my sister, I'd be here too." She reaches for the water jug, pours them each a glass. "Look, I know you must be feeling anxious but travelers go missing all the time then turn up. It's so common, you wouldn't believe." She looks directly at Julia. "However, the backpack, the passport, it's not a good sign."

Julia feels a lump in her chest. "The backpack might have been stolen. Toni could still be out there with no money stuck on some border."

Christine gives her a sympathetic look.

"You don't know my sister," insists Julia. "It's exactly the type of stupid thing that would happen to her. She can be careless like that. I can't tell you how many times she's asked me for money because she lost her wallet or gave it all away to some street person."

"Like I said, we're considering all possibilities. But I want to be frank with you. There are some uncomfortable scenarios that we might have to entertain. For one, Turkey is a well-established white slavery route. We've had instances of girls being kidnapped and shipped off to Eastern Europe to work in brothels or internet pornography. Believe it or not, sometimes they're even smuggled into the States for the same thing. And not long ago a US citizen was killed by a vagrant. Her body was found after a three-day search."

"Toni isn't dead," says Julia flatly.

"I'm sorry," says Christine. "That was insensitive of me."

Julia's forces herself to relax her shoulders. "There's no need for apologies. I just ask that you keep an open mind."

"Of course."

"What can you tell us about the investigation so far?"

Christine nods toward Detective Muhtar. "We're working as closely as we can with the Turkish authorities."

Julia raises her eyebrows. "The American embassy isn't running the investigation?"

Christine shakes her head. "Strictly speaking, we're in Turkish jurisdiction so it's the Turks' investigation. We're supposed to have a supporting role only." Christine shoots Detective Muhtar a smile. "But Detective Muhtar has been letting us help where we can, haven't you?"

He nods but says nothing. Julia's dislike for the man is growing. There is just something off about him.

"Forgive me, Detective," she says. "But what exactly is being done to find my sister?"

He pulls on his earlobe and studies the ceiling. "We check morgue, hospital, and correctional facilities to see if she arrested in another part of Turkey. This is hard because communication between regions not so good. We also check overland borders. But this takes much time."

Christine interjects. "And what I can tell you, Julia, is that the embassy is also making inquiries on your behalf. So far we have nothing from intel, but we haven't utilized all our avenues yet."

Julia suddenly feels exhausted. There's so much to absorb.

"Try not to worry," says Christine. "We'll keep you up to date every step of the way. Detective, I understand you have some questions for Julia?"

"That is correct," he says, reaching for the manila folder on Christine's desk. He takes out a document.

Julia glances at the file and wonders what else is in there.

He looks at the paper. "Your sister travels a lot."

"Yes."

"What does she do for money while she travels?"

Julia hesitates. "I'm not sure. Waits tables, cuts hair, probably."

"Okay." He purses his lips. "You were foster children. That is hard life, I think."

Julia feels a tug in her gut. "How did you know about that?"

"US records," says Christine. "It's best that we give the Turkish authorities as much information about Toni as we can."

Detective Muhtar continues. "Your sister returned to United States three years ago. She did not go anywhere for one year. Did you have contact with her when she come back to America?"

Julia's heart beats a little faster. "I'm not sure what that's got to do with her disappearance," she says, carefully.

Detective Muhtar glances up at Julia. "You do not wish to answer?"

"Detective Muhtar is just trying to get a better picture of Toni," says Christine.

"And I understand that, but that trip back home was over three years ago."

Detective Muhtar rubs his chin. "Did your sister have a mental issue?"

Julia looks at me. "What do you mean?"

"Was she depressed?"

Julia sits back in her chair. "What are you implying? That she might have committed suicide? Toni would never do that."

"They're just discounting possibilities, Julia," says Leo, trying to be reassuring. He looks at Christine. "Maybe that's enough for one night."

Julia shakes her head, irritated. "I'm fine, Leo. Please continue, Detective."

Detective Muhtar delves into the file, pulls out a photograph, and slides it across the table.

"You know this?"

Julia picks up the image, looks closely. The saturated backpack lies discarded on the sea rocks like a piece of trash. By the looks of the wear and tear around the edges, the backpack had seen a lot of miles, and what was once probably a vibrant teal is now a faded, grubby beige. A tiny knitted Chinese girl doll the size of a key ring, with black plaits and red pajamas, hangs from one of the back straps. Typical Toni. A little girl at heart.

Julia swallows. "Was this it? Toni's backpack?"

Christine nods. "It was fished out of the water on the rocks on the western side of Galata Bridge."

Detective Muhtar shows Julia and Leo a drone shot of where the backpack was situated on a sea wall at the opposite end of the ferries and piers.

"And her belongings? They were still in there, along with her passport and wallet?"

"That's correct," says Detective Muhtar. "The pack was full of her personal items."

"Including her phone?"

Christine frowns. "Phone? I wasn't aware she had one."

"I bought it for her the last time I saw her. She used it to Facebook, email, whatever. As far as I know she still had it with her."

Christine turns to Detective Muhtar. "What does it say on the inventory list?"

He scans the file, finds the list, reads. He looks up.

"No phone," he says.

15

The drive back to the hotel with Detective Muhtar is a silent one. No one is much in the mood for polite conversation, especially Julia. After being dropped off, Leo insists they eat something before turning in for the night. Julia reluctantly agrees so they opt for the tired-looking restaurant inside the hotel and order from the menu. But Julia does nothing except push tomato wedges around her plate.

"We could get them to make you something else," offers Leo. "A grilled cheese or something?"

Julia shakes her head. "I'm not hungry."

"The cell phone was a good pickup. Maybe they can triangulate, whatever. Track where she went."

"Assuming it didn't simply fall out somewhere." Julia spears a cube of feta, breaks it in half, leaves it there. "That detective, I don't know."

"Oh, he's all right."

"I swear I smelled alcohol on his breath."

"Really?"

She looks up. "There were other signs. Broken capillaries on the nose and cheeks, yellowing of the sclera in the eyes."

Leo stuffs a lump of lamb into his mouth and chews. "Lots of cops drink. Doesn't mean they aren't any good at their jobs. Besides, there's not much we can do about it if he does. We're kinda at their mercy. At least there's Christine Fletcher. She's switched on. You like her?"

Julia shrugs. "She seems competent, I suppose."

He puts down his fork and looks at her.

"What?" she says.

"I know you're used to being in control, but you're going to have to let the experts do their jobs. Have some trust in other people for a change."

That stings and she looks away.

Leo stares at her. "Why didn't you tell them?" he says.

"It's none of their business."

"They need to know everything about her. Good and bad."

"They'll just make assumptions."

"Julia."

She gets to her feet. "I need a shower."

16

Julia slips from the hotel room just before daybreak, clutching the tourist map in her hand. She's heading for the waterfront and the port of Eminonu, a ten-minute walk from the hotel. Pausing at the brick wall boarding the railway, Julia squints at the line Ada had drawn in ink on the map. In the pale dawn light Julia can barely make out Ada's chicken scratch. Taking a calculated guess, she continues west until she finds the train station, then exits through a set of bifold doors, emerging in a busy area called Sirkeci. She follows a set of tramlines past the Burger King and KFC until she gets to a main road heavy with morning traffic.

She looks across the road and sees the quarter-mile-long Galata Bridge, the primary link between the historic and modern districts of Istanbul. Despite the early hour, fishermen are on the bridge bent over the railings and dropping lines into the water. She needs to go left of the bridge toward the bus depot.

When the traffic lights change, Julia crosses the road and reaches the paved promenade along the waterfront. Continuing past locals queuing for the ferries, she ignores the call of a passing vendor with a basket of pretzel bread balanced on his head and keeps heading west, searching for the Galata Bridge underpass leading to the bus depot and the sea wall beyond that.

She thinks of the drone photograph of the backpack. Piers and ferries at one end, Toni's backpack on a sea wall at the other.

Julia looks around as she walks, conscious she could be following in Toni's very footsteps. It's an eerie feeling and Julia tries to quell the growing sense of anxiety. But disturbing questions pop into her mind regardless. If Toni had come this way, was it voluntary or had she been forced? Was she frightened? Had she reached out for help from a passerby only to be ignored?

Julia thinks of when they were kids, and how Toni would be off talking to strangers in the grocery store or in the park or the street. Anyone who smiled or looked Toni's way would get peppered with questions. *Where are you from? Do you have any kids? What's your favorite food? Do you have a dog?* Julia would have to pull her away. *You don't even know that person, Toni. You've got to be careful. There are people out there who want to hurt kids like you.* And Toni would say, *But they're nice. I just want to say hello.*

Julia carries on and before long sees the bus depot. Feeling a sudden sense of urgency, she picks up pace, half-jogging until she reaches the sea wall. She stops. In front of her, around a rusty railing, a length of torn police tape flaps like a streamer.

Taking care not to slip, she descends the crumbling concrete steps until she reaches the top of the rocks. She looks down, hair a frenzy in the ocean breeze. Just below is a pink circle of spray paint on the rocks, the same spot in the photograph where the backpack had been. A chill runs through her. She stares at the pink circle for a long time, then turns and walks away.

17

"Where the hell have you been?"

Julia looks up and sees Leo standing in the corridor outside her door. She nudges past him, slipping the key card into the lock.

"I didn't realize I'd be gone so long."

Leo waves the crumpled *Be back soon* note she'd pushed under his door earlier.

"You can't just disappear like that," he says, following her into her room. "What was I supposed to think?" He looks down at his socks. "What the hell."

Julia follows his gaze. He's standing in a wet puddle.

She sighs. "God, the fridge. The buzzing was keeping me awake, so I turned it off. The ice must have melted."

She goes into the bathroom, returns with a towel, and crouches to mop up the puddle.

"Listen, Julia," says Leo. "I'm here to help you. I'm just as worried as you about Toni. She's like my little—"

"Sister?" Julia hears the bitter undertone to her voice, immediately hates herself for it.

Leo's face falls. "You're never going to let it go, are you?"

They stare at each other.

"You want me to leave?" he says.

Julia looks at him and feels a stab of regret. "I went to the place where they found Toni's backpack."

"Oh."

"I had to see it for myself."

He gives her a sympathetic look. "That must have been tough."

"I thought it might make me think of something."

"And did it?"

"No."

Leo reaches for her hand but she pretends not to see. She dumps the wet towel in the bathtub, then returns to check the stack of flyers in her satchel.

"I hate this," she says. "This lack of facts. Someone must know something." She stands, shouldering her bag.

"Where are you going now?"

"I arranged to meet Yasmin. She's the one who reported Toni missing."

Leo frowns. "You think that's wise? The Turkish police might think you're interfering with the investigation."

She throws her hands in the air. "We can't just sit around here and do nothing."

Leo stares at her.

"I just want to talk to her, Leo. Where's the harm in that?"

"Fine," he says, exhaling. "But at least give me a chance to change my socks."

18

They follow the tramline past shop windows piled high with pyramids of pink and lemon Turkish delight and pistachio-encrusted baklava dissected into perfect rounds. Restaurants are opening for the morning, and the aroma of freshly brewed Turkish coffee drifts out onto the street. It's not long before the hill levels off and Istanbul's two most famous mosques come into view. The Blue Mosque and the Aya Sofiya. Julia and Leo stop and stare at the glorious structures. The staggering size of the Blue Mosque is breathtaking and like nothing Julia has ever seen before. Constructed from beautiful gray-blue stone and marble, the central dome is flanked by four semi-domes and surrounded by six minarets that soar into the clear morning sky. At the other end of the paved promenade sits the majestic Aya Sofiya. Although smaller than the Blue Mosque, the Aya Sofia is no less impressive, with its exquisite white and rose-colored marble and intricate detailing.

Julia looks around. Despite the early hour, the promenade is already busy with tour groups and vendors selling chargrilled corn on the cob from red and white carts.

She points to a paved walkway. "According to the map, the hostel area should be down there somewhere."

They descend the cobbled pathway and make their way through a tangle of tiny roads, catching glimpses of the sparkling Bosporus as they go. The mostly three-story buildings surrounding them are well-kept, with wrought iron flower boxes beneath pretty sash windows and big stone pots with olive and palm trees straddling the front doors.

They turn left and the area changes. Buildings become rundown. Paint peels off in leaves. Plaster crumbles in places. Power and phone lines are tangled in nests at the top of their wooden poles.

An old woman in a blue head scarf and PVC scuffs emerges from one of the decrepit houses. She squints at Julia and Leo then shuffles off down the road toward a red-bricked railway bridge.

Leo points to a small white sign. "Hey, what does that say?"

They move closer. *Cankurtaran.*

Julia examines the map. "We've come too far."

They circle back until they find a street lined with bars and restaurants, most of which have outside seating sheltered beneath awnings decorated with fairy lights and hanging lamps. Clearly, the nightlife area. Most of the establishments are empty given the early hour; the only signs of life are the blinking big-screen TVs inside. Julia and Leo continue on and soon the bars and restaurants give way to buildings converted to hostels and guest houses. Julia stops outside one painted a strange shade of yellow. She tucks the map into her pocket and turns to Leo.

"Let me do the talking," she says and opens the door.

19

The hostel, aptly named The Hostel, is a little rundown with a pokey unmanned reception area. Definitely for travelers on a budget, Julia thinks, looking around at the drab décor. She's about to ring the service bell when a beautiful, long-limbed African American woman appears at the top of the staircase.

"Julia?" she says, with a slight southern accent. "I'm Yasmin."

Julia smiles at her. "I'm so sorry we're late, we got a little lost."

Yasmin shrugs an impossibly elegant shoulder. "It happens around here."

When Yasmin reaches the bottom of the stairs, there's an awkward pause because no one's quite sure whether to shake hands or embrace. Finally, Yasmin moves in for a quick cheek-to-cheek and squeeze of the arm, and does the same for Leo.

"There's a seating area on the roof. The others are up there already."

"Others?"

Yasmin nods, holding her hands loosely in front of her. "A group of us usually travel together. I thought you might want to speak to them, too."

"Oh, thank you. That would be very useful," says Julia.

They follow Yasmin up the stairs and through a wooden door, emerging on the rooftop. Leo whistles.

"I know, utterly beautiful, isn't it?" says Yasmin, gazing out at the spectacular view.

The Blue Mosque is so close that Julia can see the black webbing on the feet of the gulls circling the stone turrets. Beyond that, the beautiful sunlit waters of the Golden Horn sparkle between the dusty-orange terracotta rooftops and earthy-stone terraces. Julia has to agree with Yasmin: it's one of the most spectacular vistas she's ever seen.

She looks around at the rest of the rooftop. The seating area is the typical backpacker set-up with a mismatch of furniture—a few tables, fold-up chairs, and a couple of dingy couches. Over to the right, there's a trestle table with a water cooler and stainless-steel hot water dispenser, containers of instant coffee and tea to the left.

Four people, three women and one man, sit together on a sofa near a low table covered with a vinyl red gingham tablecloth. Yasmin introduces them to Julia and Leo. There's Conner, an Irish redhead with a pasty complexion. Sally, a short-haired Australian in cargo pants and red plaid shirt. Nicole, a lean, athletic Canadian eating sunflowers seeds from a ziplock bag. And Debbie, a short, plump woman from Norway.

Yasmin glances at the door. "And Daniel should be here soon. He didn't get in until late."

Leo and Julia take a seat opposite.

"Thank you so much for meeting us," says Julia. "I really appreciate you taking the time."

"We all knew Toni and want to help in any way we can," says Nicole, earnestly.

"Toni was such fun. *Is* such fun," says Debbie, unpeeling a wrapper from a granola bar and taking a bite. "She has this thing, you know, a gift, where she would hold us all spellbound whenever she'd tell us one of her crazy travel stories, but I'm sure you already know that, being her sister."

Sally rolls her eyes and reaches inside the front pocket of her shirt for a pack of cigarettes.

"Let's not deliver her eulogy just yet," says Sally, placing a cigarette between her lips. "Perhaps she just got sick of you lot."

"Gosh, Sal," says Nicole, eyes darting toward Julia and Leo. "You could show a bit more sensitivity."

Debbie chimes in. "Yes, we all need to keep a positive frame of mind. Send good vibes out into the universe."

"Kumbaya my Lord, someone's singing," groans Sally under her breath.

Julia catches Leo's eye and he returns her look. He's clocked the interesting group dynamic, too.

"So how did you all know Toni?" asks Julia.

Yasmin pushes back her fringe. "I met Toni six months ago in Thailand. Daniel and I had just come off a week-long elephant trek in Chiang Mai and were resting up in the hostel when we saw her—the cool girl with crazy hair playing pool in the common area. Toni and I got talking and realized we were both from the States."

"Is Daniel from the States, too?"

"Ha!" says Conner. "Don't let him hear you say that. That man has the Union Jack tattooed on his heart."

"Daniel's English," Yasmin explains, somewhat proudly.

Julia nods. "I see."

"Yeah, we're practically the United Nations of travelers," says Sally, wryly.

Yasmin takes a sip of her coffee before continuing, "Toni was heading to China, and so were Daniel and I, so she decided to join us."

"You get to know each other in hostels," explains Debbie. "You might decide to tag along then drop off when another place catches your eye, or you get work like a teaching gig or hospitality, in which case you'll stay behind to earn some money and organize to meet up again somewhere down the track in a few weeks' time."

Yasmin pushes her gold bracelet up her arm. "When Toni, Daniel, and I reached the Vietnam-China border there was a storm and dreadful flooding, so we found a rundown guest house and these guys were there."

"We were holed up in that flea pit for a week," says Debbie, munching.

"Come on, Debs, it wasn't that bad," says Nicole.

"Let's just say we got very good at playing mahjong."

Yasmin looks out at the view wistfully. "After the storm passed, we all got as far as Beijing, then some of us decided to go our separate ways and meet up in Istanbul to travel around Turkey together. Everyone agreed to meet up here in The Hostel by last Sunday."

"I had a friend who's an art major living in Beijing so I stayed there and flew into Turkey last Friday," says Nicole. "Debbie, Conner, and Sally wanted to go to Chengdu, you know, the panda place, so they left the group and arrived in Turkey last Saturday."

Sally stubs out her cigarette. "I do have a tongue, you know."

"Do you ever," says Conner.

"And you'll never know the pleasure of it, carrot top," she says, giving him the finger.

Yasmin looks at Julia and Leo. "I guess the point is that we were all supposed to be here by last Sunday, and all of us were, apart from Toni."

The door swings open.

"Hello there."

Julia looks up and feels herself redden. The tall dark-haired man standing in the doorway is very good-looking. In a casual sort of way. Wavy hair in need of a cut. Stubble. T-shirt and jeans. Capable and friendly. Daniel, she presumes.

Yasmin jumps up to greet him with a kiss. "Hey, babe. I thought it better to let you sleep." She threads her arm through his and turns to Julia and Leo. "This is Daniel Bambury. Daniel, this is Julia and Leo."

He shakes their hands.

"Any news?" he says, frowning.

"Nothing so far."

Daniel runs his hand over his handsome face. "Lord, you must be worried."

"Yes," says Julia. "Very. Yasmin, you were telling us about Toni?"

Yasmin nods, reclaiming her position on the sofa, this time with Daniel settling in beside her. "Toni wanted to have a look around Greece before meeting up in Turkey. Daniel and I were supposed to go with her but we had to pull out at the last minute."

"It was my fault," says Daniel. "I got a call-up for an orphanage in Bulgaria."

"Daniel's a doctor," says Yasmin, gazing up at him in adoration. "He works with kids, delivering vaccine programs with NGOs."

Daniel waves her off. "It's nothing. My job, that's all."

"Ah, such modesty," jokes Conner.

"Daniel has a strong humanitarian streak," says Yasmin. "But doesn't like to admit it."

He looks young for a doctor, Julia thinks. Even so, she can visualize him with his sleeves rolled up, white coat billowing out as he strides through the maze of refugee tents administering to sick infants.

"I went to Bulgaria with Daniel," says Yasmin. "We arrived in Istanbul last Sunday in time to meet everyone else. The only person not here was Toni."

"And she never checked in at reception?" asks Julia.

Yasmin shakes her head and starts getting emotional. "I honestly thought she'd got sidetracked in Greece but by Tuesday, I knew something wasn't right. No email, no Facebook, no Insta. Nothing. I mean Toni posted every day, multiple times a day." She blinks back tears. "That's when I contacted you."

The group falls silent.

"You must get close traveling together," says Leo.

"Yeah, you look out for each other. Share food, tampons, whatever," says Debbie.

"Have the police spoken to you yet?" asks Julia.

"They came yesterday," says Nicole. "Some old dude."

"Detective Muhtar," says Leo.

"Yeah, him."

"I'm not sure I trust the man," says Julia.

Sally picks a thread of stray tobacco off her tongue. "That's one thing you learn traveling—sometimes the systems aren't what you expect them to be. There's a lot of corruption in these countries. Everyone wants a cut. They think you're a rich tourist and don't understand you're traveling on a shoestring budget, eking out a stale loaf of bread to last for the week."

"That's for sure," says Conner. "You don't know how many US dollars I've had to slip in my passport just to cross a border legally."

"Yeah, money definitely talks," says Debbie, nodding.

"But you've got your consulate working on the matter, I take it?" says Daniel.

"Yes," says Julia. "But our representative made it clear the Turkish police are leading the investigation."

Daniel looks at her softly. "Julia, I'm sure I speak for everyone here when I say that if there's anything you need, anything at all, we'll do our utmost to help. We all love Toni and, like you, we're all praying she's found safe and sound."

"Hear, hear," says Conner.

"Absolutely," says Yasmin.

20

Julia and Leo leave the hostel and head back toward Sultanahmet Square.

"What do you think?" says Leo, sidestepping a stray cat.

Julia exhales. "I'm not sure."

"I don't like the look of that doctor," says Leo, pulling a face.

"Who? Daniel Bambury?"

Leo shoots Julia a sour glance. "Huh, thought so."

"Thought what?"

"He charmed you."

Julia laughs. "What?"

"You couldn't take your eyes off him."

Julia laughs again. "That's not true."

"Hanging on his every word."

Julia stops to face him. "I don't believe it, you're jealous."

"Bullshit," says Leo. "I'm just saying, don't be so easily fooled."

Julia carries on walking. "This is stupid. We're here to find Toni, not fight because of your sad little ego."

Leo looks away, jaw clenching. They fall silent and continue on up the pathway toward the mosques.

"At least we know more than we did before," Leo says, finally. "Effectively no one has seen Toni since China."

Julia purses her lips. "Or so they say."

Leo frowns. "What do you mean?"

"They could be making it all up, holding the line to an agreed story."

"What? Concocted a cover story? The whole lot of them?"

Julia nods. "It's possible. We can't trust them, Leo. We barely know them."

"But what would they have against Toni?"

"Oh, I don't know," says Julia, sighing deeply. "God, I feel so useless."

Leo touches her shoulder. It feels good. Reassuring. "Hey, don't give in to that. We're going to find her." He taps her satchel. "Now let's hand out these flyers and see what we can shake from the tree."

*

They focus on the shops and hotels in the Sultanahmet district first. Most of the owners are polite. Even with the language barrier, they can tell the seriousness of the situation. A foreign girl is missing, possibly the victim of foul play. They study the photo of Toni, taking in the unconventional hair, the septum piercing, the disarming smile. But time after time, they lift their gaze to meet Julia's expectant face and shake their heads no. Most agree to put a flyer in their windows, although a few refuse—displaying a photograph of a missing foreigner in Istanbul's prime tourist area isn't exactly good for business.

After five hours of exhausting leg work, Julia and Leo decide to head for the famous Grand Bazaar, an enormous covered market, before stopping for the night.

"Oh, Jesus," says Leo, stepping through the stone-arch entrance way.

The sheer scale of the place is dizzying. Rows of cluttered little shops, possibly thousands, overflow with all manner of things. Persian rugs. Turkish ceramics. Jewelry. Leather goods. Bolts of cloth. Luggage. Beaded slippers.

The bazaar is jammed packed full of people, too. Tourists. Locals. Shopkeepers. It's overwhelming and Julia feels her energy levels sag.

"You look beat. Maybe we should hit this tomorrow," says Leo.

Julia shakes her head. "I'm fine." She gestures left. "Let's start down there."

Shouldering their way through the bustling crowds, they navigate the labyrinth by focusing on one shop at a time, taking care to note each row as they go to avoid inadvertently missing a section. But it's impossible to cover every single one. There are simply too many. Two hours later, they're lucky to have covered even a third of the place.

Leo suggests they take a break and grab something to drink. They find an exit and step out into darkness.

"And day becomes night…" says Leo, looking up at the sky. "You could go an entire month in that place and never know it. Hey, over there."

Julia follows Leo's gaze and sees the café in an alcove filled with secondhand book shops. They go inside, buy some bottled water, and take a seat by the window.

"This is a total waste of time," says Julia, twisting off the bottle cap. "We've been at this all day and no one has seen her."

"Yeah, it's disappointing," says Leo. "We got lots of flyers distributed, though. That's a good thing. Someone might recognize her and get in touch."

"It seems like such a long shot," says Julia, glumly.

Leo gives her leg a shake. "Hang in there. We're doing all we can."

She looks down at her shoes. "It doesn't feel like enough."

"Oh, is that a challenge I hear?" says Leo, playfully. He guzzles down the last of his water and gets to his feet. "You asked for it then, Dr. Norris. One more hour and we'll call it a night."

21

Nearly out of flyers, they search for somewhere to print off more and manage to find a small supply shop with a lone photocopier for public use in one of the streets behind Istanbul University. Julia feeds the photocopier Turkish lire as it spits out a fresh ream of flyers. The color is slightly off, giving Toni a reddened complexion and turning her hair a nasty shade of chartreuse, but it's better than nothing.

By the time they step outside, most of the other shops have pulled down their grates for the night.

"Looks like we're calling it quits, whether we like it or not," says Leo.

They head through the dark and empty streets, passing by rows of closed shops. Behind dusty picture book windows are large cardboard boxes filled with buttons, belts and zippers, and stacks of clothes bundled with string.

"Where the heck are we?" says Julia, looking around.

"Garment district? Wholesalers maybe?" says Leo. "I think the hotel is this way."

Julia's doubtful. "You sure?"

He flashes her a smile. "Reasonably."

"Oh, I forgot how hilarious you are."

"And just getting better with age…"

They turn left and try to locate the main road with the overland tram. If they could just get a fix on that, they could follow the tracks back to their hotel or at least get a cab. They continue up the road toward a slight hill and turn the corner. There are more people and cars.

"We must be close to the main center," says Julia, encouraged.

They walk on and the crowd gets thicker.

"What the hell is that noise?" says Leo, halting.

They stand listening. Somewhere nearby people are chanting.

"Sounds like a protest," says Julia.

"Oh, boy," says Leo. "We don't want to get caught up in that." He grabs her hand. "Let's get out of here."

They cross the road, turn left, and halt.

"Holy shit," says Leo.

The street is filled with people, mostly young, waving flags, thrusting signs, thumping drums.

"I guess we can forget that cab."

Julia raises her voice over the racket. "I think they're heading for the Galata Bridge. Let's follow and see if we can make our way back to the hotel along the waterfront."

Julia and Leo weave in and out of the crowd, holding tight to each other's hand. The chanting and drumming grows louder, and Julia feels it reverberate inside the walls of her chest.

"Stick close!" Leo yells.

They half-jog through the throng. A girl no more than nineteen with the Turkish flag painted on her cheek grabs Julia's arm as they pass.

"The prime minister is in bed with terrorists!" she shouts.

Sirens flash up ahead. Stationary police cars and men in combat gear are lined up in front of a barrier blocking the Galata Bridge.

"Oh my God, Leo, guns!" shouts Julia.

The combat men are clutching heavy-duty weapons and look like they mean business. Suddenly, behind Julia and Leo there's a surge and they are catapulted forward into a mosh pit of angry politically charged youth, all pushing forward toward the bridge.

Leo pulls on her arm. "Jesus, Julia. We gotta get out of here."

"Wait!" Julia points into the crowd. "Isn't that Detective Muhtar? Has he been following us?"

Next to her, a guy with a goatee and lip piercing shakes her arm.

"Cover your face!" he shouts in broken English.

"What? Why?"

Julia watches with growing dread as the protesters pull bandanas and rags from their pockets and tie them around their heads covering their noses and mouths.

The goatee guy shoves a cut lemon and two rags into her hands.

"Put the lemon on the rag. It will help with gas."

But before Julia can do so, a volley of shots rings out from the bridge. Police are firing into the crowd. A hissing canister lands right by her foot.

"Leo, we've got to get out of here!" she yells.

But when Julia turns around, Leo isn't there. Her eyes begin to stream. She presses the rag to her face and tries to breathe. The protesters surge forward. Police shoot a warning round into the air. That's a live round, Julia thinks, they are actually shooting live rounds. Julia scrambles up some steps and frantically looks across the crowd for Leo. She calls out for him but her voice is lost in the chaos.

Police fire again and protesters scatter. Through blurred vision, Julia sees a white substance oozing from people's eyes. At first she's horrified, then she realizes it's milk, that people are pouring milk into each other's eyes. A sudden, hard push from behind and her satchel is torn from her shoulder. Flyers tumble out and quickly get trampled underfoot. She bends, reaching for the satchel, then feels a shove, an elbow in her back, between her lower two vertebrae, and she's pushed to the ground hard and fast.

The stone step hurtles toward her and everything goes black.

22

Julia blinks awake. She's back home in her apartment, safe in her own bed. But something isn't right. Groggy, she lifts her head, wincing from the pain in the back of her neck. She looks around. She's in bed, dressed in a hospital gown. The night before comes back in a rush. The protest. The tear gas. The foul-smelling smoke. She sputters a cough and plunges a knuckle into her suddenly watery eye.

"How are you feeling?"

She squints at the figure in the doorway. Two figures. Detective Muhtar and Christine Fletcher.

Detective Muhtar has a plaster above his right eye. A memory shudders into place.

"You were following us," says Julia, sitting up.

He doesn't say anything.

Julia turns to Christine Fletcher. "Did you know about this?"

"Detective Muhtar helped you," says Christine. "It's lucky he was there at all. Things could have been much, much worse, Julia. Believe me."

"You mean I should be grateful he was spying on us?" says Julia, throwing off the blanket. "This is unbelievable."

She swings her feet out of bed, sways precariously. Detective Muhtar catches her before she falls.

"Get your hands off me."

Then she remembers Leo. Her eyes dart to Christine. "Where's Leo?"

Christine holds up a hand. "Leo's fine. Just a nasty bang to the cranium. A few stitches. Nothing serious."

Julia lowers herself to the edge of the bed, exhaling.

Detective Muhtar looks at her. "You want to help. This is understandable. But you must let police do their jobs. This type of thing diverts resources from the investigation."

Julia stands and this time she's prepared for the rolling wave of nausea and remains steady on her feet. She reaches for her clothes folded on a chair.

"If we were back home people would be tying yellow ribbons around lamp posts and doing ground searches."

"Please, Dr. Norris, you must rest," says Detective Muhtar, hovering close.

"Detective Muhtar's right," says Christine. "Your concussion could be serious. You need to be cleared by the doctor before you go anywhere."

Julia pulls on her jeans. "Oh, that would suit you perfectly, wouldn't it? Problem sister kept out of the way."

Christine shakes her head. "It isn't like that, Julia. Believe it or not, I do understand what you're going through."

Julia pulls on her sweater. "Oh, you have no idea."

Christine pauses. "I lost my husband in the World Trade Center. It took two months to confirm he was in the number two tower."

Julia stops what she's doing and looks at Christine. "Oh God, I'm so sorry. That is truly terrible."

Christine looks at her wedding ring. "Yes, it is, and that's why I do what I do. Working as a diplomat in places like Turkey opens up lines of communication between countries, fosters relationships and builds bridges. It helps keep Americans safe from other attacks like 9/11." She pauses. "Julia, we've been doing some background checks on Toni."

Julia feels heat rise in her cheeks.

"You should've told us."

"What background checks?" says Julia, heart thumping.

"It serves no purpose to pretend. We're not here to judge," says Christine, kindly.

Julia lowers herself onto the bed. "It's not an easy thing to talk about."

"I can't imagine that it would be."

"Toni was always into everything, even as a kid. After the early life we had, it wasn't exactly a surprise she turned to drugs."

"Heroin?"

Julia nods. "And the rest. Three years ago she stayed with me and Leo. Got clean. She doesn't use anymore." Julia looks at them. "I know what you're thinking, but Toni wouldn't get caught up in drug trafficking."

"Addiction can make a person do unthinkable things," says Christine.

"I told you already, Toni was clean."

"We don't know that."

"So that's it?" says Julia, throwing up her hands. "You're going to stop looking now that you think Toni is just some junkie?"

"No one is saying that," says Christine. "It gives us other lines of inquiries to explore, that's all."

Julia feels her eyes water but manages to hold it back. "Don't give up on her. Toni's a good person. She needs us to keep looking."

Detective Muhtar bends down, picks up Julia's shoes, and holds them out for her.

"And we will," he says.

*

Leo's in slightly worse shape than Julia. A heavy-duty plaster and gauze are stuck to his forehead. There's also a nasty black bruise on his left cheek that must hurt like hell. Julia waits for him to get dressed, turning to look out the window of his hospital room as he disrobes.

"What a night," he says. "I feel like I've been hit by a bus."

"They know about Toni."

"Oh."

"Yeah."

Leo slips on his shoes. "It was bound to come out in the end."

"They'll stop looking now."

"They won't. They have a duty to locate her. We'll keep on at them, ramp up the pressure. Go to the media if we have to."

He joins her at the window, taps the bandage on his head, checks the pads of his fingers for blood.

"I could use a hot shower," he says. "Let's go back to the hotel, get a change of clothes, grab something to eat, and regroup."

Julia doesn't move.

"Julia?"

She wipes a tear from her eye.

"Hey," Leo places a hand on her shoulder. "It'll be all right. You'll see. We'll find her."

"I turned my back on her, Leo, when she came to me for help. You were the one who convinced me she could do it. And she did. Toni got clean. You were right."

"It was a team effort."

Julia stiffens and pulls away, remembering that wasn't the end of the story.

"We should go," she says.
Then her cell phone begins to ring.

23

They head out, turning left through the wrought iron gates of Gulhane Park and up the winding pathway that dissects the park in two. It's a lovely space, shrouded by towering cypress trees and the pale stone walls of the Topaki Palace, the former residence of the Ottoman sultans, now a museum. Given it's mid-morning, the park is busy with locals strolling along the winding pathways. Older thick-waisted women with colorful headscarves tied under their chins talk loudly together as they walk, while here and there, gray-haired men sit on wooden benches dotted around the park, twirling worry beads and contemplating the pleasant morning in silence.

"Any sign of her?" says Leo, looking around.

"She said to meet her by the statue of Ataturk."

They keep going, past a fountain and a lone gardener turning over soil in a flowerbed, and locate the bronze statue of Turkey's former president. Sally is there, dressed in the same plaid shirt and army fatigue cargo pants as the day before.

"Not here," she says, pushing herself off the squat cinderblock wall.

Leo and Julia follow her out the park gates, up the main street, and into a bustling teahouse. The place is crammed floor to ceiling with enormous glass jars filled with all sorts of exotic spices, most of which Julia would have trouble naming, apart from one jar near the counter that contains the distinctive flame-colored threads of saffron.

Sally nods at a table near the back corner. "Take a seat over there. I'll order us coffee."

They do as she says and it's not long before Sally returns carrying a kebab rolled up in a paper napkin.

"Coffee will be here in a bit," she says, sitting down. She holds out the pita. "Want some?"

Leo and Julia both shake their heads.

"Suit yourselves," Sally says, chomping into the doughy pita. She looks at Leo. "What happened to your head?"

He reaches up to touch the plaster. "We were caught up in the protests."

"You're lucky you didn't get shot," says Sally, chewing. "The police around here aren't exactly shy about testing out their machinery on the general population."

The coffee arrives. Leo takes a mouthful and gasps. "God, I think my heart's about to explode."

Sally grins, lobbing the last of the kebab into her mouth. "They say that once you have Turkish coffee, you'll never go back."

"You said you have some information?" says Julia.

Sally nods, using a paper napkin to wipe the yogurt dripping down her arm. "I do." She pauses, looking from Julia to Leo and back again. "Don't trust Yasmin."

Julia's surprised. "What's Yasmin got to do with this?"

"There's something off with her. We really had to push her into reporting Toni missing. She kept delaying, saying we'll give it another day, until finally I put my foot down and told her to make the bloody call. Embassy first, you second."

"Why was Yasmin given the job of reporting it?" asks Leo.

Sally looks at him like the answer is obvious. "She's a Yank. Toni's a Yank. It made sense for her to do it."

"How do you know Yasmin wasn't being genuine trying to hold off for a few days?" says Julia.

"I think there was some bad blood between Yasmin and Toni. When I heard her yesterday telling you they were bosom buddies, all teary-eyed, I could have puked. They were friends at first, it's impossible not to like Toni, you know that, but something happened out there on the road. I don't know what, but something definitely went down. They were barely talking to each other at one point."

"You must have some idea," pushes Julia.

Sally shrugs. "Nothing I can prove."

"Humor us," says Leo.

She pauses. "Maybe Toni got too close to Daniel."

"Yasmin's boyfriend Daniel?"

"Don't get me wrong, Danno's a nice guy, but he has a tendency to go for the injured bird thing and Toni had injured bird written all over her."

Julia feels herself tense. "You think Toni was sleeping with Daniel?"

Sally shrugs. "I don't know for sure. But if she was, you can bet your boots that Yasmin would be spitting about it. I'm not sure if you noticed but she's a little possessive when it comes to her darling Daniel."

Julia tells herself to relax, but there's no denying the anger she's feeling for Toni right now.

"But you have no proof, right?" says Leo, shifting uncomfortably in his seat. "What you're saying is just a guess?"

Shut up, Leo, Julia wants to say. Just shut up and don't make it worse.

Sally exhales. "Like I said before, I don't know for sure."

Julia puts down her coffee cup and looks at Sally. "So your thinking is that Yasmin may have had something to do with Toni's disappearance because Toni was having a relationship with Daniel behind Yasmin's back?"

Sally places her hands on the table and spreads them out. "Look, I want to be straight with you guys, I've never got on with Yasmin. I've always thought she was a stuck-up rich bitch. Daddy is some academic bigwig at Brown University, Mommy's a judge, and I'm pretty sure there's a mansion in Rhode Island somewhere in there, too. But Yasmin likes to pretend she's just one of the gang, eating instant noodles, scraping a few dollars together for a bed, getting down with the peeps, but everyone knows her parents pay her AMEX every month. There's something in her past, too. I remember Toni telling me that Yasmin was involved in some incident in college and left America right after."

"Did Toni say what it was about?"

Sally shakes her head. "Toni felt bad for even telling me that much. She didn't like to stab people in the back." Sally shoots them a smile. "As you can see, I don't have that particular problem."

"Was Toni on drugs?" Leo asks suddenly.

Julia stiffens. "Jesus, Leo."

Sally shakes her head. "Toni didn't touch the stuff. She told me about being hooked in the past. She didn't even smoke weed anymore. Which is no mean feat in the backpacking lifestyle."

Sally gets to her feet. "That's all I got. I just wanted you to know before I left."

Julia's startled. "You're leaving? But you need to tell the police what you've told us."

Sally shakes her head. "No way. I don't do cops. Besides, I need to grab my gear at the hostel before my bus leaves for Egypt."

"Come with us to see Christine Fletcher from the embassy then," implores Julia. "We'll make sure you're back in time for your bus."

Sally holds up her hands. "Sorry. No can do."

"Please, Sally. We've got so little to go on."

Sally gives Julia a sympathetic look. "I really hope you find Toni. I like her. But I'm not getting involved." She shoulders her bag. "Good luck."

With that said, she walks out the door.

24

Google is the obvious choice so both Leo and Julia return to the hotel business center, a room the size of a broom cupboard housing two ancient desktop computers complete with tube monitors.

"Can't you just use your phone?" says Leo, blowing dust off the keyboards.

Julia shakes her head. "I hate doing internet searches on such a tiny screen. It hurts my eyes."

Thankfully, the desktop still works and it's not long before Julia has success.

The first link is to a newspaper article about Yasmin mother's election as a state supreme court judge. Accompanying the article is a photo of Yasmin and her mother and father, taken in an exquisite rose garden outside what could only be described as a mansion.

Leo whistles. "Not short of a buck then."

The second link is about Yasmin's father, a dean at Brown University, receiving some prestigious medal for his work in physics. There's a small photo of Yasmin and her mother sitting in the front row of the ceremony.

"Providence, Rhode Island, country club all the way," says Leo. "No brothers and sisters, just Yasmin and her four-poster bed and wisteria balcony."

Julia scrolls down the page. She stops when she sees a link. *Dean's daughter implicated in freshman's suicide.*

"Huh," says Leo, peering at the screen over her shoulder. "That looks interesting."

Julia clicks on the link and they sit reading. Yasmin had outed a nineteen-year-old freshman as a lesbian. As a result, the Idaho native, who came from a devout Christian family, had thrown herself off the fifth floor of the chemical lab. The article included vitriolic Facebook postings about the young woman's sexuality all traced back to Yasmin and her sorority sisters. What was worse, though, was that Yasmin, the head of the sorority, had deliberately befriended the young woman only to later expose her in what Yasmin had described in reports as a "prank." Yasmin had secretly filmed the young woman in an encounter with another girl then posted it online. Yasmin escaped criminal charges but was expelled.

"That's pretty cruel stuff," says Julia, printing off the article. "If Yasmin can do that, who knows what else she might be capable of."

Leo's doubtful. "I don't know, Julia. It's a big leap to say she's involved in Toni's disappearance."

"At the very least, it shows form, don't you think, Leo? Besides, it's the best lead we've got."

Julia does a search on Facebook for Yasmin, but her page is set to private. Daniel's comes up though. He's smiling in his Facebook profile.

"Ah, the good doctor," says Leo.

Julia scrolls through his timeline. There are shares of posts about UNICEF, Doctors Without Borders, the World Wildlife Fund. Fun photos of him eating tarantulas in Cambodia, deep fried crickets in Laos, and tossing laughing kids into the air in a remote Northern Vietnam village. There's a photo of Toni that Julia hasn't seen before. She looks happy. Her blue eyes are bright and healthy. The slight hint of sunburn on her shoulders. In the caption below, Daniel had written: *Please help us find our friend. Toni Norris went missing on September 29th. Any information please contact the Turkish police or get in touch with me.*

Leo tugs on her arm. "Julia."

She looks up and follows his gaze to the door. Christine Fletcher and Detective Muhtar are standing there, both looking somber. Julia's chest tightens.

Her chair scrapes against the floor as she stands. "What is it?"

Christine steps into the room. "You might want to sit for this, Julia."

Julia's heart crashes in her ears. "Is it Toni? Have you found her?"

Christine's eyes shift to Leo, recruiting an ally.

He touches her arm. "Julia, why don't you do what Christine says and sit down for a minute."

Julia stands completely still and stares at Christine. "Just tell me."

Christine exhales, her expression solemn. "We found a body and we think it's Toni."

25

A body. The words clang, off-kilter, inside Julia's head. She's half aware of Leo behind her, guiding her into the armless chair. She wants to push him away, tell him she's not a child, but she can't speak.

"A restaurant worker was dumping lard illegally after hours when he found the body in the drain." Julia tries to focus on what Christine Fletcher is saying. "We came right away."

Then Christine stops. As if there's nothing left to say.

Julia feels their eyes on her, wishes she was any place but here. Imagines she's back at the hospital and the buzz of a triple bypass surgery when she doesn't have room to think about anything but the patient's heart pulsating in her hand.

"In a drain? How is that even possible?" she says.

Christine Fletcher has no answer. Julia wonders if she's had to do this before. Inform a US citizen of a relative's death. She wonders whether there are embassy courses or workshops with role plays for delivering such terrible news.

"Where was she found?" says Leo.

"Taksim," says Detective Muhtar. "On the other side of Galata Bridge."

Leo frowns. "Why would Toni be all the way over there?"

"We don't know," says Christine.

"But you think it's her?"

"Everything fits. We'll know for certain when we run DNA."

"Where is it now? The body, I mean," says Julia.

"The hospital morgue."

Julia stands. "I want to see it."

Detective Muhtar shakes his head. "Not possible."

"I'm her next of kin."

"The body's in no condition for a viewing, Julia," says Christine, softly. "She's been submerged for days and the rodents…well, to put it bluntly, the face is a mess."

Julia feels sick. She stares at the gold medal encased in a Perspex square hanging on the wall. The Golden Horn Hotel won best budget hotel of the year in 1988.

"But we don't know for sure it's her, correct? Until the DNA checks out?" Julia says.

"That's right. But I think you should prepare yourself. Everything fits that it's Toni. I'm sorry to be blunt but I don't want to offer you false hope," says Christine.

"When will the DNA be processed?"

Detective Muhtar speaks up. "A week to ten days."

Julia's shocked. "You expect us to wait that long? No, that's absolutely not okay. I want to see the body, maybe I can identify the clothes or something." She looks at Christine. "Can you take me to the morgue?"

Christine doesn't answer.

"Please, Christine. She's my sister. I need to do this."

26

They drive in silence. Julia stares numbly out the window as the local population goes about their ordinary day in their ordinary clothes living their ordinary lives. Julia wonders if any of them ever had to bury a sister.

"I'm so sorry, Julia," says Leo. He's been quiet since the hotel. Hurting too.

Julia can't speak. It's taking all her effort to not simply fall to pieces. All she can offer him is a solitary nod of acknowledgment as she continues to stare out the window. She shuts her eyes and the awful image of a coffin being rolled into the cargo hold of a plane comes to her. She imagines sitting in the airplane cabin, the other passengers oblivious to the fact that in the undercarriage beneath them lay a dead body, her sister's dead body. She feels sick at the thought.

She takes a breath and tells herself to relax. Not yet. Don't go there yet, not until we know for sure it's her. After all, it could all be one giant mistake.

They reach a monolithic building and drive directly into the underground car park, get out, and take the lift to the basement. When the lift door opens, they're faced with a narrow corridor lit with ugly fluorescent lighting. At the end of the corridor is wall-to-wall glass, behind that the morgue.

Julia's palms begin to sweat.

"How are you doing?" asks Leo.

"Okay."

He squeezes her hand, then lets it fall away. They carry on, following Detective Muhtar and Christine up the corridor, stopping when they reach the end. Behind the glass the area is divided into two distinct sections. On the left side, the entire back wall is made up of stainless-steel cubby holes with drawers like an industrial filing cabinet. On each door is a padlock.

To the right is what appears to be the area where they carry out the autopsies. There's a hose on a reel in a corner for washing away blood and other bodily fluids through the narrow drains that run lengthwise across the room. Even from behind the glass, there's the faint scent of cleaning solvent.

Julia's eyes fall on the lone stainless-steel gurney. There's a body in a cadaver bag on top. It hits her then, really hits her, that the body in the bag could be Toni.

"I want to go in and see her," says Julia.

Christine shakes her head. "I can't let you do that. Like it or not, Toni's body is evidence now. Besides, you'll never recover."

"Christine's right," says Leo, gently.

Julia can tell by the tone of his voice that he's crying. But she doesn't turn to look. She can't cope with that right now.

"I need to be with her."

Julia feels a hand on her shoulder, Christine's. "We should head back to the hotel. Give you some time to rest, take it all in."

Julia doesn't move. She can't tear her eyes away from the body bag. All she can think is how final this is, and that there is nothing she can do to fix it. Suddenly she finds herself lunging for the door and pulling on the handle.

She's surprised how easy it opens, how easy it is to slip inside and shut the door tight behind her before the others can get in. Just below the handle there's a turn lock and she flicks it closed.

On the other side of the glass, the others stand looking at her in stunned disbelief. She quickly turns away, ignoring their warbling voices, the thumping on the door. She faces the gurney and her hands begin to shake. She wants to be sick. But she has to do this, she has to see, has to be sure. Julia steps forward and unzips the bag to the sternum. Glimpses red and yellow cloth. A T-shirt filthy with blood and dirt. Torn at the breasts. Flesh as gray as a fava bean. Oh, Toni.

Behind her a rattle on the door, a key in a lock.

Julia keeps going. Even though it hurts, she keeps going. She unzips the bag right down to the hips and spreads the canvas apart. Her hand flies to her mouth. The face is nothing but a cave. The hair, red and bloody. Missing ears, too.

She forces herself to keep looking. But there's no way to know from the face whether it's Toni or not. Julia steps closer, toward the end of the gurney, near the feet. She touches the left leg and lifts it up. The weight of it sickens her in a way she isn't expecting. She nearly gives up and walks away. Instead she swallows down her fear. She has to do this. She has to know it's not a mistake. She lifts the leg higher, checks behind the knee, lowers it.

When she turns, Leo, Christine Fletcher, and Detective Muhtar are there, the door wide open behind them.

"It's not Toni," she says.

"What do you mean?" exclaims Leo, eyes darting to the body. "Are you sure?"

"There's no strawberry birthmark behind the knee."

"Toni has a birthmark?" says Christine.

Leo nods. "Shaped like a clover. Big, about the size of a fist."

Christine frowns. "You never mentioned that before."

Julia's legs are shaking. "You put us through that for nothing."

Christine's lost for words. "Julia, I'm sorry, I don't know how this happened."

But Julia doesn't believe her.

27

Julia and Leo stand outside the hotel entrance as Detective Muhtar pulls away in his dented Fiat.

"Do you want to talk?" says Leo.

"I'm fine."

"No, you're not. How could you be? That was as traumatic as hell."

She looks at him. The bruise on his forehead has turned a nasty shade of gray.

"That looks sore," she says. "Do you need pain relief? There's ibuprofen in my suitcase."

Leo crosses his arms. "Don't do that."

"Do what?"

"Dodge my question."

She squints at the sky. "Yes, all right," she says. "For a minute, I did think it was Toni and it wasn't very nice."

She considers telling him about her gut feeling that something is off with Christine Fletcher but she doesn't have anything concrete so decides to keep it to herself for now.

She glances over her shoulder. "I need to get some air, walk around for a bit."

"I'll come with you."

"I'd rather be on my own."

Leo jams his hands in his pockets. "Suit yourself." He turns to go inside the hotel but changes his mind. "You always do this," he says.

"Do what?"

"Freeze me out."

"I'm not freezing you out."

"Aren't you?" he says. "Have you ever thought that sharing how you feel might actually help?"

"You're blowing things out of proportion."

He shakes his head, exasperated. "You don't trust me, I get that, God knows you've made that crystal clear, but holding things in isn't healthy either."

Julia feels a sudden burst of anger. "Are you sick of this, Leo? Is that it? You want to go back to your comfortable life? Missing your power tools and Monday night football?"

He shakes his head. "You're not listening, Julia."

She raises her voice, knows she should stop but can't. "You're here to soothe your own conscience, Leo, nothing more. We both know that's how you operate. Face it. You look after number one and always have."

Leo bangs his fist into his palm. "One time, Julia. One mistake. Years ago. It cost me my marriage. Are you going to hold it against me for the rest of my life?"

Julia bites her lip.

"I'm tired of this," she says, walking away.

"Where are you going?" he calls after her.

"Like you care."

"For Pete's sake, Julia."

"Go to hell, Leo."

It feels good, making him suffer.

*

Julia moves through the narrow streets at a fast clip, doing her best to ignore the tightness in her chest. She chides herself for losing control. Emotion had hijacked her usual self-restraint, and the mean and petty words spilled from her mouth before she could stop them.

She turns right, and men with mustaches selling leather jackets and Turkish rugs call out to her with their best offers. Ignoring them, she carries on, stopping to buy a drink from a vendor wearing a T-shirt stained with pomegranate juice. She cracks open the bottle and takes a mouthful. Cold. Wet. It makes her feel better. She sits on a bench shaded by an olive tree where two dogs are playing rough and tumble on the grassy area in front of her. Strays. White coats dirty and gray. Thin but fed.

She watches them. She can't remember the last time she'd had fun like that. Maybe with Leo a few years ago and the jet boat ride he surprised her with for her birthday. The freezing water nearly blistered her skin, but she'd never felt so exhilarated. Then Toni came back, gaunt and bedraggled, begging for help, and everything changed.

At the time, Julia couldn't quite put her finger on it. There was something different but she didn't know what. She began noticing little things. For instance, whenever she walked into a room, Toni and Leo would somehow always be on opposite sides. And the times the three of them ate together, Toni and Leo would never look at each other. There was also the incident when Toni tripped over the rug in the kitchen and fell to the floor and Leo didn't go to help her up.

Then one day they both came to her.

"We need to talk," said Toni more serious than Julia had ever seen her before.

At the time, a myriad of things had popped into Julia's head. Another debt? Criminal charges? A relapse? Then Julia realized they were both looking at her like she had cancer and didn't know it.

"I can't do this," Leo had said, turning to leave.

Toni stopped him. "Leo, she deserves to know the truth."

Julia had shaken her head, confused. "What truth? What the heck are you two talking about?"

Toni grabbed Julia's hand with tears in her eyes. "We made a mistake. A terrible mistake. You have to forgive us."

Then the shoe finally dropped. The two people Julia loved most in the world had betrayed her in the worst possible way. A three-month affair right under her nose.

Thinking about it now, she feels sick, all those months of pain she endured, the heartbreak she never thought she'd get over, how goddamn stupid she had felt. Julia lifts her head and watches one of the stray dogs bound over to a stranger holding out a chunk of bread. She wishes she could be like that dog, living from one moment to the next, no betrayals from the past to hold her back. She stays there a while longer, thinking about how emotional wounds run so much deeper than physical ones and how they could ruin your life if you let them.

28

It's growing dark by the time Julia returns to the hotel. The foyer is empty and Ada is nowhere to be seen, despite her playing cards being laid out in their familiar pyramid pattern on the glass-topped coffee table. Julia heads for the elevator, halting when she spots Leo glued to a computer screen in the business center.

She steps into the doorway. "Leo, I want to put it behind us."

He looks over his shoulder. "Oh, hi."

"I mean it," she says.

"Okay."

"I'm sick of thinking about it," she says.

He turns around to look at her properly. "I don't know how many times you want me to say I'm sorry, Julia."

Every day for the rest of your life, she thinks. But she bites her tongue.

"Losing you was the worst thing that ever happened to me and I'm sorry I hurt you," he says.

She knows he means it, but it still doesn't help.

"It happened and it hurt but there's nothing we can do about it now so let's just move on."

"Julia."

She turns away. "I don't want to talk about it anymore."

Leo presses his lips together and gives her a perfunctory nod. "If that's what you want."

She looks at the computer screen. "What are you doing in here anyway?"

"Research."

"Research?"

"I might have found something." He hands her a stack of printouts. "I did a search on missing women in Turkey. What Christine Fletcher says is true. Organized crime syndicates are active in the area as far as human trafficking is concerned, women in particular, but also kids. It's possible that Toni could have been taken by one of the groups. She's pretty, still young enough to be a money earner, and although Sally said that Toni was off drugs, we both know there's also a chance she wasn't, which means Toni could've been in contact with some unsavory types. On the other hand, the kidnapping of an American tourist for the purposes of white slavery is rare. These syndicates tend to target and recruit girls from Eastern Europe and Asia. They trick the girls into coming abroad to work as models or hostesses, which is probably exactly what happened to thar poor girl back there in the morgue. And the dumping of Toni's backpack…it just doesn't feel right. Her money and passport were still in there and the kidnappers like to hold onto passports as a way to control the girls."

"So no to a white slavery kidnapping?"

Leo nods. "Yeah, I think it's unlikely."

"What then?"

He clicks open a tab. "I found this. I'm not sure it means anything."

He leans back and lets Julia read. The news article is from an online Turkish newspaper report three years ago. An unsolved rape of a western woman in Istanbul. Barely a one-liner.

"I did another search and pulled up four more cases, again small mentions, two a year. The last rape was three months ago."

"You think Toni could have been taken by a serial rapist?"

"Who knows? There may be no connection but at the moment anything's possible." He lifts a piece of paper. "I sent an email to the reporter pretending to be another journalist asking for her to get back to us."

Julia's pleased and she's about to suggest they search for the journalist's telephone number so they can contact her directly when Julia's cell phone rings. She looks at the screen. Local number. She picks up.

"Julia speaking."

The male voice on the other end is muffled, like he's walking against the wind. There's a thick Turkish accent, too. Julia can barely make him out. She manages to catch three words. *Information. Missing. Girl.*

Julia shoots Leo a hopeful look. "You have information about Toni Norris?"

"Yes." The line is clearer now. "Best information. You come to Karakoy. One hour."

"Karakoy? Where's that?"

Leo frowns, shakes his head no. He points to the floor and mouths. "Hotel. Here."

"Can you come to my hotel instead?" says Julia.

"No hotel. We meet on Karakoy only."

Julia shakes her head at Leo.

"Let me speak to him," whispers Leo, holding out his hand for the phone.

Julia turns her back on him and faces the poster of Anzac Cove in Gallipoli.

“Okay, we’ll come to you.” She hears Leo curse behind her. “Where exactly in Karakoy do you want to meet?”

The line goes silent and for one anxious moment Julia thinks she has lost him. Then she realizes he’s put his hand over the phone and is talking to someone else. He comes back on the line and gives her an address. A place by the waterfront. She repeats it back to him and Leo writes it down.

“How will I know who you are?” she says.

“Come alone,” he says and hangs up.

29

Istanbul's overland tram system, Julia is quickly learning, is efficient, reliable, and the best way to get around. The tram, which looks more like a highspeed modern Japanese bullet train than the old-fashioned trolley trams she's used to back in San Francisco, appear at regular ten-minute intervals and stop in the main areas, including over the Galata Bridge to Karakoy, where she and Leo need to go.

After changing some Turkish lire into orange plastic tokens at the self-service vending machine, Julia and Leo squeeze into the full tram. Julia stands near a young Japanese guy in a Cure T-shirt, working his way through a tube of strawberry Mentos. She keeps a close eye on the LED screen displaying the name of each approaching stop. There are four stops before they need to disembark and Julia doesn't want to make a mistake and end up miles from where they are supposed to be.

She glances at Leo, who's wedged between an overweight teenage girl and a middle-aged woman laden with grocery bags. He looks tired. They both are. She's heading into a third night without proper sleep and she can feel her skull shrinking around her brain by the minute. She knows they should both rest, especially after last night's drama with the protests and the knocks to the heads they had taken, but she has to keep going for Toni. With any luck, this caller might just have what they need for a breakthrough.

She knows Leo is doubtful. Earlier at the hotel, he'd made it clear he didn't think it was a good idea to meet the man.

"How do you know it's not some sort of scam?" Leo had said.

"We don't. But we don't know it's not either, and that's why we put the flyers up, isn't it? To get information?"

"We should call Christine Fletcher or Detective Muhtar and let them handle it."

"No."

"Why not?"

She deflected, not yet ready to share her misgivings about Christine Fletcher. "We'll tell them afterward if we get any worthwhile information."

"You're a doctor, Julia, not an investigator. It could be dangerous."

"We'll let Ada know our plans. If we're not back by eleven p.m., she can call Detective Muhtar and give him our location."

But when Julia told Ada where they were going and why, Ada looked concerned.

"You should not go there."

Leo had crossed his arms. "That's what I said, but she won't listen to me."

Ada looked serious. "Bad area of Istanbul. Very unsafe."

Julia felt her gut clench. "I understand, Ada, and thank you for your concern, but we'll be careful and I still think it's worth the risk. We're all assuming the caller has bad intentions, but what if he doesn't? What if he has critical information that leads to Toni? I'm not passing up that opportunity. Leo, you have every right to stay here if you want. The choice is entirely yours."

He studied her face. "You're killing me here, Julia."

In the end, he gave in and came with her and she was grateful. She hadn't relished facing this unknown caller on her own.

Julia bends to look out the window as the tram crosses the Galata Bridge, busy with traffic and pedestrians at this time of night. Julia pushes her way through the crowded carriage until she reaches Leo.

"We need to get off at the next stop."

When the tram pulls into the platform, they disembark. Most of the other passengers get off here too and Julia and Leo stand watching as the crowd heads uphill.

"What's up there?" says Leo.

Julia looks at the map. "It must be the open-air mall called Istiklal Caddesi. We, on the other hand, need to go left." She glances up. "Down there," she says, pointing.

Leo hesitates. "Are you sure about this, Julia?"

"With you here to protect me, Leo, what have I got to worry about?"

He looks at her then gives her a playful pinch. "Funny girl."

"Come on, we don't want to be late."

Julia and Leo cross the road and dip down into a street lined with pokey little hardware shops closed for the night. Julia glances at the dusty windows as they walk. There's a huge variety of items sorted separately into individual timber crates ready to be wheeled out in front of the shops the next morning. Steel faucets. Bike pedals. Nails and screws. Hammers. Kitchen sinks. Steel tubing. Showerheads. Light sockets. Door handles.

Given it's not a residential area and the businesses are shut, the streets are almost empty, apart from a few men talking and smoking outside on the curbs. Julia looks down at her phone. They need to make a turn somewhere ahead but Google Maps is struggling to account for the little alleyways and no-name streets.

Julia enlarges the screen and tries to get a fix on their location.

"This way," she says.

They turn right, down what could hardly be called a road. There's no street lighting so Julia takes care navigating the bumpy, unsealed pathway using her phone light to illuminate the ground as they go. They emerge in a tiny postage stamp of a park overlooking the old side of Istanbul. Across the water, the mosques in the old quarter are bathed in golden light, their silhouettes glimmering on the surface of Bosporus.

In contrast, the park is dark and utterly empty. Just over the squat sea wall, there's a clutch of small fishing boats. The tide is out and the boats are half-resting on the rocks, hulls exposed, ropes creaking against their wooden moorings. The stench of discarded fish is strong.

"You sure this is it?" says Leo, looking around.

Julia points to the EXXON tanker. "He said he'd meet us over there."

They cross the patch of dead grass and stand next to the tanker and wait.

30

"I feel like a sitting duck," says Leo.

Julia looks at her watch. "He should be here by now."

"Try calling the number."

She does. No answer.

"I don't like this," says Leo.

Julia feels nervous, too. Considers abandoning the whole thing. Then remembers they've got nothing else to go on.

"A few more minutes."

A man appears from the laneway. Tall and lanky. Dark-haired and unshaven. Younger than Julia had been expecting. He makes a beeline for them, glancing once over his shoulder before cutting across the dead grass.

"This doesn't look kosher," says Leo.

"Let's see what he has to say first."

When the man reaches them, his dull eyes land on Leo.

"You police?" he says. "I don't like police."

Julia shakes her head. "He's my friend. Leo. I'm Julia. The girl in the flyer is my sister, Toni, and we're all very worried about her. Anything you can tell us would be of great help, no matter how small."

The man thrusts his hands into the pockets of his dirty denim jacket.

"Money first," he says.

"Money?" says Leo. "You said nothing about money on the phone. Did he, Julia?"

The man's eyes harden. He scratches the inside of his elbow.

"I am student," he says. "Tuition is very expensive."

"You're no student," growls Leo. He turns to Julia. "Let's get out of here. This guy's a scam artist."

Julia ignores Leo. "Of course we'll pay you for your time."

"Julia, don't be an idiot. He could make anything up."

Julia gets out her wallet. "How much do you need? A hundred dollars?"

"Two hundred," says the man, wetting his lips. "US."

Julia counts out the bills. "Here's two hundred fifty dollars."

The man reaches for it. Leo grabs his wrist. "Give us something first. So we know you really saw Toni."

The man stares at Leo, then spits on the ground.

He points to his own wrist. "Tattoo. Here."

"That's Toni," says Julia, mouth instantly dry.

"What's the tattoo?" presses Leo.

The man frowns. "I don't know how to say."

Leo rolls his eyes. "I bet you don't."

The man's face suddenly clears and he makes the victory sign with his fingers. Julia's heart leaps. She looks at Leo, who is also surprised. They both know that Toni had a peace sign tattoo done the day she turned eighteen. Leo releases his grip and the man slips the money into his front jeans pocket.

"Where did you see her?" says Julia.

"At a club last Saturday night."

Saturday. Nine days ago.

"What club?"

"Asena."

"Where's that?"

"Istiklal Caddesi, near the mall."

"What time was she there? Did you speak to her? How did she seem to you? What was she doing?"

The man pauses. "That's all."

"What do you mean—that's all?" says Julia.

"I know nothing else."

Julia's throat tightens. "But if you saw her, you must remember the time." Julia fumbles with her wallet. "Do you want more money, is that it?"

The man shifts on his feet. "No more questions."

Julia looks at the man, alarmed. "There must be something else you can tell us."

The man pulls out a knife.

"Wallet," he says. "Watch. Jewelry. Everything you have."

Julia freezes. The blade is about four inches long and as thin as a credit card. But Julia's not fooled by its diminutive size. She knows how much damage a weapon like this can do. She's performed heart surgery on at least twelve stabbing victims over the years, the majority of which involved small, easily concealable knives exactly like this one.

"Do what I say," says the man, agitated.

Leo takes a step forward. The man thrusts out the knife. "Do not move!"

Julia tries to keep her voice even. "Leo, please, just do what he says."

She kneels down and places her purse on the ground, slips off her ring, puts that there, too.

"See?" she says, standing and holding up her hands. "We don't want anyone getting hurt. Leo, please do the same. Your wallet and watch."

Leo hesitates, jaw flexing in anger, but does as she asks, reaching inside his pocket for his wallet and placing it on the ground. He tries to take off his watch, but has trouble with the catch.

The man waves the knife at him. "Hurry! You take too long!"

"Here," says Julia. "Let me help."

She moves forward to assist Leo and is suddenly knocked to the ground. It takes a moment for her to register exactly what's happening when she sees Leo launch himself at the man.

"Leo, stop!" she cries out.

It's too late—he's already upon him, smashing the man in the jaw. The man lashes out with the knife, nearly slicing Leo across the side of face. Undeterred, Leo charges again and there's a sudden hard thud as both men stumble backward and fall on the ground beside Julia. Scrambling out of the way, she screams at them to stop. They ignore her and continue to wrestle in the dirt, the blade flashing threateningly between them. For a minute, it looks like Leo might have the upper hand, but the man, younger and fitter than Leo, gets the better of him and incapacitates Leo with an armlock across the throat in three simple maneuvers. Eyes bulging, Leo sputters and gasps against the man's unyielding forearm, his fingers desperately digging into his flesh.

"Stupid American," says the man, breathing hard.

"Let him go!" cries Julia. "He can't breathe!"

There's a commotion to the right. Someone is running across the grass toward them, shouting in Turkish. God, he has an accomplice, Julia thinks, both she and Leo are dead for certain. Then she sees the frame of a woman, long hair bouncing, small dog clutched to her chest. The woman is more of a girl, a teen really, in the late stages of pregnancy.

When the girl reaches them, she is crying. The man's face softens when he sees her. He utters something gently to her in Turkish, and she replies in kind, pleading for him to stop. Leo makes use of the distraction and lands a punch to the side of the man's head. The man is momentarily dazed but recovers quickly, angrily throwing Leo to the ground and aiming the blade at his throat.

"Stop! Oh God, please stop!" cries Julia.

Julia hears a police siren and turns her head to see the flash of blue as a police car barrels across the dead grass toward them. The car halts and Detective Muhtar leaps from the driver's seat, gun drawn.

The man stares wide-eyed into the glare of the headlights, fear alive in his eyes. Sobbing, the girl pleads with him to drop the knife. She softly calls his name, "Suleyman." Breathing hard, the man looks at her, hesitating. She touches her pregnant belly. "Suleyman." He swallows, glancing at her belly, blinking back the perspiration dripping into his eyes. They stare at each other for the longest time. "Suleyman," she says again. Finally he nods and drops the knife to the ground.

31

Julia and Leo sit on the sea wall while Detective Muhtar briefs the patrol officer who's arrived to take the girl and man called Suleyman into custody. What sea fog there was has lifted and the park has transformed from an eerie gloom into a startling blue thanks to the churn of police lights.

Julia hugs herself to warm her bones against the chill boomeranging off the sea. It's also the shock, she thinks, the terrible thought of what might have been had Detective Muhtar not turned up when he had. Julia had since learned that Ada had been so worried about them coming here, she'd phoned Detective Muhtar not long after they left. Thank God she had. Two minutes more and Leo could've been dead.

Julia glances at him now. He hasn't said a word since the patrol car arrived. She looks at his neck, still red from the headlock.

"You should get that checked out."

"It's nothing," he says, voice hoarse.

"You nearly lost consciousness."

He looks at her testily. "I had the son-of-a-bitch."

She hugs herself tighter and looks at the harbor. "It was a stupid thing to do. We should have just given him what he wanted."

"A simple thank you would be nice."

She snorts. "Thank you? You're joking. You could've been seriously injured."

He grits his teeth. "I was trying to protect you, Julia."

"Well, I'd rather you didn't get yourself killed by being macho."

"Yeah, I get it, Julia," he mutters. "You don't need looking after. You're a perfectly capable and independent woman, blah, blah, blah..."

Julia feels her blood pressure rise. "Stop being a child. And for the record, what just happened wasn't about me, it was about you. You didn't want another man getting the better of you, pure and simple. You wanted to conquer, compete, and control."

He turns to her sharply. "Really, Julia? Really? You think so little of me? That I'm just some caveman who can't control his emotions?" He pauses. "I was worried that when that lowlife pulled the knife, he might rape you."

She's shocked. It was honestly something she hadn't thought of.

"I know you think I'm just this uneducated, dumb shmuck who works with his hands, but believe it or not I do have a brain."

She swallows. "I know you do."

They fall into silence. Curious onlookers are beginning to gather along the grass boundary.

"You're okay. I'm okay. That's what's important," she says. "And we have a lead. Toni was at a nightclub on Saturday night."

Leo takes a breath, calmer. "Assuming Suley-what's-it over there is telling the truth."

This catches Julia off guard. "What do you mean? He knew about Toni's tattoo. He must have seen her."

Leo shrugs. "Maybe there's a Facebook post somewhere showing Toni with it or..." he says, drifting off.

"Or what?"

He pauses. "He could actually be involved in Toni's disappearance. Responsible for it, even."

Julia shudders as she has a flash of the man abducting Toni at knifepoint down some dark alleyway. She looks over to where the patrol officer and Detective Muhtar are talking separately to the man and the girl.

"What about her?" she says. "What do you think her involvement is?"

Leo rubs his jaw. "Difficult to say. I don't think she knew about the knife though, given her reaction."

The patrol officer places his hand on the crown of Suleyman's head and guides him into the backseat. Next, he turns to the girl but she refuses to get in the car. Crying, she pleads with Detective Muhtar and points to Julia and Leo.

Julia gets to her feet. "Something's up."

"She's just pissed they got caught."

"Maybe," says Julia. "But maybe she knows something."

Julia strides over to Detective Muhtar and the girl.

"What's she saying, Detective?"

To Julia's surprise, the girl answers in English. "I did not know Suleyman was planning that. I thought he would just get the money for the information. Please, he is not a bad person. He is a soldier from the war. He has mental problem now because of the war." She grabs Julia's hands and holds them between hers. "Please tell them to let him go. They will listen to you. He is the father of my child."

"Enough of this," growls Detective Muhtar, grabbing the girl's upper arm. "You have caused these good people too many problems already."

"Wait," says Julia. "Where did Suleyman get the information about my sister?"

The girl hesitates.

Julia pushes. "Is Suleyman responsible for Toni's disappearance? Does he know where she is?"

The girl shakes her head. "No, no, you have it all wrong. Suleyman never met your sister. My best friend works at Club Asena. She's the one who see your sister."

"Why didn't she come forward herself?"

"She did not want to be involved."

Leo looks disgusted. "So you thought you'd steal the information from your best friend to make a quick buck?"

The girl lowers her eyes. "We are poor. The baby come soon."

Julia pauses, thinking. "If we help Suleyman, will you take us to your friend?"

Detective Muhtar gives Julia an exasperated look. "Dr. Norris, we cannot help him. He is a criminal. He tried to rob you."

The girl starts to weep. "It is the war. It turn his mind. He saw things, terrible things. He scream at night like a small boy."

Julia pulls Detective Muhtar aside. "Surely there's something you can do. This nightclub worker may have valuable information."

He lets out a breath and turns to the girl. "Get your friend to talk and I will let the judge know about your help. That is all I can do."

Julia looks at her. "Do we have a deal?"

The girl casts a longing glance in Suleyman's direction and then turns to Julia.

"Yes, we have a deal."

32

The girl, whose name it turns out is Miray, rides in the front with Detective Muhtar, cradling the sleeping dog in her arms. On her left wrist, there's a pretty pewter charm bracelet that jangles whenever it brushes against her pregnant belly. Julia watches from the backseat. She can't imagine what it would be like to be so young and expecting a child. At thirty-seven, she still doesn't feel ready. Not that she currently has any choice given the lack of likely father candidates. When she and Leo first got married, they'd had the "baby" conversation. He'd wanted kids but they agreed to wait until Julia finished med school and was established in her career first. But the timing never seemed right and Julia never seemed ready. Then it was too late and they were divorced.

Julia glances at Leo and feels a pang of guilt. He would've made a great father. Who knows, maybe if they'd had a family, the incident with Toni might never have happened and they'd still be together. Julia turns back to the window. Too late for what-might-have-beens now. She needs to focus on what family she has left.

"I have something for you," says Detective Muhtar, reaching down in the front seat to retrieve a folder. "They have identified the body. They matched her to a missing person's report filed a year ago by her mother."

He passes the folder to Julia and she opens it to see a photograph of a pretty, blue-eyed fair-haired woman dressed in a white shirt with an embroidered collar of crimson roses. Unrecognizable compared to the body which now lies in the morgue.

"She was from Romania. They tell her to come to Turkey to work in a restaurant but put her to work in a brothel instead," says Detective Muhtar, his distaste evident.

"That's awful," says Julia.

"At least her family can put her to rest now," says Leo.

"Yes, that's something."

Julia returns the photograph to the file and feels the stir of disquiet. The entire incident with the body is strange. Something doesn't fit. But she isn't sure what.

Detective Muhtar doubles back through the web of streets then travels uphill toward Galata Tower, where the road for vehicles ends and the pedestrian-only entrance begins. He pulls into a side park and they get out, following Miray uphill past a clutch of shops selling traditional musical instruments. Julia's eyes sweep the store fronts as they pass, noting the exquisitely carved Turkish teardrop mandolins hanging in the windows like art installations. There are darbuka drums too, animal skins on either end, small enough to place between the knees. Leaving the music shops behind, they crest the hill and the area opens out to Istiklal Caddesi, a sprawling open-air pedestrian mall that stretches well into the distance. It's just after 9 p.m. on a Friday night and the place is bustling with people. There's an almost festive atmosphere as the noisy crowds peruse the big-name chain stores or hunt for a bite to eat in one of the restaurants or bars in the lanes branching off from the main mall. Julia smells lamb cooking over coals and her mouth waters. But there's no time to stop. Miray has picked up pace, forcing Julia, Leo, and Detective Muhtar to fight their way through the shoulder-to-shoulder crowds in order to keep up.

Miray takes a sudden left down one of the laneways and drops out of sight.

"We're going to lose her," says Julia, pushing her way through the crowd.

"I knew we should not trust her," growls Detective Muhtar.

They half-jog through the throng of people and turn into the laneway and see Miray waiting for them beneath a neon blue sign in the shape of a wolf, the word *Asena* emblazoned across the bottom in fancy, looping script. Brisk techno beats leak out from behind an imposing black door.

When they reach her, Miray says, "Let me speak to Clara first."

Detective Muhtar shakes his head. "Not possible. We are coming in with you."

"You cannot. She will know you are police. She will not tell you anything if I do not explain first."

"You are making me wonder about this girl Clara very much," says Detective Muhtar, eyes narrowing. "It seems she has something to hide. Should I be arresting her?"

Miray bites her lip. "Clara is a good person."

"You said that about Suleyman, too. You are not the best judge of character, I think."

Julia shoots Leo a look. She doesn't like where this is heading.

"Maybe Miray is right, Detective Muhtar. We don't want her friend to clam up," says Julia.

Miray glances at the club door. "Clara is from Lithuania. She does not want to go back there. That is all."

"She's an illegal immigrant?" says Detective Muhtar.

Miray exhales. "Yes. But she is a good person. She work's hard to send money home for her little boy."

"We are wasting time," says Julia. "Let Miray go in and talk to her friend."

Detective Muhtar lets out a breath.

"Five minutes only, then we come in."

33

They wait outside beneath a withering cypress, trying not to look too conspicuous. Detective Muhtar pulls a cigarette from a softshell pack and lights up. Julia realizes she must be frowning because he takes two sidelong steps to keep the smoke downwind.

"What's with the wolf?" says Leo, looking up at the blue-coated canine above the doorway.

Detective Muhtar follows his gaze.

"The wolf is the holy animal of Turkey. There is a famous Turkish legend that Asena, a she-wolf, found an infant boy and nursed him back to health. Asena was impregnated by the boy and gave birth to ten half-wolf, half-human cubs, from which the Turkic people are born."

Leo raises an eyebrow. "Sure beats the bald-headed eagle."

Detective Muhtar glances away and Julia's reminded of the first time she met him and his aura of lingering sadness. She eyes his wedding ring, thinned out by time.

"Do you have children, Detective?"

He looks startled then rearranges his face to something more passive. "A daughter."

"Is she involved in police work, too?"

"She died."

"Oh, I'm sorry."

He grinds out his cigarette. "Yes. It was a great tragedy." Detective Muhtar looks at his watch. "That is long enough."

"A few more minutes."

He shakes his head. "I give her more time than I first said. We go in now."

Before Julia can object, he opens the door to the club. Inside there's a dimly lit corridor and a muscle-bound doorman sporting an earpiece. The doorman's eyes land on Detective Muhtar and remain there. He takes a step to the left, crosses his arms, blocking their path.

Detective Muhtar barks something harshly in Turkish but the doorman's unimpressed. Detective Muhtar reaches into his pocket and holds his ID up to the doorman's nose. "Okay?"

The doorman stares a beat longer then finally steps aside and lets them pass. They walk up the corridor and reach another door, where there's a smiling hostess in a pink sequined bustier and scarlet lipstick. She opens the door with a flourish and they are instantly transported into another world. A world of crisp Armani suits, bejeweled throats, and multicolored cocktails.

Leo whistles under his breath, looking around. "Beverly Hills, eat your heart out."

Floor-to-ceiling glass doors lead out to a large, softly lit balcony with a spectacular glass bottom floor. The floor is partially submerged in the ocean, floodlit to enable the best views of the sea life below. Tiny fish dart in all directions. Jellyfish billow. Julia even spots what she thinks is a baby shark. The effect is both mesmerizing and disconcerting and Julia feels mildly seasick.

She drags her eyes away to take in the rest of the surroundings. To the left, there's a horseshoe-shaped bar, a dance floor, and a large seating area with table and chairs. To the right, low-slung couches provide a more relaxed zone where beautiful women and equally beautiful men recline, sipping exotic cocktails and sucking on bubbling hookah pipes.

Julia can't imagine what a backpacking traveler like Toni would be doing in a glitzy place like this. Leo nudges her. She follows his gaze. Just west of the bar, Miray's involved in a heated exchange with a blonde woman.

"Looks like we found our mystery witness."

34

Clara Domitrovich. Strikingly beautiful. Early twenties. Long blonde ponytail sitting high on the crown of her head. Her sparkling chandelier earrings swing violently as she gestures wildly with her arms. Clara is not happy. She shouts something at Miray, turns on her heel, and slams through a side door.

"Oh boy," says Leo.

Miray sees them and comes over. "She will not talk to you."

"Try harder," says Detective Muhtar.

"I have. She does not wish to be involved."

"If you want to help your boyfriend, you have to get Clara to talk," says Leo.

Detective Muhtar nods. "That is correct. Tell your friend we can do this here or I can arrange for her to be sent back to Lithuania."

Miray looks distraught. "Please, no. You can't."

Detective leans close to her. "I can and I will. Go back and get her to talk."

Miray raises her eyes to the glittering skyline and takes a deep breath. She's on the verge of tears and Julia feels sorry for her but they need that information.

"I will try again."

She dumps the dog in Detective Muhtar's arms and disappears through the side door. Five minutes later she emerges, shaking her head.

"Clara won't change her mind. She is angry with me for bringing you here. I'm sorry. Please still help Suleyman," she says, miserably.

Detective Muhtar utters what is likely to be a Turkish obscenity, passes the dog back, and makes a beeline for the side door. Julia catches his arm.

"I'll go."

She squeezes past him before he has a chance to object.

*

Julia finds Clara in a small utility room, sitting on an upturned crate. She's even more beautiful up close, with fine features and high cheekbones and remarkably green eyes. Those eyes cloud with fear when she sees Julia and she makes a move to flee out a side door.

"Don't be afraid. I just want to talk. Do you speak English?" says Julia.

Clara pauses, hand hovering on the door handle.

"Please, Clara, just for a minute."

And then, to her dismay, Julia bursts into tears. She's horrified. But she can't control it. The pent-up emotion of the last few days comes out in a flood.

"God, I'm sorry. I don't know what's wrong with me." Julia sniffs, wiping the tears from her eyes.

She digs inside her satchel for some tissues but can't find any. Clara backs away from the door, opens a cupboard, and hands Julia a roll of paper towels.

Julia tears one off and blots her face. "Thank you. You're very kind."

Clara remains standing, saying nothing.

"Won't you sit down?" says Julia.

Clara glances at the crate then at Julia, considering.

"Please."

Clara gives in and takes a seat, folding her hands in her lap.

"Miray says you have a little boy?'

Clara reaches for the locket round her neck.

"How old is he?" says Julia.

"Four."

"You must miss him."

Clara looks sad. "Yes. Very much."

"My sister is my only family."

Clara looks away and studies the top shelf laden with supplies.

"Did you see her, Clara?"

Clara hesitates.

"Imagine if it was your family member…your little boy," presses Julia.

Clara looks down at her shoes. "She was here on Saturday night."

Julia's heart races. "What time?"

"After midnight. She looked like she was waiting for someone."

"Why did you think that?"

"Many guys hit on her but she ignore them and she keep looking at her phone."

"What happened after that?" says Julia.

"I work out on the balcony for a time, an hour maybe, and when I return inside to get clean glasses, she is gone."

"Did she leave with anyone?"

"I do not know."

"What time was this?"

"About one thirty a.m."

"When you served her, how did she seem?"

Clara thinks for a moment. "Worried."

"Worried?"

Clara nods. "Not happy. No smile. She like this—" Clara frowns.

"Was she intoxicated?"

Clara considers this. "I don't think so. I serve her two sodas and lime. No alcohol."

"What else?"

"Nothing more." Clara stands. "I have to get back to work."

Julia stands, too. "Are you sure? There must be something else you can tell me."

"No."

Julia studies her closely, believes she is telling the truth.

"Do you have video footage? Cameras? Anything like that?"

Clara laughs. "You must be joking." She lifts her finger to her nose and pretends to snort drugs. "Boss does not like cameras. Not good for business."

*

Julia waits until they've exited the club before filling the others in.

"This is good," says Detective Muhtar. "We will interview patrons, other staff, see if we can get more information."

Julia nods, pleased. For the first time in days, she feels hope. "Toni was due to meet Yasmin the next day. Sunday. Something must have happened between the time she was here and the next day. We need to find out exactly what that was."

Detective Muhtar waves a taxi over and issues instructions to the driver to take Miray home.

Julia looks around for another taxi. "Leo, we should go to the hotel, get some flyers, come back and hand them out to surrounding business."

Leo frowns. "Don't you think we should call it a night? It's getting late. Detective Muhtar can take it from here. We can always come back in the morning and do the flyers after he's done his interviews."

Julia thinks about arguing. But he's right, she needs rest, and so does he.

"I guess that makes sense," she says, finally.

Leo's distracted by something across the road.

"Are you even listening to me, Leo?"

He points to a shop.

"There."

A small hair salon. A lone hairdresser is closing up for the night.

"You want a haircut?"

"Above the doorway."

Julia follows his gaze. Perched to the left, beneath the ancient rusty spouting, is a tiny CCTV camera pointing directly at the club.

35

The hairdresser is an older woman with enormous brass hoop earrings and a nose ring. They catch her as she's about to leave. Despite this, the woman is welcoming and invites them into the small but tidy three-chair salon, complete with a single hair dryer and sun-faded posters of glamourous Turkish women with thick, luxurious hair.

"She offers us tea," says Detective Muhtar, translating.

Julia hesitates. She's desperate to see what's on that camera.

"It would be impolite to refuse," Detective Muhtar presses.

Julia turns to the hairdresser. "Thank you. You are very kind. Of course, we would love some tea."

The hairdresser smiles and ducks behind a gold curtain separating the working part of the salon from a small staff kitchenette. Soon there's the hiss of water and the clatter of cups. They don't have long to wait before she emerges with a tray of hot tea and a plate of lemon cake.

Balancing the petite tea glass in one hand, Detective Muhtar fishes a flyer of Toni from his back pocket and shows the hairdresser. She studies the image intently then shakes her head.

Undeterred, Julia turns to Detective Muhtar. "Please ask her about the camera."

He relays Julia's request. The hairdresser replies in a rapid, thick stream of Turkish. She sounds angry. Detective Muhtar nods sympathetically and waits for her to finish before translating.

"She's had break-ins. They steal the dyes for their hair. That's why the camera."

"Does she have any footage from Saturday?"

Detective Muhtar points to the laptop on the little half-table near the cash register and says something to the hairdresser. She nods, opens the laptop, and taps on the keys. She stands back to let them see.

Julia looks over Detective Muhtar's shoulder at the grainy, black-and-white footage. Although the camera's wide-angled, it doesn't catch the front of Club Asena. Detective Muhtar zooms in and catches the laneway to the left of the club. But even though the laneway is busy with people, it's impossible to see any human features. It's simply too far away. Detective Muhtar fast forwards until just before midnight, the time Clara said she first saw Toni at the club.

"Stop!" cries Julia. There's a figure, a woman in dark jeans and boots. "That could be Toni. She walks a lot like her."

Leo studies the image. "Julia's right. She does."

"It is Toni, I know it is," says Julia, heart racing.

Detective Muhtar speeds up the footage until he reaches 1:30 a.m. then slows it down frame-by-frame.

Julia points to the screen. "Wait, there she is again."

They watch the footage in two-second increments. This time the woman's body language is different. She glances twice over her shoulder, back toward the club, then hurries away.

"She looks scared."

She reaches the corner then stops abruptly. There's a sports car on the side of the road, a yellow Lamborghini.

The driver appears to be speaking to her through the unwound window. It's a man, but they can't see his face.

The hairdresser says something, looking concerned.

"What is it?" says Julia. "Does she know who he is?"

The hairdresser raises her voice, upset, and points to the door.

"She wants us to leave," says Detective Muhtar.

Julia's alarmed. "What? Why?"

Leo taps on the computer screen. "Hey you guys, look."

They turn back to the screen. Toni gets in the car with the man. In the next frame, the car is gone and so is she.

36

Christine stares at the footage on the laptop. "Where did you say you got this?"

"At a hairdressing salon across the road from the nightclub," says Julia.

They fall silent as they watch Toni get into the Lamborghini and see the car drive away. Julia feels her throat close. She's never felt so powerless.

Christine sits back in her chair. She seems shaken. Julia catches Leo's eye and he returns her look. He's clocked Christine's strange reaction, too.

"You recognize him? the man?" says Julia.

Christine gets to her feet and crosses the floor. "This bar worker, Clara, did she see who Toni was with?"

Julia shakes her head. "She said Toni was alone, but then Clara had to move to a different part of the club and lost sight of her, so I guess it's possible Toni did meet someone inside without Clara noticing."

Christine frowns. "And you're sure she's telling the truth?"

Leo crosses his arms and stares at Christine. "You never answered Julia's question."

"Sorry?"

"About the man in the car. The hairdresser had a strange reaction when she saw the car, too. Kinda like yours, actually."

But Christine doesn't miss a beat. She offers an apologetic smile.

"Sorry," she says, picking up her satchel. "I'm tired. There's a developing international incident in Cairo. I've been up all night." She glances at her watch. "Which reminds me, I've got a plane to catch." Christine ejects the flash drive from her laptop and slips it into the inner pocket of her satchel. "I'll take this, see if I can get it enhanced to make out the number plate and the driver."

Julia looks at her, startled. "You're leaving? What about Toni? This is the first real break we've had. You can't leave now."

Christine shoulders her bag. "Don't worry, I'll be back in the morning."

"But we can't afford to waste any time. Who knows what this man has done with her. We need to check for other footage immediately," says Julia, her panic rising.

Christine's heads for the door. "Agreed, and Detective Muhtar will take care of it."

He nods from the corner where he's been oddly silent.

Christine pauses and looks at Leo and Julia. "Listen, we have to be careful not to speculate or jump to conclusions. There could be an innocent explanation for why Toni is getting into that car."

"You're kidding?" says Leo. "What kind of innocent explanation could there be?"

Christine's cell phone rings. She looks at the screen. "I have to go. I'll be in touch."

Then she walks out the door.

37

Julia waits until after Detective Muhtar drops them off at the hotel and they're back in her room before turning to Leo.

"What the heck is going on, Leo? Christine knew that man. I swear it. And what's wrong with Detective Muhtar? He could barely look me in the eye."

"Yeah, something is definitely up."

Julia shakes her head in frustration. "They're deliberately keeping us in the dark. We have a right to know what's going on. We're the family, for God's sake." She pauses and looks at him. "We should get a lawyer."

"A lawyer? What good's a lawyer going to do?"

Julia stares at the carpet where Leo is standing. Spreading out around his feet is a wet patch the size of Canada.

"For Pete's sake," she snaps. "How many times have I told Ada that fridge needs fixing?" Julia goes to the bathroom, gets some towels, dumps them on the wet carpet, and stomps on them. "This fucking country."

"Leave it, Julia."

Julia tosses the sodden towels aside, kneels down, and reaches in behind the fridge. "And her solution is to simply turn the damn thing back on. It defies logic."

Julia finds the switch, along with a handful of dust bunnies, and pulls out the plug.

"I'll go get Ada," says Leo. "She can get you a new fridge or put you in a different room."

Julia sits back on her calves and wipes her dirty hands on a wet towel.

"Forget it."

They sit in silence.

Julia exhales and blinks at the ceiling. "Sorry. This isn't your fault."

Leo rubs his hand over his face. "It's late. We're both too tired to think straight. Things will be clearer in the morning."

"I don't think I can sleep."

Leo sits on the end of the bed and takes off his shoes.

"You're going to have to try because there's jack shit we can do at one a.m. in the morning in a country where we don't speak the language." He lies down on the bed with his clothes on and closes his eyes. "Christine's back tomorrow. We'll go to the embassy and wait outside her office. All day if we have to, and we won't leave until we get answers."

Leo falls asleep on her bed. Julia doesn't have the heart to wake him, so she moves to the tub chair by the window and logs onto her computer to check her work emails. Two from Sue wanting to see how things were going. One from the cardiothoracic team committee secretary, complete with the minutes and PowerPoint presentation from the meeting Julia had walked out on. Another from Brian Harvey, chief surgeon and her boss, asking when she could be expected back to work. Twelve more from hospital admin notifying her of forthcoming out-patient appointments and surgery schedules.

She stares at the messages. Was it really only less than a week ago she was living a normal life? A life that now seemed to belong to a totally different person. She closes her laptop. It just doesn't feel right to be doing ordinary things like checking emails with Toni still missing.

She opens the curtain a crack and looks out at the dark night, her mind drifting. She thinks about what she and Toni have been through together. The many nights as kids waiting in their beat-up Honda while their mom disappeared down an alleyway to do tricks to feed her habit. The foster homes and change of schools. The lonely, unstable, patched-up, hand-me-down life. It had been hard, but at least they'd had each other.

The last time they'd been together, Julia had screamed at Toni to get out of her house and to never come back. *You're a drug addict. A whore. Just like our mother.* Now Julia wishes she could take it all back. Every cross word she has ever spoken. Every cold shoulder she has ever turned. All the dumb and pointless and petty things she has ever done to teach Toni a lesson.

She closes the curtain. She should sleep. There was still much to do in the morning. She lays her head back on the rim of the chair and shuts her eyes. But sleep doesn't come. All she gets is the grainy, anxious figure slipping inside the Lamborghini playing on repeat.

38

Julia wakes up with a start. Leo is standing over her holding a blanket.

"You looked cold."

She blinks at him through rough, dry eyes. "What time is it?"

"Early."

Leo lowers the blanket over her then heads for the counter where he turns on the kettle. He tears open two coffee packets, shaking the contents into two mugs.

Leo glances at the crumpled bed. "You should've woken me and kicked me out."

Julia sits up. "It's okay. You were tried."

He pours hot water into the mugs, hands her one and takes a seat. They lapse into silence. Somewhere above them there's a flush of a toilet followed by the creak of wooden boards as someone crosses the floor.

"We're making progress. It's only a matter of time before we find her," he says.

Julia cradles the mug in her hand, comforted by the warmth.

"I wish I could believe that."

"Don't lose hope."

She sighs. "I'm not. It's just that this whole thing is like three steps forward, two steps back. And I'm not sure who's on our side."

Leo blows on his coffee. "You were talking in your sleep before."

She looks at him. "I was?"

He smiles. "Something about Chuck E. Cheese."

Julia gets a flash of a happier time. "Toni's favorite restaurant as a kid. Mom used to take us there sometimes. I must have been dreaming."

"You've never talked much about when you guys were kids."

She swallows. "I try not to dwell on it. It makes me angry and I don't want to live my life in anger."

"Anger at your mom?"

She nods. "And myself, I suppose."

Leo frowns. "What have you got to be angry at yourself for? You were just a kid."

She stares into her coffee, old memories shuddering into place. "I never told you, but after we were sent to foster care when Mom died, Toni would have these terrible nightmares. She'd yell out for Mom in her sleep and end up waking the entire house. The foster parents would get annoyed so I would stay up all night watching her and shake her awake if it looked like she was having another nightmare. I did that for years." She looks at Leo. "I resented her, Leo. I was supposed to be doing kid things but I was the mom. I sometimes wished Toni had died too. I used to think that if there was just me, I would stand a better chance of getting adopted by a nice family and be a regular kid. What a terrible thing to think, to wish away my own sister like that."

"We all have selfish thoughts."

Julia blinks back tears. "God, Leo, what if that man did something to her?"

"We're going to find her."

"What if she's dead?"

"Hey, stop this," he says, softly.

He picks up her hand and kisses it. They stare at each other. Something inside her stirs. Desire. A memory of him holding her when they were married, his skin against hers.

Leo leans in and kisses her. It feels good. She returns the kiss, the heat of the coffee mug on her thigh. She pulls back.

He looks at her. "I've never stopped loving you, Julia."

She stares at him for a beat. "It's not the right time, Leo."

He glances away, hurt.

"I'm sorry," she says.

Without facing her, he rises from the bed.

"Leo," she says.

But he says nothing and returns to his room.

39

Julia pours herself another cup of coffee while she waits in the hotel restaurant for Leo. Her third of the morning, even though it's not quite 8 a.m. yet. She needs it. Her energy levels are already flagging and the earlier incident with Leo is still playing on her mind. She feels bad for hurting him. There are clearly still unresolved feelings there, on both sides, something she finds difficult to admit. But right now, she just doesn't have the emotional bandwidth to cope with that on top of everything else.

Julia brings the steaming cup to her lips and tries to get her thoughts in order. Approaching matters from a surgeon's dispassionate and analytical eye, she thinks about what she knows about Toni's disappearance so far. One, Toni had made it to Istanbul and was alive on Saturday night. Two, by the time Toni left Club Asena something had shaken her up. Three, Toni gets into a car with a man she does or doesn't know and the trail goes cold.

The big question is, who exactly was the man? Was he part of the backpacker group? It certainly doesn't seem likely given he had a vehicle, a Lamborghini at that. No, there's a far higher chance he's a local. Someone that the hairdresser, Christine Fletcher, and Detective Muhtar all recognized.

Julia drains her cup and lowers it. The whole thing is more than concerning. If Christine refuses to let them in on what's really going on when they see her this morning, Julia has made up her mind—she's getting a lawyer.

"Hey."

Julia looks up. Leo drops into the seat opposite, not meeting her eyes.

"Morning," she says.

He's trying not to show his hurt but every little thing plays across his face. It was something she had loved about him from the start. That he couldn't pretend. Not like her.

He looks at her plate of food. She pushes it toward him.

"You have it. I'm done. It will save you fighting the masses," she says, gesturing to the near-empty restaurant.

He picks up a boiled egg and begins to peel it. "Listen, I..."

"Coffee?" she says.

He nods. She pours him a cup.

He continues. "Julia, I just wanted to say about before..."

"I've been thinking," she says, tapping her finger on the table. "We should get in touch with Yasmin again." He stares at her, clearly irritated. She glances away, refills her coffee even though she has no intention of drinking a fourth. "We can ask about the man in the car, whether he was part of their group or not."

He puts down the egg. "Fine," he says. "Let's just bury what happened earlier just like we bury everything else."

She pretends not to hear. "I mean, I know he's probably a local but maybe there's some connection to the group. We won't know unless we ask."

He stares at her. "Sure, Julia, whatever you say."

"Good," she says. She glances at her watch. "We should get to the embassy. I want to make sure we catch Christine when she arrives."

Leo digs inside his pocket, pulls out a piece of paper, and puts it on the table. Julia glances at it. Four phone numbers. Four female names.

"I did a bit more digging on the news story about the rapes," says Leo. "I didn't want to tell you in case it turned out to be nothing."

Julia raises her eyebrows. "You found something? A connection to Toni?"

"No. Not yet anyway. You remember Craig Parker, my friend from high school? He's in IT now, works for a big telecommunications provider. I emailed him. After I explained the situation with Toni, he agreed to help. He got me their phone numbers."

"The rape victims' phone numbers?"

Leo nods. "Well, four of them at least. He couldn't track down the other one."

"Have you called them?"

Leo shakes his head. "I didn't want to go any further without you. You want to call them now before we head for the embassy? The time difference is good for the States. Otherwise we'll have to leave it to tomorrow morning."

Julia gets to her feet. "This is good, Leo. Thank you. Let's go talk to them now."

40

Leo's room is a mess, the air wet and thick with his morning shower and spray deodorant. There's a television identical to the one in Julia's room high up in the corner on a metal bracket. Unsurprisingly, it's switched to the sports channel. Leo turns down the sound, then sweeps aside a pile of clothes and a wet towel and offers the lone chair to Julia. She takes it while Leo lowers himself onto the end of the bed, smoothing out the paper with the telephone numbers.

They start at the top of the list. When there's no answer with the first number, they move on to the second. A woman's voice fills the line. Julia delivers a spiel about how Toni is missing and asks to speak to Sally Lichen about her experience in Turkey. But the woman, who may or may not be Sally Lichen, hangs up before Julia can try and talk her around.

Leo looks at Julia and raises an eyebrow. "This is going to be tougher than we thought."

He punches in the third number. A man picks up.

"May I speak with Sarah Pinkton?" says Julia.

A pause. "I'm her father. What's this about?"

Julia explains the situation. The man goes silent.

"Are you still there, Mr. Pinkton?"

There's a deep breath. "That Godforsaken country," he says, voice thick with emotion. "I'm sorry to hear about your sister, but what's that got to do with Sarah?"

"I was hoping to talk to Sarah about the incident in Istanbul two years ago."

Another pause, much longer this time. The close of a door, different acoustics as he moves to a different room.

He lowers his voice. "My daughter has gotten on with her life."

"I understand and I'm sorry to impose, but we're desperate for information. Any little connection might be significant."

He falls silent. There are muted sounds of children playing in the background.

"Did they have any suspects for your daughter's rape?" presses Julia.

The man laughs harshly. "That country is one of the most corrupt places on earth. The police didn't do squat."

"Do you know whether they got the attacker's DNA?" asks Julia.

"Sorry. I can't help you. Good luck with your sister."

He hangs up. Julia and Leo stare at each other.

"He's hiding something," says Leo.

But Julia's not listening. Her eyes are locked on the television screen above Leo's head. Detective Muhtar is escorting a disheveled man in handcuffs into a police station. Julia scans the newsfeed text below.

"Oh my God, Leo. They've arrested someone."

41

It's like the universe has shrunk to the size of a small room. Maybe it's because at that precise moment in time a small room is the only thing that matters, a room and the man sitting alone in it and what he has done to Toni. His head is bent, his thin, matchstick arms crossed on the table before him, the filthy T-shirt hanging loosely on his frame. His thinning gray hair, a disheveled, tangled mess, falls an inch shy of his collar and looks as if it hasn't been washed in months.

He lifts a trembling hand to pick something from his teeth and the light seems to sour around him. He looks about nervously, a strange leer on his face, studying each wall, the camera in the corner. Then, quite suddenly, the man holds his head in his bony hands and weeps.

In the next room, Detective Muhtar, Julia, and Leo watch him on the monitor. For the first time, Julia sees his eye. The left one. It's no more than a slit, the lid crimson, swollen like a boxer's in a fight. A mottled bruise forms on his cheek, too.

"That guy owns a Lamborghini?" says Leo. "He looks like a vagrant."

Detective Muhtar nods. "That's because he is. His name is Asen Cevik. He has prior arrest record for loitering outside steam baths. One previous conviction for filming the underskirt of a woman and putting it on internet."

"If he's not the man in the Lamborghini then why did you arrest him?" says Julia.

Detective Muhtar pauses.

"I need to show you something." He holds out a plastic evidence bag with an object inside. "Have you seen this before?"

Julia takes the bag and looks at the object. Her heart nearly stops beating. In the bag is a necklace. The same necklace that Toni never took off. The pendant is an ugly buckled penny from 1964 that Toni insisted was their mother's but from Julia's recollection was simply a discarded coin they found in gutter one time. When Toni was nine, she had asked Julia to make a hole for it so she could put it on a chain and wear it.

"Where did you get this from?"

Detective Muhtar nods toward the suspect. "He was picked up after trying to sell it at a pawn shop. He thought the penny was made of gold. You recognize it, yes? Your sister was wearing it in the photograph you gave us."

Julia feels her stomach clench. Nodding, she says, "It belongs to Toni. She wears it all the time."

A policewoman enters the interview room and gestures for the man to get to his feet.

"Wait. Where is she taking him?" says Julia.

"Back to the cells."

"But someone needs to question him."

Detective Muhtar stands and returns the necklace to the lock box. "We have completed the interrogation. He denies knowing anything about your sister and is refusing to say anything else."

"Well, you can't just accept that. You have to make him talk," demands Julia.

Detective Muhtar looks at her evenly. "Everything is under control, Dr. Norris."

Julia nods and softens her voice. "Of course. I know, and I'm not telling you how to do your job…it's just that…"

"He has a brother who lives in a village near Bursa who might have more information. I will talk to him."

"Okay, good. That's good," says Julia, nodding. "Are you going there now? Leo and I will join you."

Detective Muhtar shakes his head. "You cannot come, Dr. Norris. It would not be appropriate."

"But what if there are other items you need me to identify?"

"This is an official investigation and you are both civilians. You must stay behind," he says, firmly.

Julia folds her arms. "Leo and I can't just wait around here and do nothing, Detective. We'll hire a car, a driver, whatever, and go to this Bursa village ourselves. And maybe we'll ask a few questions of our own. Hand out some flyers. Who knows what information we might be able to dig up. Isn't that right, Leo?"

"Oh, for sure," says Leo, a smile playing on his lips.

Detective Muhtar runs a hand over his face and mutters something in Turkish.

Julia stands up straighter. "So I guess the choice is yours, Detective—bumbling, unpredictable amateurs messing up your investigation, or keeping us where you can see us so we won't get in the way."

42

They travel in Detective Muhtar's battered Fiat, heading east across the Bosporus Bridge to the Asian side of Istanbul. Unlike the European side, this side is dominated by charmless office blocks and high-density housing with rooftop satellite dishes and ugly electricity pylons colonizing the hills. For Julia, most of it passes in a blur. She can't stop thinking about the disheveled vagrant in the police station and what he might have done to Toni.

"How long before we get there?" she says.

Detective Muhtar glances in the rearview. "Three or so hours. Bursa is sixty miles south of Istanbul. The suspect's brother lives in Agri village, another hour's drive from there. The quickest route is to take the ferry to Yalova Port and travel by car. Otherwise it's a six-hour drive overland."

Three hours seems like an eternity but there isn't much Julia can do about it. Detective Muhtar turns off the highway and a body of water comes into view, tendrils of mist hovering above the surface. Beyond that there's a ferry terminal, busy with cars and buses waiting to board. Detective Muhtar pulls into the queue and they wait there until the vehicles begin moving across the gangplank and onto the front of the ferry.

Once they've boarded, Detective Muhtar points to the stairs leading to the upper deck and explains they can buy coffee or tea for the journey up there.

"I will wait here in the car," he says, putting a cigarette between his lips and settling back in the driver's seat.

Julia and Leo leave him to it and reach the upper deck just as the ferry pulls away from the dock. Despite the chill, the deck is busy with locals drinking tea, smoking, and reading newspapers. Julia and Leo look around for somewhere to sit and settle on an uncomfortable plank seat near the bow.

Julia stares at the low-lying sea mist as the ferry cuts its way across the channel and thinks of the buckled penny. It was jarring to see it there in the evidence bag. More jarring than seeing the backpack even. The necklace was such an intimate object and had lain right next to Toni's skin. Julia can't remember a time when Toni had been without it.

Julia knows that when personal items like these are found, it's not a good sign. She knows that killers take personal items and call them mementos.

Then Leo says, "Julia, maybe you should prepare yourself for the worst."

She turns away, eyes tracking a plastic bag billowing in the water.

"Toni's not dead, Leo. I would know if she was. And maybe you should keep your thoughts to yourself."

It's a spiteful thing to say, she knows that, and immediately feels disappointed in herself.

"Sorry," she says.

He offers her an understanding smile. "It's okay."

"No, it isn't. You didn't deserve that and I'm sorry."

He gives her a nudge. "Apology accepted."

Forty minutes later they disembark the ferry at Yalova and spend the next three hours driving barren highways punctuated by windowless factories and beaten-up trucks loaded with crates of tomatoes. They head inland and the terrain changes, forcing Detective Muhtar to navigate the Fiat through a set of winding, bush-clad mountains. Eventually the road flattens out, and the hills become studded with enormous olive and chestnut trees.

Julia looks out the window and feels like she's been dropped right into the middle of a pretty Turkish rural scene. On the roadside, there's an old woman carrying two buckets on a shoulder pole leading a tethered sheep with a rope. In the distance, a farmer burns off the fields for winter crops, while children play games under the shade of the trees. Julia wonders wistfully what it would be like to live such a peaceful life, away from the madness of a frenetic city and high-pressure job. Maybe that's what she needs, to slow down, simplify things, spend more time in nature, build closer relationships. She makes a vow that when all this is over, she will reexamine her priorities, herself, too. Satisfying as it may be, there is more to life than work. She just needs to make the space.

It's not long before they enter a village and Detective Muhtar follows a sputtering tractor up a dirt road. The village is mostly inhabited with rundown, single-story squat houses with terracotta roof tiles and badly cracked render. There are a few shops here and there. A barber. A bicycle repair shop. A café where men are sitting outside playing cards and drinking tea.

They carry on through the township until they reach a lane lined with green-skinned orange trees and turn left. Detective Muhtar pulls to a stop outside a set of gates. Behind the gates there's a smart-looking house set back from the lane. He turns to Leo and Julia in the back seat.

"Remember," he says, "I do the talking."

43

Julia stands looking at the house. Set on a large block of farmland with several outbuildings, the modest single-level dwelling has seen better days. The whitewashed exterior is plain but clean, and accented by a large green creeper curling its way up the drainpipes to a sloping roof ribbed with aging terracotta tiles. Six small windows, enclosed in decorative black wrought iron, lend a mildly creepy atmosphere to the place.

Julia, Leo, and Detective Muhtar approach the house on foot, their shoes rasping against the loose stone chips on the driveway. Out the front of the house there's a well-tended garden that includes a blaze of orange marigolds, rosemary shrubs, and what could be mint plants. By the looks of it, the rest of the land has been left to grow wild, and is covered in tall grass and ancient trees whose fallen, bird-pecked fruit lies scattered about the gnarled roots.

They reach the front door and knock. It's not long before the door is opened by a plump woman in her late twenties dressed in a nurse's uniform and traditional headscarf. An older, fine-boned man appears at her shoulder. There's no doubting this is Demir Cevik, the suspect's brother. He has the same hooked nose and sloping forehead.

The man and the woman listen patiently as Detective Muhtar explains the reason for the visit in Turkish.

"Certainly. Come in," says Demir Cevik in very good English.

Julia, Leo, and Detective Muhtar follow Demir through the tiled entranceway into a neat and homey living area. Huge floor-to-ceiling bookcases overflow with books and magazines. A wooden, four-stringed guitar is propped up in the corner, the strange bulbous shape similar to the guitars Julia had seen in the shop windows in Istiklal Caddesi. The only picture in the room is a photograph on a side table of a woman who looks a lot like the young woman who answered the door. Placed next to the photograph is a simple candle and an open black, leather-bound Koran.

"Please," says Demir, gesturing for them to sit on the couch.

The young woman hovers in the doorway and says something in Turkish.

"English please, Ela. Consider our guests," says Demir.

She nods. "Of course, Father. Shall I bring tea? I still have an hour before work."

Demir nods, spectacles winking on top of his head. "Yes, thank you, Ela. I am sure our guests are thirsty after their long journey. Ela is a nurse," he explains. "She works at the local hospital in the next village. I am very proud of her."

"Oh, Father," says Ela, blushing slightly.

"It is true," he beams. "Very proud."

She departs, closing the door behind her.

"So," says Demir, placing his hands on his thighs. "My brother is in trouble again." He shakes his head in disappointment. "He is a disgrace to our family. I have spent years contributing to our community and he does nothing but bring our good name into disrepute."

"We think he may have hurt my sister," Julia blurts out.

Demir looks startled.

"Dr. Norris. Please let me ask the questions," says Detective Muhtar, clearly annoyed.

Julia ignores him. "My sister has been missing for over a week, and your brother was found in possession of her necklace."

Demir Cevik looks at her evenly. "My brother is many things, madam, but I've never known him to be violent, especially against women."

"Please show him the necklace, Detective Muhtar," says Julia.

Leo shoots her a warning look. But Julia can't help herself.

"Go on," she insists. "The necklace, please, Detective Muhtar."

"Father, is everything all right?"

Ela stands in the doorway with a platter topped with homemade cookies and tea pre-poured into traditional Turkish glasses.

"Of course, Ela. Please serve our guests," says Demir. "Ela is famous for her cardamom cookies." He picks up the plate and offers it to Julia. "Please, you must try one. They are delicious."

Julia gets to her feet and pulls a flyer of Toni from her pocket. She holds it in front of his face.

"This is my sister, Toni Norris. Have you seen her?"

He frowns and shakes his head. "I have not."

Detective Muhtar rises from the couch. "Please, Dr. Norris. This isn't the way to do things."

Julia turns to Ela. "What about you?"

Ela glances at the photograph and shakes her head.

"Are you sure? You don't seem sure. Please take another look."

"Julia," says Leo.

"I haven't seen her," says Ela.

Julia looks at Demir. "How do you explain the fact that your brother had my sister's necklace?"

He shrugs. "I do not know."

Demir glances at his daughter and says something in Turkish. She leaves the room.

"It is not good for Ela to hear these things," he says. "She recently lost her mother after a long illness. Ela took her care of her until her mother's dying breath." His eyes linger on the photo of the woman on the table. "We are both still grieving."

Julia looks at him. "I'm very sorry for your loss, but please answer my question, why would your brother have my sister's necklace?"

"Asen is a liar and a gambler but he would not hurt a woman. Perhaps he simply found it on the street."

"Dr. Norris, please step outside," says Detective Muhtar.

Julia shakes her head. "He needs to answer the question."

Demir throws up his arms. "I do not know anything."

She stares at him. "You're hiding something."

Detective Muhtar steps in front of her. "That is enough, Dr. Norris."

Julia pauses and looks at her shoes. "Yes, yes, you're right, Detective. Of course you are. I apologize, Mr. Cevik. It has been a stressful time. I don't mean any disrespect. I'm just desperate for answers."

Demir nods, clearly unhappy. "I understand."

"Perhaps I could take a moment to collect myself and use your bathroom."

At first Julia thinks he's going to refuse. But after a pause, he nods.

"Ela will take you."

44

Julia follows Ela through the small but relatively modern kitchen up a hallway and into the back portion of the house.

Ela opens a door to reveal a clean, squat toilet. "Sorry we do not have a western toilet."

"It's fine. Thank you."

After Ela leaves, Julia stands at the door, heart thudding. What she's about to do is foolhardy and most probably highly illegal but it needs to be done. There's something off about this entire situation and Julia intends to find out exactly what it is.

She listens until she's totally sure that Ela is gone then steps out into the hallway. She finds the first room, Ela's bedroom by the looks of the neat single bed with the frilly bedspread. Basic with a wardrobe and a chest of drawers. All very ordinary and nothing untoward.

Julia moves on to the next bedroom, most likely Demir's given the navy terrycloth robe lying neatly at the end of a double bed. She glances around the room. There are bookcases like the ones in the living area, full of books and magazines, organized neatly in alphabetical order. Apart from that, there's only a small closet and bedside table. Again, all very normal.

She moves on to the third and final room located at the end of the hallway. She turns the handle. It's locked. She presses her ear to the door. Then something. A shuffle. A breath. She can't be sure what. Terrible things flash through her mind. Toni tied up and gagged. Drugged or beaten.

"Toni, is that you?" she whispers into the wood.

She listens again.

"Toni, it's Julia."

Putting some force into it, she tries the door handle again.

"What do you think you are doing?"

Julia spins round. Demir Cevik is standing there, the others behind him.

"She's in there, isn't she?" says Julia, trembling.

"Who? Your sister?"

"Open the door."

Demir shakes his head, angry. "This is ridiculous. Please get out of my house."

"I know she's in there. Open the door!"

Demir faces Detective Muhtar. "I have finished answering your questions. I want you to go."

Detective Muhtar pauses. Julia thinks he's about to escort her from the house but instead he turns to Demir Cevik. "What is in the room, please, Mr. Cevik?"

Demir splays his hands, palm upward. "Nothing at all. Just a spare room for storage."

"Storage?"

"Yes."

Detective Muhtar strokes his chin. "You are being evasive, I think, Mr. Cevik."

"I am not," says Demir, unconvincingly.

Detective Muhtar stares at him. "Then why not let us take a look?"

Flustered, Demir says, "Because there is nothing to see."

Detective Muhtar holds out his hand. "Give me the key, Mr. Cevik."

"I will not," says Demir.

"I have the key," says Ela.

Demir looks at her, panicked. "Ela."

"Father, we must show them the girl is not in there."

"Ela, do not interfere."

"We must, Father."

Before Demir can object, Ela unlocks the door and shoves it open. Julia pushes past her, halting when she sees the dimly lit space crowded with boxes and objects covered with drop-cloths. Four large humidifiers hum softly in each corner of the room. Detective Muhtar enters behind her and throws off a sheet revealing an enormous bronze bell oxidized with a green patina. Next to that is a marble bust of Alexander the Great. He digs through a box and pulls out swords, ancients coins, fossils, bronze figurines.

"What is all this stuff?" says Leo, looking around.

"The heritage belonging to the Turkish people," says Detective Muhtar in disgust.

Leo crouches to look at a water jug made of stone. "Oh, I read about this. Thieves going into the unsecured sites, stealing artifacts, then smuggling them offshore to sell on the black market to collectors."

Bewildered, Julia looks around the cramped space. "A smuggling operation?" She shakes her head. "No. Toni has got to be here. I heard her."

Detective Muhtar pivots to face the doorway. Ela is there but Demir Cevik is gone.

"Where is the son-of-a-bitch?" he growls.

Ela looks at him in dismay and says nothing. Scowling, Detective Muhtar mutters something and tells the others to stay put while he goes searching for Demir. He departs, his footsteps thumping angrily down the hall.

"I heard her, Leo," says Julia, moving deeper into the room.

"You can't have."

Julia pushes aside boxes, searching through the maze.

Leo catches her by the arm. "Julia, she isn't here."

She stares at him. "I heard her, Leo. I know I did." But her voice sounds hollow, even to her.

"No, Julia. You made a mistake."

She glances back at the room. Nothing but dust and lifeless objects. Her heart sinks.

"I thought she was in here," says Julia.

"Your mind playing tricks. That's all."

Julia bites her lip to stop from crying. "Are we ever going to find her, Leo?"

She searches his face for the answer. But he just stands there and looks at her like he doesn't know what to say.

45

Julia stares out the car window into the dull black night. The scene that had played out hours earlier at the village had left an unwelcome residue and she's struggling to shake it. For a brief moment, she had genuinely thought Toni had been in that room. She realizes now that was just a fantasy, her mind playing tricks, substituting wishing for reality. She glances at Leo, who's fast asleep, head resting against his rolled-up jacket against the window. He'd done his best to stay awake and offer her comfort, but Julia needed answers, not hugs.

None of it makes sense. Toni going to the nightclub. Toni getting into the Lamborghini with an unidentified male. Toni's penny necklace in Asen Cevik's possession. Demir Cevik certainly wasn't talking. In fact, he'd flashed Julia such a hateful look when he was cuffed and driven away in the back of the police car, Julia thought that even if he did know something it was unlikely he would ever share it with her.

As they stood watching the police car drive off, Leo had asked Detective Muhtar what would happen now that Cevik had been arrested.

"That depends on whether he has friends in high places," the detective said, dryly.

"You think the smuggling thing is bigger than just him?"

"Oh, undoubtedly. Cevik is just a cog in the wheel, as you people like to say in the west."

None of that mattered to Julia. Her primary concern was finding Toni and they had failed in that regard, although something in her gut told her Ela knew more than she was letting on. Julia had caught sight of the young nurse weeping in the kitchen window after her father had gone. Julia asked Detective Muhtar if she could speak to Ela alone, but he'd shaken his head and glanced up at the darkening sky and said there wasn't time because they needed to make it through the mountain pass before nightfall.

So here they were, driving through the night, back to Istanbul, empty-handed and heavy-hearted.

They'd stopped only once, just after midnight, when Julia had made the suggestion. At first Detective Muhtar had balked at the idea because he wanted to carry on uninterrupted. But Julia had insisted, and in the end, he'd reluctantly pulled into a half-empty truck stop that served, it turned out, five nondescript minced-meat dishes in barely warm bain-maries, coffee in an old-school percolator, and orange cordial dispensed from a large plastic urn. Julia and Leo had sat wordlessly under the harsh fluorescent lights pushing lamb mince and overcooked rice round their tin trays while Detective Muhtar stood outside smoking and staring into the starless night. They hit the road not long after.

She looks at Detective Muhtar now. He still seems alert despite driving for hours.

His eyes meet hers in the rearview. "Okay?"

Julia nods and returns to the window and Detective Muhtar drives on.

They reach the hotel just after 4 a.m. Julia crawls into bed and sleeps.

*

The sun wakes her. Still groggy, she lifts a hand to shield her eyes from the glare and sees Leo's silhouette hunched over his laptop.

She licks dry lips and speaks. "How long was I out for?"

Leo glances up. "She awakes."

"What time is it?"

He lowers his eyes to the time on his laptop. "Two in the afternoon."

Julia sits up on her elbows. "Oh God, that's practically another day lost."

"You needed to sleep."

There's an edge to his voice and she decides not to argue. She throws aside her covers and stands.

"We need to go see Christine Fletcher."

He grins at her. "I may have something better." He flips the laptop around to show her. It's a Wikipedia page of a female journalist named Beren Aslan.

"The reporter I emailed about the rape stories wants to meet us."

46

They wait on the marble steps of the Yeni Camii mosque, a stone's throw from the waterfront. Earlier Julia and Leo had made their way through the warren of narrow streets behind the mosque, an area that housed the Istanbul spice market, a throbbing, noisy open-air collection of shops and stalls. The exotic market sold all manner of things. Powdered turmeric. Cinnamon sticks. Chilies. Olives. Dried apricots. Dates. Figs. Shelled walnuts. Pistachios. All displayed in large hessian sacks or plastic tubs. Vendors offered Julia and Leo tasting samples as they passed, which they politely declined, concerned they were going to be late for their meeting with Beren Aslan. But when they finally located the Yeni Camii, the journalist was nowhere to be seen.

Leo looks at his watch now. They've been waiting for nearly half an hour.

"Five more minutes," he says. "Then we'll can it."

Julia studies the crowd for a woman in her mid-forties with short dark brown hair. She only hopes the Google image they are relying on isn't too outdated. They had found it on Beren Aslan's Wikipedia page, which had made for interesting reading. It seemed the outspoken reporter on Turkish women's issues had been forced to resign her position at one of Turkey's leading newspapers because of her social activism. She now runs a controversial blog, The *Bayan Guardian* (The Lady Guardian), that covers stories about such topics as a Muslim woman's right to decide whether to wear a headscarf or not; the sexual objectification of Turkish women in social media; and what Beren Aslan has herself described as Turkey's shameful record of imposing pitiful sentences for men who perpetrate violent crimes against women. Not a woman who shies away from controversy, that's for sure. Hopefully, she is also someone who will be willing to shed some light on any connection between the rapes and Toni's disappearance. But as Julia waits on the steps and glances over the faces in the crowd, she begins to feel despondent.

"With the luck we've been having lately, she probably won't even show," she says.

Leo remains silent.

Julia pauses and looks at him. "I'm being negative."

"Forget it."

"No, I'm sorry. You've been a fantastic support."

"That could be her," says Leo, eyes drifting past Julia's shoulder.

Julia turns and catches sight of a woman walking briskly toward them, dressed smart casual in a burgundy leather jacket, black pants, and ankle boots.

"Yes, that's definitely Beren," says Julia, standing.

As the woman gets closer, Julia notes the slash of plum lipstick and dark kohl eyeliner that makes Beren's large brown eyes appear even larger. The woman nods a hello then glances around.

"Not here," she says. "There are spies everywhere."

*

Beren Aslan, it turns out, is an extremely fast walker and both Julia and Leo have to half-jog in order to keep up. After crossing the public square outside the mosque, they follow her through the back streets adjoining the spice market, then turn a hard left. They continue on a few more blocks, heading east until Beren stops outside a plain building.

She swings opens the door.

"After you," she says.

Julia looks up at the staircase made of non-slip galvanized steel.

"What is this place?" says Julia, suddenly uneasy.

Beren shrugs. "You want to talk, you don't want to talk, that's fine by me."

Beren hits the stairs two at a time, leaving Julia and Leo at the bottom.

"Leo, I don't know about this," says Julia.

He grabs her hand. "Nothing ventured, nothing gained."

He pulls her up the stairs before she can object and they are both breathless by the time they reach the entrance to a rather sad-looking café. The place is mostly empty, with a pool table that doesn't look like it sees much action, a Sleepy Hollow pinball machine, and a large plant pot containing a plastic weeping willow with pink blossoms.

Beren opens another door and leads them up a short flight of stairs to the rooftop.

"Wow," says Leo, stopping to admire the panoramic view stretching out over the Bosporus and into the northern side of Istanbul.

Beren heads to a far corner overlooking a grungy rooftop patio where laundry hangs on a clothesline. She drops into one of the mismatched resin chairs, pulls out a pack of Benson & Hedges, and lights up.

"They will bring tea shortly. Take a seat and we will begin."

47

"So," says Beren, blowing out a stream of smoke from her very purple lips. "Your sister is missing."

"Can you help us?" says Julia.

"Do you have a photograph?"

Julia pulls out the flyer and gives it to Beren.

The reporter studies it closely. "None of the other girls ever went missing. Raped, yes. Missing, no." She hands back the flyer. "I have not seen her."

"All the victims were Western?" says Leo.

"Correct."

"And there were five of them?"

Beren nods. "That we know about." Beren looks from Leo to Julia. "Have you tried contacting them?"

Julia nods. "We spoke with Sarah Pinkton's father. He wouldn't let us talk to her. He said she was still traumatized by the incident. The other victims wouldn't talk to us either."

Beren purses her lips. "As I thought."

"What do you mean?" says Julia, puzzled.

Beren falls silent and watches the laundry flap in the wind.

"Can I trust you?" she says.

Julia glances at Leo, wondering where all this is going.

"Of course," she says.

Beren looks at both of them. "Because just being here talking to you is a threat to me."

"Nothing will be traced back to you," says Julia. "You have our word."

Beren pauses. "All of them have been paid off. Paid for their silence."

"Who? The victims?"

"Yes."

"How? Why? I mean who would do that?" says Julia, shocked.

Beren lights a fresh cigarette end-to-end with the old one. Her face disappears in a cloud of smoke.

"Have the police been helpful?" she says, pulling the ashtray toward her.

Julia shakes her head. "Not exactly. I'm pretty sure we're being kept in the dark about a lot of things."

Beren nods. "Corruption is everywhere. It fuels laziness. A culture of doing nothing and looking the other way. A few years ago there was a big clean-out targeting corrupt officials. Over three hundred fifty police officers were dismissed, some of them very high ranking. But, sadly, it did not change a thing." She taps her cigarette. "Two years ago I noticed one rape then another coming across my desk. Young, western, white. I wanted to dig deeper but my editor warned me against it. I went out and spoke to people at the bars. One name kept coming up. Mustafa Saat. I found a pattern. Each time he was arrested on suspicion of rape, the charges were dropped and the victim would leave the country."

"And you think they were paid off?"

She nods grimly. "I know this for a fact. I have a friend, let's just say she's sympathetic to my cause and good with computers. She provided me with some excellent information. I was able to verify the payments to the women."

"Do you have a picture of Mustafa Saat?" says Julia.

Beren removes her tablet from her leather satchel and brings up a photograph. A handsome man in his late thirties.

Julia and Leo stare dumbfounded at the screen. "Oh my God, Leo, that's the man in the yellow Lamborghini."

Beren looks at them. "That's not all."

48

Beren reaches into her bag and takes out a folder. She removes a stack of financial statements secured with a bulldog clip and a large A3-sized Venn diagram. She smooths out the diagram on the table, holding it in place with the salt and pepper shakers. As far as Julia can tell, it appears to be an analysis of different companies and various shareholdings.

"Mustafa Saat comes from a very powerful family. He is the son of a high-powered minister, Ahmet Saat. Three years ago, I was working on a money laundering case linked to Mustafa. The Saat family owns every museum shop in Turkey, which Mustafa oversees as managing director. There is a well-known rumor in Turkey that these museum shops are fronts to launder money gained from another side venture of the Saat family. Drug wholesaling, opium mostly. Trying to prove all this was another matter but I wanted to give it a try. My hacker friend helped me gain access to Mustafa's financial records and I found something unusual. Regular lump sum payments of US currency deposited by a company called Indigo Enterprises, the same entity that had deposited money into the rape victims' accounts." She pauses and looks at them. "Indigo Enterprises originates from the USA. It's a shell company used by the CIA."

Julia stares at Beren. "The CIA?"

"Yes."

Julia tries to keep her voice even. "Isn't that a little far-fetched?"

Beren gives her a look. "You believe me, you don't believe me, what do I care?"

Julia leans forward. "Listen, Beren, I don't mean to cause offense but I'm finding it hard to make the leap that my own government might be involved in this."

Beren gathers up her papers. "I guess this conversation is over then."

"Wait," says Julia. "Assuming for a moment that what you say is true, why would the CIA want Mustafa on their payroll and buy the silence of his victims?"

Beren pauses. She reaches into her bag and pulls out a photo of an impeccably dressed man and puts it on the table.

"Because of him," she says, tapping the photo. "Babak Saglam. A thirty-nine-year-old Iranian tycoon worth over thirteen point five billion dollars. The US government believes he's involved in illegal arms dealing, including chemical weapons and other weapons of mass destruction. The US has been after him for years. He is Mustafa's best friend. They socialize together. Mustafa is part of his inner circle. In other words, Mustafa has access to information that the US government wants and wants badly."

"You're saying the US government paid for the victims' silence to keep Mustafa out of prison so the CIA could continue receiving intelligence from him about Babak Saglam?" says Leo.

Beren sits back. "Precisely. He's what they call a platinum asset. The highest there is. They will move heaven and earth to protect him. Mustafa has information they want and they're willing to pay a high price for it, including covering up his crimes."

"And you can prove all this?" says Julia, rattled.

"Yes," Beren says, smiling. "Yes, I can."

49

Trust no one. That's what she used to tell Toni. Trust no one, not even me. Because you never know what's motivating a person, because they might tell you they are doing something for your benefit, when really, they're just in it for themselves.

Now, as the implications of what Beren Aslan told them begin to sink in, Julia looks at Leo as they cross the Golden Horn lobby and realizes he's the only person she can really trust.

"You believe her?" he says.

Julia lets out a breath. "I don't know. She seems credible but we really don't have any evidence apart from her say-so. That makes me nervous, and her claims just seem so outrageous."

They enter the hotel elevator and Leo hits their floor.

"I get it," he says, nodding. "Should we trust the word of an unemployed journalist who holds all sorts of grudges against the establishment? But Julia, the CIA does pay assets for information. It goes on all the time. That's how they get intelligence on individuals and groups who might be a threat to the US."

They emerge from the lift and Julia stops mid-stride. She looks at Leo.

"God, Leo. Do you think Christine Fletcher knows about this? What if she's really working for the CIA? What if our own government knows what happened to Toni and is trying to cover it up? That would explain her reaction to the Lamborghini and why she's been missing in action. Leo, are you even listening to me?"

She follows his gaze. He's staring at the door to her room, which is slightly ajar. She goes cold. Leo signals for her to stay back and uses his foot to nudge open the door. They stare dumbfounded at the state of the room. Julia's belongings are strewn all over the place. Mattress torn. Feathers scattered everywhere.

Julia picks up a crumpled flyer. "Who would do this?"

The bathroom door flies open and a man in dark clothing sprints across the room. He pushes Julia out of the way and knocks Leo to the ground. Without thinking, Julia snatches the man's jacket as he tries to flee. He tries to shake her off but she holds on tight. When he turns to face her, there's a gun in his hand.

She freezes. "Please don't shoot."

"Hey!" A shout from the doorway. Julia turns to see Detective Muhtar standing there.

The man pivots and fires the gun at him. The bullet glances off the wood above Detective Muhtar's head. He shoots again. Detective Muhtar cries out and jerks backward.

"Stop!" cries Julia. "Please stop!"

The man charges for door, knocking the detective off his feet, and takes off down the hallway.

Julia rushes over to Detective Muhtar.

"It's okay," he says, wincing. "I'm okay."

Julia examines his arm. A flesh wound. Bleeding badly.

"We need to get you to a hospital."

He grimaces and shakes his head. "There isn't time. We must leave immediately. It is not safe here."

Julia stares at him, breathing hard. "What the hell is going on? Who was that man?"

"People want you out of the country."

"*What* people?"

He hauls himself to his feet. "I will explain on the way."

50

Leo drives the Fiat while Detective Muhtar gives directions.

"Turn right up here."

They head in the same direction as the overhead train lines, passing through Sultanahmet, then east until they leave the shops completely behind. Julia looks down at her knee, which is jiggling like a piston. It's the adrenaline leaving her body. From the shock of having a gun aimed right at her face. She feels the sudden urge to throw up, and quickly winds down her window to take in some air.

"You all right?" says Leo, eyes hitting the rearview.

"Why was there a man with a gun in my hotel room, Detective Muhtar?" she says, anger simmering.

Detective Muhtar turns to look at her over his shoulder, the bloody wound on his arm shining like syrup.

"We will soon be there. I will explain everything then."

"Does this have anything to do with what's been going between Mustafa Saat and the CIA?" she demands.

If Detective Muhtar is surprised that Julia knows about the Saat/CIA matter, he doesn't show it.

He turns back to face the front. "We must get to the safe house first."

She frowns. "Safe house? What safe house?"

"You must trust me."

She shakes her head, exasperated. "Don't talk to me about trust."

He runs a hand over his face. "Please, Dr. Norris, I will tell you everything. I promise."

Julia sits back in her seat, biting down her discontent. She wants answers now, not later, but knows there's not much she can do except do what he asks and wait.

Detective Muhtar instructs Leo to go right and they enter a residential area. After driving a few more blocks, Detective Muhtar points to a narrow side street and tells Leo to park, which he does.

"Follow me," says Detective Muhtar, getting out.

They walk at a fast clip along the quiet street until they reach an entrance to an apartment building. Detective Muhtar ushers Julia and Leo inside and they follow him up to the second floor, where he inserts a key into the door on the left and shows them into a small but nicely decorated apartment.

Julia's surprised to see an older woman sitting on the sofa reading. Dressed in blue jeans and a fashionable sweater, with jet black hair tucked behind a striking green headscarf, the woman is probably in her early sixties, the same age as Detective Muhtar. She stands when she sees them, eyes widening when her eyes fall on Detective Muhtar's bloody arm.

"It is nothing, Reyhan," he says. "A flesh wound, that's all." He turns to Julia and Leo. "Reyhan, these are our guests. Please make them feel welcome."

The woman's takes in Julia and Leo, eyes narrowing. "American?"

Detective Muhtar looks at her softly. "They need our help, Reyhan."

She gives him a steely look but says nothing.

He introduces them. "Dr. Norris and Leo, this is Reyhan, my wife."

The woman nods stiffly then turns to Detective Muhtar. "Emri, your arm needs tending."

"Yes, Reyhan." He smiles at Julia and Leo. "Please make yourself comfortable. I will return soon."

Detective Muhtar and his wife disappear into another part of the apartment. After they're gone, Julia turns to Leo.

"What the hell is going on here, Leo?"

"Beats me," he says.

She's shivering. Leo removes his jacket and tries to give it to her. Julia waves it away.

"Take it," he says.

She decides it's not worth the fight and allows him to place the jacket around her shoulders. She catches the warmth of his scent and feels a little calmer.

"Now what?" she says.

They sit there and wait.

51

Thirty minutes later Detective Muhtar emerges with his forearm cleaned and bandaged. Julia does a double take when she sees him because standing next to him, holding his hand, is another man.

"This is my grandson, Turan."

More child than man, Turan is obviously intellectually disabled, and he grins at Julia and Leo through his misshapen jaw as he plucks the chest of his Incredible Hulk pajamas.

"*Merhaba*, Turan," says Julia.

Turan reciprocates with a strange kind of moan and a string of drool spills over his bottom lip. He holds something up for her to look at. It's a little toy car, gripped between his twisted fingers.

"Turan likes Matchbox cars very much," says Detective Muhtar.

Turan laughs and claps his hands. He gently wheels the toy car across Detective Muhtar's shoulders, but his fingers are too distorted to grasp the toy properly, and the car falls to the ground with a clang.

Reyhan appears. "I will give Turan his bath now." She takes Turan's hand, then pauses to look at Julia and Leo. "Please do not make trouble for us. We are good family."

"Reyhan," says Detective Muhtar, eyes gentle.

She doesn't say anything further, just gives Detective Muhtar a look, then closes the door softly behind her.

"Forgive her," he says. "She has been through a lot."

Julia looks at him. "What's going on, Detective? Why have you brought us here? Who was the man with the gun?"

Detective Muhtar sits in the chair opposite and places his hands flat on his knees.

"Yes, you have waited long enough for an explanation." He pauses and takes a breath. "I take money. I take the money from your government and it pays for Turan, this apartment, and sometimes special things like Matchbox cars and physical therapy to help with Turan's joints. His mother, my daughter, committed suicide a week after Turan was born. My wife and Turan depend on me. Only me. I am telling you this."

Julia and Leo look at each other. Any doubt about Beren's story vanishes.

"There is more," says Detective Muhtar. "The man in the Lamborghini is called Mustafa Saat. He is a very bad man. He abducts foreign women and rapes them. The US government protects him because he gives them secrets. The US government gives Turkish police bribes to keep him out of prison."

Julia shakes her head, disgusted. "By Turkish police, you mean you."

Detective Muhtar nods, grimly. "Me, others. It does not matter. It is all wrong."

Julia stands up and turns her back. There's a hard, angry lump stuck in her throat.

"That bastard did something to Toni and you covered it up."

"No. You are mistaken. At first we do not know for sure that Mustafa had anything to do with your sister's disappearance. Because his other victims were raped and let go, we never made any link between him and Toni. The first time we realized that he might be involved was the CCTV video."

Julia faces him, heat flushing through her body. "And what did you do then? I'll tell what you did, you sat on the information and did absolutely nothing."

He looks at her earnestly. "I wanted to bring him in for questioning, but those above me would not allow it."

"Christine Fletcher knows about this, doesn't she?" Julia demands.

Detective Muhtar nods. "The Turkish police take direction from her."

Julia has to sit down because she's shaking so much. "I don't believe this. You've both been deceiving us all along. Playing us for fools. You both have."

"It is not like that."

She glares at him. "Oh no? Then why don't you tell me what it *is* like, Detective, because it sure as hell feels like deception to me."

"Where does the guy with Toni's penny necklace fit in all of this?" says Leo. "Does Mustafa know him?"

Detective Muhtar frowns. "That's the strange thing. There does not seem to be a connection between Asen Cevik and Mustafa Saat."

"So Asen could have simply found the necklace on the street after all?" says Leo.

"It is possible."

"But he won't talk?"

"No."

Suddenly Leo pauses, contemplating something. "Wait a minute, do you think the US Embassy trashed Julia's hotel room? Was the guy with a gun an agent?"

Detective Muhtar shakes his head. "He was more likely to be a Mustafa's thug. Mustafa is connected everywhere. He is trying to scare you into leaving Istanbul."

"So you do think Mustafa is responsible?" says Julia.

Detective Muhtar exhales. "At the very least, he's our best suspect. Although it is a departure from his usual modus operandi, perhaps this time something went wrong. Toni could have fought back and he killed her. Or maybe he is holding her captive somewhere."

Julia stares at him. "If something has happened to Toni because of this delay I will never forgive you."

He lowers his eyes. "Yes, I am responsible. Yes, I am ashamed of what I have done. But I have been truthful with you now and I want to help you find your sister."

Julia laughs sharply. "Help? Oh, it's way too late for that, Detective."

Leo looks at them both. "I think I might have a way."

52

Beren enters Detective Muhtar's apartment just before midnight smelling of stale cigarettes and orange blossom. She has taken the time to apply a layer of purple lipstick but she's less put together than the last time Julia had seen her, dressed only in a gray T-shirt and jeans. There's a flush to her cheeks and a gleam in her eye. Julia can't blame her. She's about to break the biggest story of her life.

Beren introduces herself to Detective Muhtar and he apologizes for the late hour. She waves him away with a hand.

"Justice never sleeps."

Then Beren drops onto the sofa and pulls out her phone and opens the recorder app.

"Let us begin," she says.

The plan is simple. Detective Muhtar will be Beren Aslan's anonymous source. He will tell her everything he knows about the US government's involvement in the cover-up of Mustafa Saat's crimes and the link to Toni. Beren will then break the story, the theory being that the Turkish police and the US Embassy will be forced to arrest Mustafa, or at the very least, take him into custody for questioning.

So for the next three hours Detective Muhtar tells Beren everything he knows. Names. Dates. Places. Who. What. When. Where. How. Beren hones in on the details, circling back when things aren't clear, asking Detective Muhtar for more names and specifics, the amounts of payments and the key people involved.

The corruption reaches into the highest echelons of the Turkish police force and cabinet. The scale is far beyond anything Julia can comprehend, and the fact that her own government lies at the center makes it all the more shocking. She can tell Leo is as stunned as she is. Every now and again, he shakes his head in disbelief and utters a profanity under his breath. Because really, in the end, it comes down to one thing. The authorities, including the US Embassy, have let a serial rapist roam free to possibly kidnap and/or murder a US citizen.

When Detective Muhtar finishes downloading, a heavy silence falls over the room and they sit there and simply stare at each other. Eventually, Beren pockets her mobile phone and stands.

Julia stands, too. "This is dangerous for you. Are you certain you want to go ahead?"

Beren nods, shrugging into her leather jacket. "A friend will take me to the border. I will file my story there."

"You're leaving Turkey?"

Beren nods. "It is better that way."

Julia embraces her. "Thank you for what you are doing."

Beren returns the hug. "You are welcome. I hope it works."

*

When Julia wakes, she finds the strange lopsided man-child that is Detective's Muhtar's grandson standing over her.

"Hi there," she says. "Am I in your seat? I'm sorry. I'll move."

Turan lets out a choked laugh and shows her a red Matchbox car wedged between his stiff, unbending fingers.

"Very nice," she says.

Detective Muhtar, who's been sleeping under his jacket on the floor, stirs and murmurs something in Turkish to Turan. But when Turan doesn't move, the detective sleepily casts his jacket aside, gets to his feet, and steers Turan to the other chair where there's a tub of cars for him to play with.

Julia glances over at Leo, who's fast asleep in the chair, and feels a stab of annoyance. He's supposed to be monitoring the internet for any news on Beren's story.

"Wake up, Leo," she growls, getting to her feet.

He jolts upright. "What is it?"

"You fell asleep. Remind me never to go out on patrol with you."

Julia looks at the laptop and her heart nearly stops beating. Twitter and other live news feeds are buzzing with the story.

"Something's happening," she says.

The others join her and she clicks on one of the news feeds and sees Beren being interviewed via Skype at an undisclosed location. Ticker tape runs the length of the screen: *US government implicated in a cover-up of a serial rapist who is now linked to a missing US citizen in Istanbul. Officials have declined to comment.*

Some footage flashes up. The Istanbul police commissioner faces the camera and speaks as a translator interprets.

"We reject wholeheartedly these claims of corruption. My team has been working hard to solve the disappearance of Toni Norris and I can confirm we are now currently locating Mr. Saat for questioning."

Stunned, Julia stares at Leo and Detective Muhtar. “It worked.”

53

Waiting for news of Mustafa Saat's arrest is excruciating. As the three of them sit on the sofa glued to the laptop, the morning drags on into late afternoon. The authorities can't find Mustafa Saat anywhere, or so they say. It appears he has gone to ground. Or, worse still, fled the country. As a consequence, the sudden burst of hope Julia had felt when the story first broke is cruelly chipped away. All she can do is pray for a miracle because they are simply out of other options. On the plus side, the story has whipped the local media into a frenzy. There's that, at least, Julia thinks. That could shake some fruit from the tree and prompt a witness to come forward.

Every conceivable angle is being covered by the news outlets. The string of rapes. Mustafa's privileged childhood. His friendship with Babak Saglam. Some enterprising reporter has even managed to dig up footage of Mustafa taken last year at an opening of one of the family museums. He's a good-looking man, there's no doubt about that. With skin the color of nutmeg and a closely cut beard, he was well dressed in a fashionable taupe cashmere sweater, charcoal trousers, and expensive-looking loafers.

In the footage he's being interviewed by an attractive young reporter. Given her flushed state of excitement, she's obviously enamored by Saat. Julia can understand why. Legs crossed at the ankles, lounging back in the chair, arms causally resting on his thighs, this was a man who oozed confidence. This was a man used to getting his own way. A man who could easily lure a young woman away from a nightclub and use her for his own sinister purposes.

Earlier in the morning, newscast helicopters had done figure-eights over Mustafa Saat's ostentatious waterfront home, hoping to catch a glimpse of his high-society wife and six children. More mansion than house, the expansive three-story property is located in prime position right on the Bosporus waterfront, secured by impossibly large steel gates and two private guards toting machine guns. A five-car garage, which is no doubt occupied by a fleet of high-end vehicles in keeping with the now notorious canary yellow Lamborghini, sits at the end of a rolling driveway, a guest house with its own pool to the left. And if anyone was in any doubt about the status and wealth of Mustafa Saat, a slick, seventy-foot luxury yacht moored up close to the private jetty put paid to that.

Toni comes under close scrutiny, too. They dub her the "missing female American traveler." Posts and photos from her Facebook page feature prominently. Julia has always thought Toni shared too much about herself on social media and had warned her about it years ago. It's all too easy for someone to steal your identity these days, she had said, and there's always the possibility that some stalker type might use your posts to track you down and do you harm. But Toni would just laugh and chide Julia for being such a cynic. Not everyone is out to get everyone, sis, she would say.

The Saat museum interview comes on again and Julia feels her heart sink. "He could be anywhere. Absolutely anywhere."

Leo goes to say something, to reassure her probably, but whatever it is dies on his lips. Sometime in the afternoon,

Reyhan enters carrying a tray laden with steaming coffee, tomato slices, fresh pita bread, and feta.

"You're very kind," says Julia, staring at the perfectly cut cross-section of tomato.

But she can't face the thought of eating right now. She would be at serious risk of throwing it up. She feels terrible. Reyhan has been so hospitable. Even Turan has been a joy and, apart from a few excitable moments of hand-clapping for no apparent reason, has played quietly on the mat with a large wicker basket of colored Legos.

"Look," says Leo.

The news coverage has switched from the bird's-eye view of Mustafa's compound to a clutch of reporters camped outside the US Embassy building. They had been crossing live to reporters there every hour or so to little avail. This time, however, the camera blurs then focuses on the youthful-looking man emerging from the building. He stands on the steps, press release rattling in his hand, and recites the statement that the embassy does not wish to make a comment at this time. Unsurprisingly, Christine Fletcher is nowhere to be seen.

Leo shakes his head, angry. "Unbelievable. Our own government."

The footage returns to reruns of Toni's Facebook posts.

"What now?" says Julia.

"We regroup," says Leo.

"Regroup and do what exactly?"

A text notification chimes on Detective Muhtar's phone. He checks it. A large smile blooms on his face.

"What is it?" says Julia, standing.

His smile grows wider.

"Tell us."

"Beren Aslan has found Mustafa Saat."

54

Detective Muhtar pulls Leo's laptop closer, taps on the keyboard, and brings up Beren Aslan's live Facebook feed. Beren Aslan and Mustafa Saat are inside a car. She's in the driver's seat, he's in the passenger's. The phone camera wobbles as Beren tries to get a good vantage point. The interior light is on, glowing a rectangle of yellow, but it's not doing much to illuminate the occupants, who appear gray-skinned and bleak. It's difficult to see anything beyond the steamy, rain-streaked windows. Possibly an industrial area of some sort. But it could easily be a residential area, too.

This is a very different Mustafa Saat than the carefree one Julia has been exposed to all morning. This one is serious and drawn, with something close to outrage simmering beneath the surface. But despite the circumstances, there's still an undeniable arrogance about him. It's the way he holds his head, chin slightly elevated, and the unhurried way he blinks his eyes.

"Okay, we are live now, Mr. Saat," says Beren.

He gives her a perfunctory nod.

Beren continues. "What is it you wanted to say?"

He licks his lips and turns to look at the camera. "I wish to seek asylum in the United States."

His English is perfect. No doubt privately educated abroad.

"Let me understand this, Mr. Saat, you wish to renounce your status as a Turkish citizen because you have been an informant for the United States government?"

He shoots Beren a cross look. "It is not something I wish. I love my country with all my heart, but it is necessary given the recent events. I now have a target on my back. To stay in Turkey would be a death sentence."

Beren pushes further. "So you do not deny you were passing information to the Americans?"

"I do not wish to go into details."

But Beren isn't about to give up. "You sold information about Babak Saglam, did you not?"

Saat looks at her darkly. Beren holds the silence until he sighs through his nose.

"All right," he says. "I supplied information relating to the possible production of chemical weapons. I did not want to see them get into the wrong hands."

"How long have you been working for the Americans?"

He shrugs. "That is irrelevant."

"And the United States not only paid you, they made sure you stayed out of prison, didn't they?"

He scowls, clearly unhappy the interview isn't going his way.

Beren lets him sit in silence for a spell, then changes tack. "Tell me about the women, Mr. Saat."

Saat sits back and laces his fingers together. "They all consented. They admitted this in their settlement agreements."

"Settlement agreements arranged by the US government," says Beren, matter-of-factly.

"If you say so."

"You drug the girls."

Saat scoffs. "I do nothing of the sort."

"You are a rapist, Mr. Saat."

Julia's heart lobs in her chest. Beren Aslan is either brave or foolhardy given she's alone in a car with a known rapist, possibly killer, with no one to come to her aid.

Saat rolls his tongue over his front teeth. "That is an absurd statement. I do not need to rape anyone."

"What about the missing American, Toni Norris?"

"What about her?"

Beren holds up her tablet. "There is footage of her getting into a yellow Lamborghini outside Club Asena the night she disappeared."

He shrugs. "Mine is not the only yellow Lamborghini in Istanbul."

"What about the Civik brothers? Are you aware they had an item of Toni Norris's in their possession? A necklace?"

"I have never met those men before in my life and I do not know anything about any necklace."

"What's your connection with Agri village?"

"None whatsoever."

Beren pauses. "Where is Toni Norris, Mr. Saat?"

He doesn't flinch. "I do not know."

"Did you kill her?"

"That, Ms. Aslan, is an outrageous accusation that I vehemently deny. The very idea is abhorrent to me. I would never kill anyone, especially a woman."

"But you're saying that Toni Norris was never in your car when there is very clear evidence she was."

He exhales. "All right, I admit it. I did see her. I had just left the club and was in my car when she came out. I gave her a lift to her hotel but I never saw her again after that."

Beren raises an eyebrow. "You expect us to believe that?"

He shrugs. "Believe what you want. I am telling you the truth."

"Ms. Norris never met you before and she gets into your car, just like that?"

"I recall she was upset and wanted to get away from the club in a hurry."

"Upset? What about?"

"She wouldn't tell me. She wanted to be taken to her hotel so that's what I did."

"What hotel?"

"I don't know. Some budget hotel in Karakoy."

"Where did you go after that?"

"I don't know. A few more clubs. Home."

"To your pregnant wife and six children?"

He pauses. "Now you're getting personal."

Beren nods. "My apologies, Mr. Saat. There is no reason to involve your family. But Toni Norris has a family, too. She has a sister who loves her dearly, friends, as well. Please, for their sake, tell us what happened."

He lifts his chin, indignant. "I had nothing to do with this woman's disappearance."

"Where is Toni Norris, Mr. Saat?"

He looks squarely at the phone camera. "I'm telling you the truth. I did not hurt this girl and I do not know where she is."

55

Julia's first solo surgery was on a four-year-old boy named Jeremy Heller from Kirkland, Seattle. Jeremy had been born with a ventricular septal defect, better known as a hole in the heart. Although a VSD is typically picked up in an infant's first few days of life, it had remained undetected in Jeremy until two months before his fourth birthday when his mother had noticed he'd become uncharacteristically breathless and lethargic. She'd taken him to the family doctor, who ordered an electrocardiogram, and the VSD diagnosis was finally made. The surgery was simple and involved sewing a patch of surgical material over the hole to close it. Julia had assisted on a prior VSD surgery so knew exactly what needed to be done. All very routine. Until she closed Jeremy up and he had a massive heart attack on the operating table and died twenty-seven seconds later. Jeremy Heller, four, her first and only patient death.

"What are you thinking about?" says Leo.

They are heading back to the hotel for a shower and change of clothes after being holed up in Detective Muhtar's apartment for nearly two days.

"Jeremy."

The faces of Jeremy Heller's grief-stricken parents drop into Julia's mind. She'd told them his death had been a statistical anomaly.

"Who?"

Jeremy's mother had called her a murderer.

"A little boy. My first surgery."

"I remember."

She glances at him. She'd forgotten he'd been there. "Of course."

The administration had forced her to see a counselor, part of the hospital's malpractice procedure. When the counselor had told Julia she had unresolved issues from childhood, Julia had thanked him and told him she'd work on it. For years afterward, she'd dreamt about Jeremy's taut peachy skin, the soft sweep of his eyelashes, but she'd never cried. Julia remembers that now, not crying even though a little boy had died, even though she had probably been the cause of his death.

"What made you think about that?" says Leo, frowning.

"I'm not sure."

He stops and takes her by the shoulders. "Everything's going to be all right, Julia."

"You don't know that."

"It will be," he says, tightening his grip.

She looks at him. "Did you see the look on that smug bastard's face, Leo? He's a goddamn liar. He has Toni somewhere, I know it."

Leo lowers his hands and puts them in his pockets.

"Are you so sure about that?" he says carefully.

She's shocked. "Yes. Aren't you?"

"I'm just saying, there could be a possibility that Saat is telling the truth."

"But it's the only plausible explanation. He has a history of violence against women, and the CCTV. Toni was in his car, for God's sake."

Leo looks doubtful. "Yeah, but his pattern has been limited to drugging and raping, not kidnapping."

Julia scoffs. "But that's what happens, isn't it? These perpetrators escalate, seek more and more thrills, take greater risks. Or maybe things got out of hand. A wrong dosage. A bad reaction. Toni's system might not have been able to cope."

Leo looks away. "Yeah, I don't know. It just doesn't feel right."

"Feel right?" Julia shakes her head in disbelief. "Try employing a bit of logic here, Leo. Base conclusions on facts."

"What facts exactly?"

"Oh, for God's sake," she says, her voice rising. "I'm not attacking your intellect, so you can wipe that injured look off your face."

He looks away. "Whatever, Julia. You're right. You're always right."

Julia tosses her hands in the air. "I can't deal with you and your fragile little ego at the moment, Leo. There are more important things to think about, like my missing sister."

She strides across the tired chipped parquet floor. Ada looks up to say hello but Julia pretends not to see. Julia can't be nice, not now, not with Leo's words ringing in her ears. She enters the lift and hits her floor. She needs to be alone.

56

Water batters her skull. It's ruthless and hot and smells like chlorine but it's better than nothing. Julia reaches for the tiny hotel soap and tears the plastic with her teeth, spitting out a fleck of packaging. Lathering up, she cleans every part of herself, desperate to wash away the dirt from these past few days. She's just beginning to relax when there's a knock on the hotel door.

She pushes her face in the water and groans. "Leave me alone, Leo."

Another knock. God. She just wants some time to herself, some time to think. Is that too much to ask?

Sighing, she steps from the shower, wrapping a towel around herself. He'll just want to talk, to apologize for being so rash with his words. More knocking.

"Okay, okay." She reaches the door and yanks it open.

Christine Fletcher looks back her. "Hello, Julia."

"Christine."

Julia's eyes drop to the woman's crumpled shirt, marked with something dark on the pocket, hastily rubbed off but not entirely eliminated. She looks rough, like she hasn't slept for days.

"What do you want?" says Julia.

"Can I come in?"

Julia doesn't move.

"Just for a minute," presses Christine.

Julia lets her hand fall away and Christine steps inside. She heads to the window overlooking the sad little alleyway below and looks out.

She turns to Julia. "There are ways they can trace Saat. Sophisticated ways."

Julia puts her hands on her hips. "And who exactly are *they*, Christine?"

Christine twists her ring finger. The absent husband, lost somewhere in the rubble of 9/11.

"We never knew for sure whether Mustafa was involved. There was never anything concrete."

"What about the CCTV?"

Christine sighs. "Yes, until that. The CCTV changed everything."

"You protected him. Even after what he did to those other women? Even knowing that he could be involved in Toni's disappearance?"

"Look, I agree that Mustafa Saat is an overprivileged scumbag who deserves to be in prison for the rest of his life. But he had information critical to US security and our western allies. It's a highly complex situation, Julia."

Julia shakes her head in frustration. "So? That's good enough reason to let him get away with whatever he's done to Toni?"

Christine holds Julia's gaze. "I know this is hard to hear but there are greater forces at play here. Mustafa had information with the potential to affect thousands of lives. His friend Babak Saglam trades in chemical weapons smuggled out of Iraq in the early days of the war. Saglam has no morals. He doesn't care who he trades with—Russians, Islamic fundamentalists, whoever—the highest bidder is all that concerns him. Mustafa's latest information was about a possible chemical attack on US soil."

"But you should have done something!" cries Julia. "Toni is not just collateral damage, she's a human being."

Christine exhales. "I sympathize, Julia, I really do, but sometimes it comes down to the lesser of two evils."

Julia takes a step toward Christine. "I want to know what you're going to do about this mess."

Christine pauses. "They're sending me back."

Julia blinks. "What do you mean they're sending you back?"

Christine glances at the window. "There's a car waiting for me downstairs to take me to the airport."

"They can't do that," says Julia, heart hammering.

Christine raises an eyebrow. "Oh yes they can."

"You can't just abandon us."

Christine lowers her voice. "Listen, I shouldn't be telling you this, and I'll deny it if anyone asks, but they've agreed to give Mustafa refugee status if he tells them what he's done with Toni."

Julia looks at her. "What good is that if no one know where he is?"

"They'll make sure the message gets through to him. Like I said, they have their ways." Her face softens and she touches Julia's arm. "The point is that it's only a matter of time before Toni is found."

Christine hoists her satchel up her shoulder and heads for the door. "I need to go." She reaches for the door handle. "Someone will be in touch, Julia. You'll get Toni back. I'm sure of it."

57

As Julia gets dressed, she lets what Christine told her digest. She desperately wants to believe her. That it's only a matter of time before Mustafa is brought in and discloses Toni's whereabouts. But even if what Christine says is true and there is an offer of immunity on the table, there's still the problem of locating Mustafa, who has to be deep in hiding by now, possibly even out of the country.

Julia combs her hair and catches sight of herself in the mirror. She looks terrible. Worn down. Sick. Like her patients do when they're given news their prognosis is terminal. And something else. Julia stares at the lines on her face, the serious look of it, the way the muscles fell beneath the skin, making her seem older, a witness to some great tragedy. It strikes her then. She has the same haunted look as Christine Fletcher.

She turns from the mirror abruptly. She's not anything like Christine Fletcher. She's an independent thinker and would not simply blindly follow a chain of command. She's someone who would not lie for the so-called greater good. Julia would, and always would, put people first.

Julia frowns and digs a finger into her temple. A possible migraine is looming. She finds two Excedrin in a blister pack buried in the bottom of her bag and heads for the fridge for some water, but there's none. Ada must have removed everything when they were having issues with the leak.

Not wanting to risk a gastrointestinal issue from drinking tap water, Julia goes downstairs to find Ada. She doesn't need to go far. The older woman is seated at her usual wingback chair flipping cards on the glass-topped coffee table. Ada smiles broadly when she sees Julia then breaks into that dreadful hacking cough of hers.

After the noise trails off, Julia says, "You should see a doctor."

Ada waves a dismissive hand and swipes a watering eye with her fingertip. "I am fine."

"I'm serious, Ada."

The elderly woman gets to her feet and bends to pull up the sports socks gathered round her ankles.

"You have news of your sister?" says Ada, shooting a glance toward the exit.

Ah, Julia thinks, she must have seen Christine Fletcher.

"Nothing yet," says Julia. "May I have some bottled water please? Impending headache." She flashes the blister of tablets.

Ada's eyebrows knit together in concern. "Are you getting sick?"

"Oh, nothing serious if I catch it soon."

Ada studies her for a moment. "This is a hard thing you are going through, I think." She pauses. "Perhaps I can show you something?"

Julia hesitates. She really ought to call Detective Muhtar to see if he's heard anything.

"Okay." Julia nods. "I can spare a few minutes."

Ada smiles. "Very good. Please come."

Ada heads for the reception area, aqua-colored Nikes squawking across the parquet floor as she goes. She lifts up the counter and beckons for Julia to follow, which she does, allowing Ada to lead her through a door, along a brief hallway through another door, and into a small room.

The room is cozy and cluttered with antiques and laced with stale cigarette smoke. It occurs to Julia then that she has never actually seen Ada smoke. Now she knows why. Ada obviously comes here to do the deed.

Ada gestures to one of the cracked leather-buttoned chairs. "Sit, please."

She turns to a small fridge in the corner and leans inside, giving Julia a flash of her chubby white thighs in the process.

"Would you have something to eat?" says Ada, glancing over her shoulder. "A little meze perhaps? Some olives?"

"No, thank you."

Ada nods, pops an olive into her mouth, and passes Julia a bottle of water. She closes the fridge door then reaches inside the top drawer of a beautiful oak side-table and takes out a photo album.

"My son, Omer," she says, giving the album cover a gentle caress.

Julia cracks open the water and washes down the Excedrin. "You have children? I didn't realize."

Ada's smile fades. "Omer is gone now. For many years."

"Oh, I'm sorry."

Ada pulls her chair close to Julia's until the arms almost touch and opens the first page of the album. The album looks like something you might get in the 1980s, where the shots are displayed four to a page and wedged behind plastic sheeting that never sticks properly. Ada leafs through the pages, allowing Julia to take in what must have been Ada's son's entire life. Omer as a newborn, pink and wrinkly. Omer on his first birthday. Omer taking his first steps. Omer's first day at school. Omer at university graduation pictured with a beaming Ada and a slight man who must have been his father. There are many more photos, mostly involving the Golden Horn Hotel. Omer as a toddler hoisted on his grandfather's smartly suited shoulders. Omer as a preteen serving Turkish delight to guests. Omer as a young man behind the reception answering the phones. Then, quite abruptly, Omer as a gray-skinned corpse, wrapped in a plain cloth shroud, a wailing, tear-streaked Ada bent over him, his father standing at her shoulder looking just as grief-stricken.

"Oh, Ada, I'm so sorry."

Ada stares at the photograph. "He is in paradise."

"What happened?"

"He was a tour guide taking a group by minibus through the Parhar Mountains. A truck was coming the other way and caused a terrible accident. Omer was badly injured. They put him on the machine. Thirty-five days later they ask us to turn it off."

"God, how awful."

"His father never forgave himself for turning off the life support," she says, closing the album.

"Is your husband still with us?"

Ada shrugs. "As far as I know. I have not seen him for over ten years." She looks at Julia. "Your Leo. I think he is a good man."

Julia lowers her eyes. "Yes, well, he has his moments."

"I am thinking that he still loves you very much. Why are you still not married? Did he have an affair?"

Julia looks at her hands. "Mistakes were made on both sides."

"Life is short. This I know. It is better to love and forgive, I think." Ada pauses. "And your mother? Where is she?"

"She died a long time ago."

"I see," says Ada, nodding. "She would be proud of you, the way you search for your sister, the way you never give up."

"I don't know about that. She was lost in a world of her own most of the time."

Ada reaches for Julia's hand. "I know for certain she would be proud." Ada breaks into another cough and withdraws her hand to cover her mouth. "Sorry, sorry," she sputters.

Julia passes her the bottled water. "It's serious, isn't it?"

Ada sips the water and sits back. "A tumor as big as my fist."

"Do you have any family who can help?"

Ada's eyes land on the wall of family portraits. "This hotel has been in my family for three generations. My great-grandfather built it from nothing. Worked day and night. But now business is not good. Airbnb takes the customers and the hotel needs repairs. They cost a lot of money. It is too much for one sick old lady. I have an offer. I might take it. Go down the coast to Kas, for the sunshine, to die in peace." She looks at Julia. "What else am I to do?"

The door flies open, startling them both. Detective Muhtar fills the space.

Julia stands up. "What is it?"

He looks at her and bursts into tears.

58

"He's dead."

Ada and Julia stare at Detective Muhtar in shock.

"Mustafa Saat is dead." Detective Muhtar wipes his eyes with the heel of his hand and looks at Julia. "I'm sorry."

Julia lowers herself into the chair, not quite believing it.

She glances up at the detective. "Are you sure?"

He nods grimly. "His body was dumped on the Iranian border. His tongue pulled out by the root."

"Babak Saglam?"

"Almost certainly."

They will never find Toni now. Not with Mustafa gone.

"That's not all." His face goes slack. "They killed Beren, too."

Julia's hand flies to her mouth. "Oh, no."

"They were not as brutal as they were with Saat. No torture, just a single shot to the head."

"This is our fault," says Julia, bereft. "She was only trying to help us."

Speaking gently, Detective Muhtar says, "Beren made the decision to track down Saat on her own, Dr. Norris. She would have understood the risks."

Julia bites her lip. "That doesn't matter. If we hadn't asked her for help, she would still be alive." She blinks at the ceiling. "God, what a mess."

She gets to her feet and crosses the floor, stopping to face the painting on the wall.

Eventually, she says, "Saat was the only chance we had of finding Toni. What are we going to do now?"

"We will think of something," says Detective Muhtar.

Ada speaks. "He is right, Julia. Do not lose hope."

Detective Muhtar's phone chirps with a message. He reads it and sighs. "I am sorry. I must go."

Julia looks at him. "You're leaving?"

He nods. "Unfortunately I am needed elsewhere, but I will return later. Take some time, let the news sink in." He pauses in the doorway. "Dr. Norris, this is a setback, yes, but I will not give up on finding your sister. You have my word."

*

Julia stares numbly at the wall. She's been here for the past two hours on the end of her bed. Just sitting and staring. Staring at the flyer of Toni she had stuck there all those days ago, now slightly lopsided and curling at the edges. Like a fallen leaf gradually being dried by time. She looks at that flyer and thinks that maybe that's all she has left. That maybe it's all she will ever get.

"Hey." It's Leo at the shared door. "You know what day it is?"

She glances at him briefly then returns to the wall.

"Your birthday," he says.

Oh, her birthday. She'd forgotten. She's now thirty-nine.

"It doesn't matter," she says.

Leo hands her a steaming cup of tea. She takes it and feels a burst of warmth against her skin.

"Of course it matters," he says, sitting next to her. He leans over and kisses her cheek. "Happy Birthday." He takes a sip of tea. "How are you doing?"

"I'm fine."

He looks at the flyer then quickly glances away. "I don't know what to say."

"Don't say anything. This isn't something you can fix."

"I still can't believe they killed Saat. And Beren…"

"These are bad people, Leo. Bad people do bad things." Julia places the tea on the floor by her feet and stands. "Listen, I've been thinking, maybe it's better if you go back home, to San Francisco. I'm very grateful for your help but you must need to get back to your business. I can take things from here."

Leo gives her a look. "Julia, come on."

"I know your clients have been calling you. I never expected it to take this long. Like I said, I'm grateful but now I think it's time for you to go."

She can hear her voice. So clipped and businesslike.

"You're doing the thing with the eyes again," he says, "when you look at me but don't really look at me. It's remarkable how you can do that. Shut me out so completely."

"I don't know what you're talking about."

He takes a breath and softens his tone. "Julia, I want you to consider something."

She folds her arms. "I'm listening."

"Maybe both of us should go back."

She turns away, shaking her head. "Out of the question. I'm not going anywhere until I find Toni."

Leo looks at the water stain around the mini-fridge. "Think about it for a second, Julia. Where's our time better spent? Not here handing out flyers on street corners, that's for sure. We'd be far more effective back home, doing the media circuit, putting pressure on the government."

She scoffs. "Don't be an idiot, Leo. That won't work. No one cares. Not the Turkish government. Not the US government. Not the police. Mustafa was the only real leverage we had and now he's gone. If I leave now, Toni will be just another missing foreigner who's never found." Julia sweeps the hair from her eyes and lifts her chin. "I'm not giving up on her."

"No one said anything about giving up."

"She isn't dead, Leo. I know that's what you really think. But Toni isn't dead and I'm staying here until I find her."

59

The buzz of Julia's phone jolts her. Unable to sleep, she's been replying to work emails in an effort to distract herself, not that it was doing much good. She reaches for her mobile and answers.

"Hello."

Detective Muhtar's voice fills the line. "I have information. Important information. It could be both good and bad depending."

She sits up. "Tell me."

"We found the hotel where Mustafa Saat said he dropped Toni off. I am there now, reviewing the security camera footage. It was as he said. He let her out, he drove away, she went to her room. No problem."

"He didn't go inside the hotel with her?"

"No."

"Are you sure?"

There's some chatter in the background. "I am needed," he says. "I must go."

"Detective, wait—"

But it's too late, he's already hung up. Julia rises from the chair and knocks on the shared doorway.

"Leo."

A few seconds later, Leo appears, frowning when he sees her face.

"What's happened?"

"They found Toni's hotel. There's footage of Mustafa dropping her off then leaving right away."

His brown creases. "What? That doesn't make sense. If Mustafa left Toni at her hotel unharmed then where is she?"

"You tell me."

*

Blue and white police tape sections off the small hotel room. The room itself is basic with a single inner-sprung bed, a simple chest of drawers, and walls badly in need of paint. A dusty window overlooks a spare parts factory next door. The only thing bringing cheer to the space is a faded print of the Blue Mosque in a cheap faux brass frame above the bed.

By the time Julia and Leo arrive, forensics are busy at work. Bundled up in their paper Tyvek suits, drawstring of their hoods pulled tight around their faces. Detective Muhtar is there, donned in a paper suit too, trailing the technicians. From behind the tape, Julia and Leo watch as doorknobs and jambs are dusted, and the bed is stripped of linen, and items are placed in clear plastic evidence bags. Everything from a lamp, alarm clock, cushions, even coat hangers and the extra pillows and blankets on top of the wardrobe.

One of the technicians opens a black case and takes out a spray can and some sort of tool shaped like a paddle.

Detective Muhtar approaches Leo and Julia. "We must shut the door."

"What are they doing?" says Julia.

Detective Muhtar pauses. "Checking for blood."

Julia feels sick. "God."

Leo gestures toward the threadbare sofa by the stairs. "Let's wait over here."

Forty-five minutes later, Detective Muhtar emerges from the room shaking his head. "No sign of blood or struggle."

Julia is flooded with relief.

"But the room has been occupied and cleaned since your sister was here," says Detective Muhtar. "So we do not know for sure if any foul play has occurred in the room."

"How many nights was Toni booked in for?"

Detective Muhtar steps out of his paper suit. "She had no booking. The receptionist said Toni walked in off the street and pay cash for one night. Also interesting is that after Mustafa Saat dropped Toni at the hotel, she came to reception for a replacement key card saying she'd lost the other one. No key card was ever found in Mustafa's car. We went back to the nightclub. There was no key card found there, either."

"This doesn't make sense," says Julia.

"There is more security footage to examine. One camera just outside the hotel entrance, one in the foyer, one on each floor. None in the elevator. It will take some time to review." He looks at his watch. "It is late. You should go back to hotel. I will call you."

Julia crosses her arms and looks at him. Detective Muhtar lets out a breath.

"You want to come," he says.

"You read my mind."

60

"Hey, Julia. Wake up."

Julia stirs. "What is it?"

"You were having a nightmare," says Leo. "A pretty heavy one by the sounds of it."

A patchy memory comes to her. Toni calling out from all the dark Istanbul places. Julia searching. A body wedged between two dumpsters. Headless and limp.

Julia looks down. She's on a couch beneath Leo's jacket.

"Police station, remember?" says Leo. "The CCTV tapes? They're viewing them next door."

Julia rubs her eyes. "Have they found anything yet?"

"Not that I know of."

The door swings open. Detective Muhtar stands there looking haggard, shirt untucked, five o'clock shadow darkening his face.

"There's something you should see."

He shows them into the small, dimly lit room containing three large computer monitors. The room smells of body odor and electrical equipment left on too long. An exhausted-looking policewoman with glasses is seated at the largest monitor controlling the keyboard.

"Play it," says Detective Muhtar.

She hits enter. A timer runs across the bottom of the screen, showing seconds, the date, the time. 3:30 a.m. Three hours after Mustafa said he dropped Toni at the hotel. The footage is of the empty hotel foyer. The receptionist sits on a stool on the small desk, scrolling through a tablet, cheekbone resting on his fist.

“What are we looking for?” says Julia.

“Keep watching.”

A figure appears. Male. He strides across the foyer and heads for the stairs, confident gait, as if he belongs there. The receptionist glances up, then returns to his tablet unconcerned. The male reaches the foot of the stairs and the camera captures the side of his face.

“Zoom in,” says Detective Muhtar.

The policewoman does and Julia gasps. Staring back at her is the handsome, boyish face of Dr. Daniel Bambury.

61

Daniel lifts his hand and wipes perspiration from his brow. The woman at the car hire place hadn't batted an eyelash when he asked for a van with tinted windows. Why would she? He was simply another Brit on holiday, making his way across Turkey, spending his tourist dollars, keeping the local economy ticking over. When she asked if he wanted to upgrade to the more expensive insurance that included extra benefits to beneficiaries, should he, for instance, die in a car accident, he declined. Then he'd given her his best smile and she lowered her eyes and blushed. Women were funny like that. A little bit of attention could go a long way.

So now here he was, Istanbul long behind him, barreling down the highway heading toward Cappadocia, Toni deep in dreamland on the mattress in the back of the van.

Daniel had been surprised when he went to retrieve Toni from the hiding place how much her recovery had progressed. The caretaker had done well, administering the medication exactly as requested, tending to his little patient with a level of care that even Florence Nightingale herself would have been proud of. It was amazing what a satisfactory level of payment could do.

There's a groan from the back. He glances over his shoulder.

"All right, princess? Heat too much? It is a tad stuffy in here."

Daniel fiddles with the knobs on the old-fashioned air conditioner, flicking the lever down to blue. Perhaps he should have upgraded to a later model after all. No, he's right to be careful with money. They would need it for the journey to Laos, to set up their home in Lao Prabang. He smiles at the thought of their little house and the children Toni would bear, the fish he would catch in the Mekong.

He thinks back to that night in Club Asena, when he presented Toni with his plan for their wonderful life together.

"There's a little village where I can get work at the local clinic, my love. It is so cheap we can have our very own house and start a family."

Toni had looked at him like he was mad. "You've got to be joking, Daniel. It's over. You need to accept that and move on."

Then she walked out the door, his dream for a beautiful life together right along with her. That's when the real drama began. He never wanted her to get hurt. Not in the slightest. The entire thing had been a terrible accident. He had only followed her back to her hotel with the intention of trying to persuade her to come with him to Laos. He'd never dreamed she would run off and fall down the fire exit stairs like that. When he heard the smack of her skull against the steel barrier, he thought she was dead for sure. But by some miracle, she'd still been alive. Although he hated to see Toni so badly injured, Daniel was wise enough to recognize that the accident had presented him with a unique opportunity. One he would have been foolhardy not to take advantage of, so he had formed a plan on the fly and put it into action immediately. It was as if God the good man was pulling the strings himself.

Another groan from the back. Daniel's eyes flick to the rearview. She's waking. That really won't do. There are hours of driving ahead of them yet. Daniel turns off the highway to a remote road, pulls over, and squeezes himself through the seats into the rear of the van.

He takes out his black leather pouch and unrolls it, eyes skimming the vials of sedatives, antibiotics, malaria medication, and fresh needles, things he had appropriated from the third-world hospitals where he'd worked. Taking a syringe, he punctures the vial of midazolam with the needle, draws the full 5mg+. He fishes out Toni's arm beneath the blanket and taps a vein. He pauses to look her. His beautiful sleeping beauty, heaven sent, just for him. But he mustn't linger. They need to make it to the next village before nightfall.

He slips in the needle. Toni gasps then drifts back into silence. Daniel smiles. His beautiful sleeping beauty indeed.

62

Daniel? Julia can't believe they missed it. She'd had her initial suspicions, for sure. Not just about Daniel, but any one of the others in Toni's circle. Yasmin. Sally. Debbie. Conner.

"There's more," says Detective Muhtar.

Julia turns back to the screen. Daniel exits from the lift on Toni's floor with something in his hand.

"The keycard."

"How did he get that?" says Leo.

Detective Muhtar signals to the female officer and she pulls up different CCTV footage. The one of Toni getting into Mustafa Saat's car.

Julia frowns. "We've seen this already."

Detective Muhtar speaks. "No one thought to check what happened after Toni drove off with Mustafa Saat. I decided to take a look and found this."

They watch again as Toni exits the club and gets into Mustafa's Lamborghini. The tape runs on. Ten seconds. Twenty seconds. At forty-five seconds Daniel appears in the doorway and gets into a white van on the street and heads in the same direction as Toni.

"That confirms it then," says Leo, sitting back. "Daniel is the mystery man that Toni was meeting at the club and he somehow got hold of her hotel keycard."

"Is there any more footage of him at the hotel?" ask Julia.

Detective Muhtar shakes his head. "Unfortunately not. No cameras face the guest rooms. All we have is Daniel exiting the lift."

"And none of Toni or Daniel leaving the building?" asks Julia.

"Correct."

Detective Muhtar says something in Turkish to the policewoman. She taps a few keys and brings up a scanned copy of the hotel blueprints.

"Each floor has a fire exit to a stairwell that leads to a street exit. No cameras. It is likely that your sister and Daniel left the hotel this way."

Julia walks the length of the room. "I don't believe this. Is Daniel even his real name? Is he actually a genuine doctor?"

Detective Muhtar picks up a folder. "We are checking with Interpol. We are also retrieving his email and phone history. Both calls and texts. That will give us more information."

Detective Muhtar pauses.

"What is it?" says Julia.

He looks at her evenly. "We found blood in the stairwell."

Julia feels sick. "Oh God."

"We will test for DNA."

Leo shakes his head, confused. "But what about Daniel's alibi? Yasmin Jefferson said she was with him in Bulgaria."

Julia's face darkens. "Yasmin Jefferson is a liar."

63

Yasmin is shaking. She lowers her hands and clutches the loose-fitting fabric of her harem pants as if to steady her nerves. But it's a losing battle. Her bottom lip begins to quiver wildly and she brings her hands to her mouth and starts to cry.

Julia is also shaking. With anger. She doesn't feel sorry for Yasmin one little bit. This is the woman who led the investigation astray. The woman who betrayed them. The woman who, through her own selfish actions, put Toni's life in grave danger.

In an effort to control her emotions, Julia forces herself to shift her gaze from Yasmin to the whiteboard above Yasmin's head. She reads each word slowly. *Apple. Banana. Pear. Apricot. Orange. Monday. Tuesday. Wednesday. Thursday. Friday. Saturday. Sunday.* She does this so she does not shout and thump the table. She does this so Yasmin will tell them everything she knows.

In the middle of the room, Leo and Detective Muhtar sit next to Yasmin. The seats are arranged in a half circle, like some sort of therapy session. Julia counts them. Thirteen in total. Thirteen chairs for one teacher and twelve English students. Five minutes earlier, the twelve students ranging from teens to old-timers had trailed past Julia when Yasmin had dismissed them mid-lesson after Detective Muhtar, Julia, and Leo had appeared at the door. On their way out, the students had shot furtive glances at Detective Muhtar (he had police written all over him) and exchanged whispers as they exited down the corridor. It would be the talk of the class for weeks.

Detective Muhtar pulls a clean handkerchief from his pocket and hands it to Yasmin.

"Thank you," she murmurs, taking it.

She dabs her eyes and throws back her head and blinks at the ceiling. "God, how could I be so stupid."

"Why don't you start at the beginning," says Detective Muhtar.

"When I first met Daniel?"

"Yes."

Shaking, Yasmin reaches for the water bottle on the desk behind her and takes a sip. She lowers the bottle.

"Okay. I can do this," she says.

Pausing again, she brushes the fringe from her eyes. She looks up. "I met Daniel eighteen months ago in Hanoi. I'd just returned from a three-day trek in Myanmar. I met him in the hostel there and we clicked right away. I was going through some heavy stuff at the time and he really helped me through that."

Julia and Leo exchange a glance. The freshman suicide.

"Heavy stuff?" says Detective Muhtar.

Yasmin's face grows tense. "There was an incident back home. Someone died and I felt partly responsible, which is why I went overseas in the first place. To get away from it all. It was a terrible time."

"And you fell in love with Daniel?"

"Absolutely. He was everything I could want in a man. Kind, considerate, handsome."

"And he loved you too?"

She studies her hands. "I thought so. There was talk of him meeting my family."

She trails off.

"What happened?" prompts Detective Muhtar.

Her mouth twists into a wry smile. "Toni happened." She glances at Julia then lowers her gaze. "Daniel and I were on a local bus in southern China. We were heading to the Lonji rice fields; autumn is supposed to be the best time of year to go because of the changing colors and the final harvest. At the last stop before the bus went deep into the mountains, this girl gets on with this crazy pink hair, ear stretchers, totally funky. She sees that Daniel and I are the only other foreigners on the bus and comes over to talk to us. I liked her right away. She was really funny and told us about her recent trip through India. We got to talking and decided we would do the trek through Lonji together, just the three of us. The trek started off well enough but she gets sick on the third day. I don't know, ate something bad, whatever. And Daniel plays doctor."

She falls silent. For a moment, Julia wonders if that's all Yasmin intends to say.

"And?" says Julia.

Yasmin looks at Julia, the misery clear on her face. "I had no clue. Or maybe I just refused to see. Looking back there had been signs. The lingering hands, the smiles. Daniel meant everything to me. He was the one, you know. I felt it in my bones. I wanted to marry him and have his babies. He told me that's what he wanted, too."

She begins crying again, hard.

"I didn't know they were having an affair for sure until I called Daniel at the Bulgarian orphanage and the staff told me he'd cancelled. When I tried to reach Toni in Greece, I found out she wasn't there either. That's when I realized they must be together for some alone time before the group trip across Turkey. I confronted Daniel when he arrived in Istanbul. He admitted that he and Toni had been having an affair. He told me they had met in Istanbul and he broke it off with her."

"And you believed him?"

Yasmin nodded. "I did."

Julia glares at her. "You lied to us. You told us you went to Bulgaria with Daniel and you both arrived together in Istanbul on Sunday."

Yasmin lowers her eyes. "Daniel asked me to. When Toni didn't show he got nervous. He said it would look bad if everyone knew he had met Toni right before she went missing. They might think he had something to do with it. He said something like that could ruin his career."

Julia's stunned. "So you just went along with it?"

Yasmin nods. "I trusted him. There was no way I thought he would have done anything to Toni."

"Why didn't you tell us this earlier? All this precious time wasted!"

"I'm sorry. I truly am."

"Really? You're sorry?" says Julia. "Is that all you've got to say for yourself?"

Yasmin weeps into her hand. "I didn't want to believe he had anything to do with Toni's disappearance. I still can't believe it. He's a good person. Apart from his fling with Toni, he's never done anything to hurt me. He's a doctor, for God's sake."

"You turned a blind eye."

Yasmin shakes her head vehemently. "No! It wasn't like that."

Leo interjects. "Do you know where he might have taken her?"

She looks at him. "I have no idea."

"Are you sure?"

"I really don't have a clue."

Julia bends down to face Yasmin. "There's something you're not telling us."

"I don't know where he is. Honestly, I don't."

"Oh, stop this, Yasmin," says Julia. "How can you still protect him after what he's done?"

Yasmin buries her face in her hands. "Please. I don't know anything."

"You've got to think, Yasmin," says Detective Muhtar, gently. "Is there anything that might give us a lead? Anything at all?"

Yasmin takes a breath. "There was a text."

"Between Daniel and Toni?"

Yasmin shakes her head. "No. I snuck a look at his phone in the days after Toni went missing. There was a text between him and a car rental place. He rented a vehicle. He told them he needed it for a cross-country trip to Lebanon."

"Was it a white van?"

"I don't know."

"Where did he rent it from?"

"I don't know."

"Think, Yasmin," presses Detective Muhtar. "What was the name of the hire place? You must have seen it."

Yasmin studies some midpoint in the air then nods to herself. "Supercheap Rentals, maybe?" She turns to look at them. "Yes, that's it. Daniel rented the vehicle from a place called Supercheap Rentals."

64

The trouble with big sisters, Daniel ponders, is that they meddle. Oh, they think they're doing their little sisters a favor by mothering them and getting involved in matters that are none of their business, but what Julia doesn't know is that underneath it all, Toni is fully on board with starting a new life with him.

Julia doesn't understand Toni. Nobody does, not like him. But that's big sisters for you, thinking they know best, thinking they are somehow superior just by age alone. His own sisters were the same, worse even. Half-sisters to be more precise. How dreadfully they had treated him when he went to live with his father as a small boy after his mother died. Those hurtful little bitches had told him he was nothing but a pub fuck. Your mother's no better than the town bike, they snickered. That stung because he knew it was true. Just like he knew it was true that his father didn't want him there, and that his stepmother viewed him as little more than something distasteful on the bottom of her shoe.

Daniel shoves aside those horrible memories and focuses on the journey ahead. The van is doing well. He hadn't been sure it would make the journey overland to the border, but by and large, the vehicle was performing well above expectations. Thankfully the main roads in Turkey are pretty good, not like the unpaved, rocky, dirt roads of Southeast Asia, where you could encounter slips every five minutes, especially in monsoon season.

The downside of Turkey is the dust you get from the arid landscape. A fine tawny powder that covers the dash and puts half-moons on the windshield. Daniel has to jet the glass with water at regular intervals to heighten visibility. He tries that now but the water is running low and a tiny squirt barely reaches the glass. He turns on the wipers regardless, and the dust smears, then blurs, until the windshield partially clears.

He needs to replenish supplies, check the status of the oil, and refill the water tank. Not yet, though. Daniel wants to log as much distance between him and Istanbul as possible. He had seen the reports and knew the police were looking for them. They had no clue as to where he was though, and he wanted to keep it that way.

Careful to keep his eyes on the road, he unscrews the drink bottle and takes a pull of the tepid water. If he keeps to this trajectory, he'll hit Iraq then Pakistan and India, all suitable places in which to disappear. But those countries do not appeal to him as much as Southeast Asia, where westerners are held in high regard and the cost of living is dirt cheap. Not to mention the skirmishes and wars that break out in this part of the world. No, that would not do at all. Daniel and Toni needed a safe place to raise their children.

Tomorrow, before the last run to the border, he will have to stop and stock up on food and water. There's no telling when he'll be able to get more once they cross the border into Iran. He needs to be careful with money, too. He has a healthy wad of US dollars but that must last because it's anyone's guess how many bribes he will need to dish out at the border.

A nasty smell filters through the car.

"Oh dear. Did we have an accident?" says Daniel, winding down the window. "Never fear, my love, we will have you sorted out in a bit."

He scans for somewhere to pull over. But everywhere is too exposed. He bears the stench for another twenty minutes until he finds a small bush-clad layby on the outskirts of a small village.

He parks and gets out. Making sure he's alone, he circles round to the back of the van and pulls a lever to lower the seat and enters the area where Toni is sweating beneath the nest of blankets. He peels back the layers. He pauses there, brushing his hand across her forehead, bending to graze his lips with hers. But the smell soon has him moving. He lifts her dress, exposes the adult diaper, and unfastens the sticky strip on either side.

It's nothing to him. He's dealt with all manner of bodily fluids and human detritus for years. Still, his nose wrinkles as he folds the soiled diaper and puts it in a plastic bag for later disposal.

Opening the cylinder of antibacterial wipes, he withdraws two sheets and wipes her clean.

She groans.

"There, there, I know it's cold."

Daniel smooths hydrocortisone ointment on her inner thighs where a red rash has formed, then slips a fresh diaper under her hips, fastening the sticky strips and pulling her dress back down.

"What did I tell you, my love? Fresh as a daisy."

He glances at his watch. She's not due for another shot for an hour yet so he leaves her there and gets out of the van to study the darkening horizon. Should they stop for the night? Or perhaps it is better to keep driving, put as much distance between them and the authorities as possible? It is only a matter of time before he is recognized by some local.

No, he needs rest. He's no good to Toni if they have an accident. He thinks of the small town they just passed. Perhaps he could rent a room there. But Daniel quickly dismisses the idea. It's better to sleep in the van. Doing otherwise risks identification.

He tips his wrist to look at his watch. One more hour of driving and he'll stop. He returns to the van, reaching behind the driver's seat for his duffel bag. He digs inside, can't find what he's looking for. He turns on the interior light and peers into the bag, then tips the contents out on the seat next to him and sorts through it. He sits back, staring at his things, heart hammering. It isn't there. The map, the one upon which he had so carefully penciled out his route, is missing.

65

"His full name is Daniel George Bambury," says Sergeant Mager, the bleary-eyed Greater Manchester police sergeant. "He—"

Sergeant Mager's voice cuts out, his face becomes pixelated, and the video conferencing screen goes black. Detective Muhtar reaches for the remote and looks at the buttons helplessly. Suddenly Sergeant Mager's face flashes up and the screen returns to normal.

"Can you hear me now?" says Sergeant Mager, raising his voice.

"Loud and clear," says Leo.

"Grand."

Sergeant Mager lifts the coffee cup to his mouth and takes a chug. His bald head shines as a beam of morning light pulses through the window behind him. He has a kind face, one that has seen too much pain, and Julia guesses he's been a cop for his whole life and is nearing retirement.

Sergeant Mager sets his coffee down. "We questioned Bambury in relation to the disappearance of Annabel Newsome, his girlfriend of two years."

"When was this?" asks Detective Muhtar.

Sergeant Mager consults the file in front of him. "Five years ago now. To give the bloke credit, he was very obliging. He seemed every bit as concerned as everyone else about his missing girlfriend. At first, I didn't think he had anything to do with it, but Annabel's mum and dad insisted he must be involved. They said Annabel had ended the relationship and he couldn't let it go. Annabel caught him following her on more than one occasion. He called the house all the time. There were frequent break-ins in the Newsome residence, too. Nothing would be taken. But the message was clear—I can get you any time I want."

Julia's eyes drift to the lower righthand corner of the screen where there's a mug shot of a smiling Daniel, his sincere blue eyes locked on the camera. It could have easily been mistaken for a snap in a high school yearbook.

"Did her parents say why they broke up?" she says.

"Textbook possessive boyfriend stuff. Had to know where she was every minute of the day, told her what to wear, who she could see."

"And violence?"

"Mum said she'd sometimes overhear heated verbal arguments and saw bruises on Annabel's arms. But Annabel denied Daniel was physically violent—not uncommon for victims of abuse, unfortunately." Sergeant Mager's face grows dark. "On the night Annabel disappeared, she'd been at a pub with friends in the few days before Christmas. At first, we thought she might have drowned in the canal—there had been a spate of incidents involving intoxicated patrons falling into the water—but her parents insisted Annabel wasn't a heavy drinker and her friends stated she only had one pint all evening." Sergeant Mager runs his palm over his bald head and looks at them. "I believe Bambury killed Annabel and hid her body somewhere, but we were never able to prove it."

Julia exhales. "God."

"This is a man who likes to be in control. If things don't go his way, there's no telling what he'll do."

"Was he investigated for anything else?"

“Nothing official, but there was another girl he was involved with when he was sixteen who went missing. She was a neighbor. I made some inquires when I was looking into Annabel’s case. The girl’s name was Sheila McFadden, if I remember rightly. The word on the street was that Daniel and Sheila had been quite friendly. Then one day she turns up dead in a field not far from the school they both attended.”

“What makes you think Daniel was involved?” says Julia.

“He was the one who found her body. There were other things too, an alibi that didn’t quite add up, and he was overly helpful to the inquiry, always checking in with lead investigators to see how the case was going, which was strange for a sixteen-year-old kid. But no proof really, just suspicions.”

“How did Sheila die?”

“Strangulation. A ligature round her neck. Her school stockings, I believe.”

“What about Daniel’s background?” says Detective Muhtar.

Sergeant Mager drains his cup of coffee and gets up to pour himself another. “He told everyone he knew he was adopted, but in actual fact Bambury’s mother abandoned him when he was five. She dumped him with a man who didn’t believe he was Daniel’s real father. Consequently, Bambury was treated little better than a slave by the household and was subjected to terrible abuse. There were frequent calls to child services by neighbors but Bambury was never removed from the father’s care. When I was questioning Bambury about Annabel’s disappearance, I asked him about the abuse and while he accepted it had occurred, he refused to admit that his real mother had abandoned him. He insisted she'd died of cancer when he was five and that was the reason he was sent to live with his father. Even when I told him we had tracked his mother down and she was alive and well and living in Bournemouth, he still wouldn't accept it."

"Is he really a doctor?" says Julia.

"Oh, yes," says Sergeant Mager, nodding. "And by all accounts he worked very hard to get there, held down two jobs while studying and kept an A average. He's a very bright boy. He wanted to make something of himself, despite his rough upbringing."

"And what's your take on the situation with Toni?"

Sergeant Mager looks thoughtful. "You think he abducted the victim from her hotel?"

Detective Muhtar nods. "And according to records at Supercheap Rentals, a man fitting Daniel's description hired a van for a month using a fake license in the name of Craig Pullman."

Sergeant Mager looks thoughtful. "So he's planned for it—he was going to take her whether she decided to go with him voluntarily or not."

Detective Muhtar nods. "I agree. A search is underway. We are running number plate recognition software over our national traffic cameras. But Turkey is a big country. Also, with the time that has passed, he could have crossed borders already."

Julia turns away, despondent. "It's like looking for a needle in a haystack."

Sergeant Mager takes a breath. "Look, I'll be frank with you. This guy's no dummy. He's a man with a plan and he's well-resourced. You've got your work cut out for you.

But don't lose hope. Go back and review all the evidence. You never know what that might turn up."

66

They take Sergeant Mager's advice and go back to the start. Right to the beginning and review everything. Every document, witness statement, cell phone record, CCTV image, social media account, and piece of physical evidence they have. While the intention is to find any clue about where Daniel has taken Toni, Detective Muhtar urges Leo and Julia to keep an open mind and examine the material with fresh eyes. With all the twists and turns in the case, another relevant lead could easily be buried there.

Detective Muhtar organizes a discreet breakout room for them. It isn't exactly orthodox to have Julia and Leo assist him in this way and he explains he's not keen to draw attention to that fact. Julia's just grateful he's letting them help at all.

The plan is to work systematically through everything in chronological order, writing down any possible further leads on Post-it Notes and sticking them to the whiteboard as they go. From there they'll prioritize which areas to pursue first.

The entirety of the investigation is contained in two files and six clear tamper-proof evidence bags. They're a pitiful reminder of what Toni's life has been reduced to. A few boxes and plastic bags. It doesn't seem much to Julia. Not for all that has gone on.

She glances at the largest evidence bag containing Toni's backpack, the childish crocheted doll key ring squashed up hard against the clear plastic, and feels ill. She had only ever seen the photograph of it washed up on the rocks near the sea wall. That was bad enough, but seeing it now, a three-dimensional object right in front of her, is jarring, especially given she now knows it was Daniel who tossed it in the water after he took Toni from the hotel.

Leo glances at her. "You up for this?"

"I'm fine."

Leo slides the laptop across the table. "Why don't you take the social media accounts and I'll take the physical items."

"Thanks, Leo, that's thoughtful, but I'll be okay. Let's just get this over with."

Julia opens the plastic bag containing the backpack and is met with the salt-laden odor of the Bosporus. She bites back sadness at having to handle what is, for all intents and purposes, the total sum of Toni's worldly goods. The canvas feels brittle and stiff to the touch, the sea having done its best to claim it. She checks the bag thoroughly, probing pockets and compartments, prying open zips and snaps now beginning to show signs of rust. Nothing but grit and the dregs of what is probably seaweed.

She scribbles on a Post-it Note: What happened to the pack's other items? Clothes, toiletries, etc.? She sticks the note on the whiteboard then turns her attention to Toni's passport, flipping through the water-damaged pages, the immigration stamps now little more than inky streaks, the tiny passport two-by-two-inch photo of Toni faded and unsmiling. Toni's hair is much shorter and not pink. Exactly like the last time Julia saw her in the flesh on the day Toni confessed to sleeping with Leo. A few weeks after that Toni left the US for good and Julia never saw her again. She writes another note: How can they exit country without passports? Bribes at the border?

Next, Julia turns her attention to the wallet and examines the contents. Two expired credit cards. Forty US dollars in two twenties. Toni's US driver's license. A printed receipt in Chinese for one item that cost $40RMB. Three used bus tickets. One for a journey from Athens International Airport. The other two for one-way trips in China and Thailand.

Julia thinks that's all there is when she notices something wedged in the tight space behind the vertical credit card pockets. Pinching the corner, she wriggles out a photograph folded into quarters. She opens it and gasps.

Toni, Julia, and their mom, happy and young. Toni about three, Julia around seven. Toni is perched on their mom's hip, her tiny hand clasping some impossibly pink cotton candy. Julia stands on the other side, her mother's arm protectively around her shoulder, holding her close. Looming in the background is a giant Ferris wheel and rickety-looking roller coaster. This was not the fractured miserable family unit that Julia remembered. This was a loving family unit out for a fun day at the State Fair. But what's more remarkable is Julia's mother, with waves of black, glossy hair cascading over her sun-kissed shoulders, eyes as bright and blue as the sky above her head. Julia has never seen her look so healthy. She tries to remember the day the photo was taken but draws a complete blank. It might as well be another family entirely.

"What is it?" says Leo.

Julia shows him. He smiles.

"Wow. You guys look happy."

"Yeah. We do," she says, eyes watering. "Toni kept it all this time."

Leo hands back the photograph. "It's really special, Julia."

Julia folds up the image and returns it to Toni's wallet. "I miss her, Leo."

He gives her a sympathetic smile. "Me, too."

Julia returns to the job at hand, picking up the final item. The penny necklace. The most troubling piece of evidence of all and a major loose end. How did it get from Toni's neck to Asen Civik? A simple coincidence? Had the necklace come loose when Daniel kidnapped Toni from the hotel and Civik found it? It's impossible to know because Civik is still refusing to talk. Julia writes a note: Re-question Civik? Examine CCTV footage for Civik in Toni's hotel area?

She places the penny necklace on the table next to the other items and stands back to look at everything in its entirety. She tries to clear her head of misconceptions and approach things with a dispassionate, clinical eye. It's like a puzzle. Much like when Julia was studying for her medical degree, when she had to make sense of the disparate parts of a human body and how they all fit together. The bones (two hundred and seventy at birth decreasing to two hundred and six at death), the organs (approximately seventy-nine, five of which are vital), blood vessels (made up of arteries, veins, and capillaries), and tissue (the core types being epithelial, connective, muscular, and nervous). Everything is relevant and connected. Everything is interdependent and necessary. Together everything makes up an entire whole that is a single human body.

But here? Well, here nothing fits. There's no cohesion. No interdependence. No single story to tell.

She puts down her pen and glances up at her notes. Five Posit-its is all she has. Not much. And nothing to indicate where Daniel may have taken Toni.

Julia looks over at Leo and Detective Muhtar, both of whom have yet to write anything.

"How are you two going? Anything of interest?"

"Nope," says Leo, cheekbone planted on his fist, staring at the laptop.

Detective Muhtar lifts his eyes from the cell phone spreadsheet data and shakes his head.

"Nothing new here."

Julia feels a pinch of disappointment. She picks up the stack of witness statements. Maybe she'll have better luck with these.

67

By the time the three of them have picked over everything, there's a healthy number of tiny orange flags on the whiteboard, which is both disconcerting and reassuring, because although it shows just how much they don't know, at least they have defined what they are looking for and can get on with finding it.

"What now?" says Leo, sipping the coffee that Detective Muhtar had arranged.

"We prioritize," says Julia, opening a window to let in some air. "Work out what things to pursue first. Before that, let's give each other a brief rundown of what we've found."

Leo goes first. He tells them he's checked Yasmin's, Toni's, and Daniel's social media accounts, as well as performed a thorough Google search.

"One useful piece of information I found is that Daniel banks with Barclays, or did in the past. Could be handy in case we want to check his bank records to track his spending. You know, follow the money sort of thing. Assuming he's not just using cash."

Julia nods. "Good. Anything else?"

"That's it."

Detective Muhtar picks up where Leo left off, walking them through a summary of the cell phone data. He tells them there's nothing in the texts to indicate where Daniel is taking Toni, no flights or hotel accommodations arranged. The only people to appear in Daniel's contacts are Yasmin, Toni, and the organizations he worked for.

Detective Muhtar goes on to explain that he's checked the location data relating to Daniel's cell phone, but apart from some pings on cell towers around Istanbul, there's been nothing in four days.

"Do you think he ditched it?" says Leo.

Detective Muhtar nods. "Almost certainly. This is an intelligent man, I'm sure he would know we can track him. He is probably using a burner."

Julia fills them on her review.

"The accounts of Sally, Debbie, Conner, and Nicole are pretty much exactly what they told Leo and I," she says, touching the stack of statements. "The only thing I can think of is to re-interview them and ask if they can recall Daniel mentioning a favorite part of the world."

"Are they even still in Istanbul?" says Leo.

"Probably not, but we have their email addresses," says Detective Muhtar.

"Then we should definitely try," says Julia. She pauses, looking at the whiteboard. "So that's everything?"

They nod.

"I think we should review everything one more time, just to be sure."

Detective Muhtar and Leo stare at her.

"We've been at it for hours already, Julia," says Leo, finally.

It's a big ask, she knows. "Please."

Leo lets out a breath and reaches for his laptop. "Whatever you need."

*

They work well into the night, each of them beyond the point of exhaustion, searching for the needle in the haystack they might have overlooked.

Just before dawn, Leo sits up. "I've got something."

He shows them his laptop.

Julia looks at the screen. "Daniel's Facebook?"

"Yeah."

Leo clicks on a post about Daniel's medical volunteering. There's a photo of Daniel standing outside a white medical tent in some dusty, parched part of the world. Julia looks at the sign fixed to the tent's front canopy. Viva Volunteer Medical. There's an insignia, too—a sun and a stethoscope.

Julia frowns. "I've seen that somewhere before."

Leo smiles. "Indeed."

"Are you going to tell us or do we have to guess?" she says.

Leo clicks on another dated two years ago. "Tell me what you see."

Another photo of Daniel. This time he's listening to a little boy's chest with a stethoscope, surrounded by children and parents, mostly mothers and nurses.

"There, in the background, do you see her?"

Julia scans the photo again. Nothing registers. "See who, Leo?"

Detective Muhtar leans in and points to a dark-haired woman in the background in a nurse's uniform.

"Ela Cevik."

68

It is too much of a coincidence to be a coincidence, as Leo had put it, and after some checking by Detective Muhtar, that turned out to be more than true. Daniel and Ela had both worked for Viva Volunteer Medical, a state-funded entity that employed local nurses like Ela and recruited offshore doctors like Daniel. Records show that Daniel had undertaken three assignments for Viva Voluntary Medical in Western Turkey in poverty-stricken Kurdish areas. So had Ela. In fact, she'd been Daniel's senior nurse on all three assignments so there was no doubt the two knew each other extremely well.

"That's not all," says Detective Muhtar. "We checked her phone number against Bambury's and there were calls between them the Saturday night Daniel took Toni."

Julia's stunned. "You're joking."

"Three calls in total," says Detective Muhtar grimly. "The first was for ten minutes at one forty-six a.m., the second was half an hour later and two minutes in length. The final call was three hours later and lasted for thirty seconds."

Julia picks up the file and stares at Ela's employee photo, the full implications dawning on her.

"She helped him."

"Yes."

"Do you think that's where Toni was kept? At Ela's house?" says Leo.

Julia frowns. "But I went through the entire house and Toni wasn't there. I'm certain of it."

Leo shoots her a sympathetic look. "Everyone was so distracted with all the ruckus about the artifacts, we could've missed other rooms. Besides that, it's a big property with barns and other outbuildings, Toni could have been hidden in one of those."

"But the police would have searched everywhere."

"Let us focus on what comes next," says Detective Muhtar.

"That's obvious, isn't it? We need to arrest Ela and get her to tell us everything she knows," says Julia firmly.

Detective Muhtar shakes his head. "Much of our conclusions are speculation. We need hard evidence for an arrest warrant. We will never be granted one on what we have."

"Surely the phone calls are enough?" says Julia.

"It's circumstantial, so it is not likely." Detective Muhtar pauses. "Arresting Ela may not be our best strategy anyway."

Julia looks at him. "What do you mean? She's our best chance of finding out where Daniel is going."

Leo interjects. "Detective Muhtar's right, Julia. Ela could refuse to talk, like her uncle and father did, then where would that leave us? No. We need her to cooperate. Treat her with kid gloves."

"My thinking exactly," says Detective Muhtar.

69

Ela Cevik's eyes widen when she opens the front door.

"*Merhaba*, Ela," says Detective Muhtar. "May we speak with you?"

Her eyes pass from him to Julia then Leo and back again. "What do you want?"

"It would be better if we come inside."

She pauses. "You have news of my father?"

Detective Muhtar shakes his head. "This is not about him."

She bites her lip. "They refuse to let me see him."

"His charges are very serious."

She falls silent. Somewhere in the distance a cow moans.

"We're not leaving until you talk to us, Ela," says Julia.

Ela meets Julia's eyes briefly, then quickly looks away. "I have nothing to say."

She looks over Julia's shoulder and her mouth tightens. Julia turns to see two women standing at the top of the driveway, staring.

Julia says, "Surely you would rather talk inside, Ela, the village must be gossiping enough already."

Exhaling, Ela eventually nods. "Very well. We can talk in the living room."

She turns to trudge the length of the hallway, the others following. When they enter the living room, Julia's shocked by the state of it. The place is a mess and looks like it hasn't been cleaned since the day of Ela's father's arrest. Packaging and debris litter the floor from when the artifacts were seized by police. The curtains are drawn against the sunshine, only adding to the gloom, and there's an unpleasant odor of meat left too long on the kitchen counter.

"Please sit," Ela says, tonelessly, taking a seat herself.

No tea this time, no home-baked spiced cookies, just a blank stare at some midpoint in the distance.

Detective Muhtar leans forward, lacing his hands together.

"What can you tell us about Dr. Daniel Bambury?"

Ela's face remains passive, artificially so. "Who?"

Detective Muhtar plays along. "He worked as a doctor with Viva Volunteer Medical."

She shrugs and says nothing. Julia notices the slight tremor in her hands.

"You worked there also, I think?" says Detective Muhtar.

"Occasionally."

"But you never met a Dr. Bambury?"

She shakes her head. "Not that I recall."

Julia's sighs, exasperated. "Ela, stop this. We know you knew each other."

Detective Muhtar digs in his pocket for his cell phone, unlocks it, and shows Ela the photograph Leo found of Ela and Daniel on Facebook.

When she looks, a flush of red creeps up Ela's neck.

"That's you, isn't it, Ela? With Daniel Bambury?" says Detective Muhtar.

She lifts her eyes. "Yes, I may have worked with Dr. Bambury a few times, I do not believe that is a crime."

"Five," says Detective Muhtar.

She frowns. "Five what?"

"You worked with Dr. Bambury on five occasions."

"Oh, I don't think it was that many," she says weakly.

"According to your employment records at Viva it was."

She stands, shaking. "I would like you all to leave."

Julia doesn't move. "We're not going anywhere, Ela. Tell us what happened. Toni was here, wasn't she? Did Daniel ask you to hide her?"

"Please leave."

"Ela, it's pointless denying it. We have evidence."

"Your evidence is incorrect. I haven't done anything."

"Sit down, Ela," says Detective Muhtar.

Ela licks her lips. "Am I in trouble?"

"That depends on your level of cooperation."

She stands there, not moving.

Julia says, "We have phone calls, Ela. We know he was in touch with you the night Toni disappeared."

Ela swallows. "I was scared."

Julia frowns. "Why were you scared?"

Ela drops back into her chair and holds her head in her hands. "You have to believe me. It wasn't just about money. Yes, he paid me, but he threatened me also. I did something very stupid while I was working at Viva and he said he would tell."

"Daniel blackmailed you?"

Ela nods. "They dump medication close to its expiration date. We are not meant to take it but sometimes I do. Sometimes I take it to sell to make a little money." She looks up. "You must understand. Life is very hard. My father is a learned man and has no job because of the economic climate. We do what we can to survive. Daniel said if I did not help him, he would tell the medical board and I'd lose my license. I would be without my livelihood—"

Julia raises a hand. "Okay, okay, slow down, Ela. Take us back to the beginning."

Nodding, Ela takes a breath and interlocks her restless hands. "I had not heard from Daniel for over a year when he called me nearly two weeks ago and asked for my help. He said he had a friend who had injured herself and needed a place to stay."

She hesitates.

"Go on," says Julia.

Ela stands. "It is better that I show you."

Julia exchanges a look with Leo and Detective Muhtar. "Show us what exactly?"

"Come."

Ela crosses the living room to the rear door and retrieves a set of keys from a rusty hook. Julia, Leo, and Detective Muhtar follow her outside to a courtyard with whitewashed walls and pomegranate trees bending with fruit. In the distance, half a dozen cattle graze in the fields. Ela takes a stony path around a corner, pausing when she reaches a disused wine barrel. She rolls the barrel to one side exposing a wooden access with a latch to some sort of underground area. Bending, she unlocks the access to reveal a set of stairs plunging into the darkness below.

"Wait here," she says.

She descends the staircase, and it's not long before a light comes on.

"Please come down now," she says, looking up at them.

Julia goes first, heart thumping wildly. When she reaches the bottom, she finds herself in a tiny, damp room. On the floor, a mattress, pillows, blankets. A sweater and pair of jeans crumpled up in the corner. Something catches her eye. An IV stand. A box of bandages. A bag of syringes.

"He came and took her," says Ela.

"When?" says Julia.

"Yesterday."

Julia picks up the bag of syringes. "How badly was she hurt?"

Ela lowers her eyes. "He said she had an accident. That she fell."

"You didn't answer my question," says Julia, fingers tightening round the syringes.

"She was unconscious."

"A head injury?"

Ela nods. "He gave me medication to give her."

"What medication?"

Ela hesitates.

"Ela, what medication was it?"

Ela kneels down and reaches inside a box and pulls out some vials and shows Julia.

Julia's heart races when she sees what they are. "These are tranquilizers, Ela. Why would you do this? You must have known what you were doing was wrong. You're a nurse, for God's sake!"

Ela's eyes fill with tears. "She was safe here. I looked after her."

Julia shakes her head, incredulous. "Looked after her? You kept her drugged when she should have been in the hospital!"

"The penny necklace," says Leo. "How did your uncle get it?"

Ela's eyes flick to him. "I gave it to him. I thought it was gold. He was going to sell it and we were going to split the money. Father knew nothing of this."

Detective Muhtar interjects. "Did Bambury say where he was going?"

Ela shakes her head.

"He never told me anything." She pulls out something from her apron. A piece of paper. "But he left this behind."

Julia takes it. A map. With a hand-drawn route and annotations.

She looks up at Leo and Detective Muhtar. "They're heading to Laos."

70

For the first time in a long time there is hope, real hope. They have a map outlining Daniel's entire escape plan in meticulous handwritten detail. He had predetermined precisely what route he would take from Istanbul to Laos. Recorded well-considered and specific annotations in the margins. Estimated the various times it would take him to get from A to B. Noted where he could stop for gas along the way.

The level of detail was simply staggering: he had left absolutely no stone unturned. If that wasn't chilling enough, seeing all this written down in Daniel's tiny neat penmanship—definitely not the usual chicken scratch of doctors' handwriting—was a sure sign to Julia of how calculating, organized, and in control he was.

Julia lifts her eyes from the map and looks at Detective Muhtar.

"Any idea where he would be by now?" she says.

"He'll be past Ankara for certain. He's most probably here in Cappadocia or here in Malatya," he says, pointing to two of Daniel's markings on the map.

Detective Muhtar's phone rings and he excuses himself.

Julia looks at Leo. "You did good, by the way."

"I did?"

"Finding the image of Ela and Daniel on his Facebook was a really nice pickup."

"Oh, that."

She drops into a chair. "Tell me we're close to finding her, Leo."

"Yes, I believe we are. I can feel it in my bones."

Detective Muhtar rushes in, phone pressed to his chest. "There's been a development. Please come quick."

*

The sound of her voice is jarring. Even though Julia hasn't spoken to Toni in over two years, her sister's voice is unmistakable. Breathy. Slightly expectant. What's new, though, is the hint of a slur.

Initially there's confusion because the emergency police operator does not speak very good English.

Toni: "I'm Toni Norris. I'm an American citizen. I was abducted from my hotel in Istanbul by a man named Dr. Daniel Bambury. Please hurry."

Operator: "What is this word abducted?"

Toni: "Kidnapped, taken against my will. Please hurry. I got away from him but he's

close by. He's going to find me."

Operator: "What is your location?"

Toni: "I don't know. A small town. We have been driving for a long time."

Operator: "Are there any road signs?"

Toni: "They're in Turkish. I don't understand them."

Operator: "Can you ask someone where you are?"

Toni: "I can't, he'll see me." A breath. "It's a desert place. There's a billboard advertising hot air ballooning. Oh, please hurry. He's going to find me."

Operator: "Where is the man now?"

Toni: "Looking for me. I can hear him calling my name." Pause. "He's coming. I have to go."

She hangs up. Detective Muhtar clicks off the recording.

"The call came in this morning. We traced it to Göreme, a small town located in the Cappadocian region. We go there now, okay?"

71

The strangeness of the Cappadocia landscape is the first thing to strike Julia as she looks out the window of the six-seater charter flight. The barren terrain is utterly mesmerizing, something like a cross between Mars and the moon—arid and desert-like, with clusters of weird cone-shaped volcanic rock formations pirouetting into the sky. In the distance, the Southern Taurus Mountains loom majestically, while in the east, large tracks of sandstone dominate the land.

Julia spies a cluster of houses and single-story buildings in what must be the Göreme township where Toni's mobile was tracked to. The small town is surrounded by more of the cone-shaped pillars, although these have cave-like houses and churches carved into the rock.

"Fairy chimneys," says Detective Muhtar, raising his voice over the twin turbo prop engines. "They were created over centuries. People still live in them today. Inside they are like normal houses with kitchens and bedrooms and bathrooms."

"Remarkable," says Julia.

The pilot says something in Turkish.

"We land now," says Detective Muhtar, buckling his seat belt and gesturing for everyone to do the same.

Julia looks out the window and feels her throat tighten. How the heck is the pilot expected to land among these towers of sandstone?

She glances at the others—Leo, Detective Muhtar, the two Istanbul police officers, Officer Koc and Officer

Dogan, whom Detective Muhtar had managed to enlist to help with the search—and wonders if they're as nervous as her.

She looks back out the window at the rock formations, which seem precariously close, and has a flash of the little plane exploding into pieces.

"You all right?" says Leo.

She nods and says nothing, eyes glued to the window. Thankfully the pilot seems to know what he's doing and expertly threads his way through the towers of rock, and before long they are rolling to a stop on a small landing strip.

Julia takes three deep breaths to steady her nerves. That was not an experience she would like to repeat every day.

Detective Muhtar ushers everyone from the aircraft and into a rental car for the fifteen-minute journey to the outskirts of Göreme, the place where the cell tower is located. It's also the area where all the hot air balloon operators have their businesses, which makes sense given Toni had seen a billboard advertising hot air ballooning.

Detective Muhtar turns right off the main road, drives a short distance inland until they reach a cluster of prefabricated buildings, and comes to a stop.

"This is it," he says, cutting the engine. He points out the windshield at the man-made tower jutting into the sky. "That's the cell phone over there, and these are the hot air balloon operators."

The place seems eerily empty.

"Where is everyone?" says Leo.

"Hot air ballooning is done at dawn. Given it is now late afternoon, we will be fortunate to find any operators still here but Officers Dogan and Koc and I will go and check.

Dr. Norris, it would be good if you and Leo could look around and identify any place that fits the description Toni gave on the phone about where she was hiding."

Julia nods. "Of course."

They exit the vehicle, and Leo and Julia stand watching as Detective Muhtar and Officers Dogan and Koc head toward the prefab buildings.

Leo looks around at the parched landscape. "Which way do you want to go?"

Julia gestures left. "This is as good as any."

They make their way across the dusty plains, the sun beating down on their shoulders. As they walk, Julia's struck by the stillness of the place, along with the profound sense of quiet. Maybe it's the lack of trees or absence of wind; whatever the cause, it feels as though they've been dropped into the middle of nowhere.

They cross a small rise and find nothing on the other side. Julia stands looking at the horizon and feels her heart sink. It's just so sparse out here. With only clusters of vegetation. Barren hills and valleys. Nowhere to hide. When Toni made the phone call it was near dawn. 4:52 a.m. At that time of morning, it would have been terrifyingly dark and lonesome. Julia glances at the quiet road leading into the Göreme township.

"Are we thinking the same thing?" says Leo, staring at the road too.

"Daniel pulled up the van to sleep here and Toni slipped out."

Leo nods. "Yeah."

Julia exhales and looks around. "But where did she go?"

Leo raises his hands to shield his eyes and studies the landscape. "What's that over there?"

In the distance, there's a group of buildings. A ramshackle house and a couple of barns. Possibly a ranch. Julia and Leo look at each other.

"Let's go get Detective Muhtar," she says.

72

Despite the two horses tethered to a hitching post, it turns out the place is not a ranch at all but an artist's abode, a potter by the looks of the stacks of glazed earthenware through the window. When a knock on the front door of the main house brings no response, Detective Muhtar, Julia, and Leo decide to check the two outbuildings.

They locate the potter in the first barn. The petite woman in her late fifties is busy at a foot-propelled potter's wheel, shaping a mound of slippery wet clay into what might have been a water jug. She's so absorbed in her work that she doesn't notice them standing at the open door.

Detective Muhtar clears his throat. The woman looks up, her face clouding over when she sees them. She stops the wheel with her hand and the object lies there, half-finished, as she listens to Detective Muhtar explain the situation.

"I speak English," she says. "My father was a teacher. My name is Lucinda."

Lucinda gets to her feet and rinses her hands at a sink.

"So," says Detective Muhtar, continuing in English. "Did you see anything unusual last night or this morning?"

She dries her hands on a cloth and heads for the door. "You should speak to my son."

They follow Lucinda to the adjoining barn that houses a wood-fired kiln and shelving stacked with jugs, plates, and ornaments, some glazed, others not. The sight is impressive. Lucinda is clearly not only talented but industrious too.

Julia spots a shirtless man on his back beneath the southern end of the kiln, a toolbox lying open beside him.

"Jayar," says Lucinda. "They are here about the girl."

The young man of about twenty slips out from beneath the kiln and gets to his feet. There's a black smear on his face. Detective Muhtar introduces himself, Julia, and Leo.

"You saw something?" says Detective Muhtar.

Jayar nods. "I start the firing work around five a.m. when it's still cool. When I got here this morning, the door was open." He points to a pile of broken pottery. "Someone had been in here. They knocked the table over but I could not see anything stolen. Then I hear yelling. I go outside and I see two people over by the road. A man and a woman. Foreigners."

Detective Muhtar shows him the flyer.

"Was this the woman?"

Jayar shrugs. "It was dark. They were very far away."

"Was there a vehicle?"

Jayar nods. "A white van."

"It's them," says Julia, looking at Leo.

"Could you hear what they were saying?"

"Not really. I thought they were tourists having an argument. I watched them for a while. Then they got in the van and drove off."

"Which direction did they go?" says Detective Muhtar.

The man points to the road. "East, toward the township."

"What time was this?" says Detective Muhtar.

"Between five fifteen and five thirty a.m."

Julia looks at her watch and feels disappointment wash over her. It is now after two in the afternoon.

"They'll be long gone," she says.

"But at least we know she has a phone," says Leo. "She may try and contact us again."

"Show them, Jayar," says Lucinda.

Jayar wipes his hands on a rag and heads for a cabinet. He takes a key from his pocket, unlocks the first drawer, and opens it. When he turns around, there's a cell phone in his hand.

"They left this behind."

73

Daniel lifts his eyes and stares at the hospital entrance. He's been here for over an hour, watching. It's more of a clinic than hospital, by western standards at least. But he's satisfied it will serve his purpose. He can't believe he'd been so stupid as to leave the map behind. What a silly, amateur mistake. There's a chance the authorities don't have it, that he has paid Ela enough to buy her silence, but that is unlikely.

No, by now the authorities would most probably have made the connection between him and Ela, and he doesn't doubt for one second that she'd throw him under the bus to save herself. Consequently, he has to assume that his entire route is now in possession of the police, forcing him to change his plans.

His current thinking is that since Laos is now out of the question, they will go to India instead. There are plenty of places to disappear there. While he has no contacts in India, he is clever and resourceful and has no doubt he can find Toni and him a suitable place in which to live and raise children. So instead of heading for Iran, they will go through Iraq and Saudi Arabia, then cross the water into India.

But first he needs to get inside that damn hospital. He continues to watch the entrance waiting for the right time. He's desperate to get on with it but can't risk getting caught. Patience, he tells himself, the opportune moment will arise.

He's here because of mistake number two. He had let Toni escape. Even now, he can't believe how it had happened. Yesterday, the map's loss had thrown him off so badly he had driven well into the night, becoming dreadfully fatigued and nearly causing a head-on collision with a semi-trailer. Consequently, he'd been forced to pull to the side of the road to rest. He'd intended only to nap lightly for an hour or so, then get back on the road so they would make it to the border, but he fell into a deep sleep instead. So deep, in fact, that he never even heard the sound of the back door of the van opening.

When he finally awoke and saw it open, he thought he'd been robbed. Then the dreadful realization hit—Toni was gone. She'd outsmarted him. She had kept so quiet that he'd missed her shot by an hour and she had seized the opportunity to flee.

He knew she could not have gotten far with her injury, and as it turned out, it took him less than thirty minutes to find her. It was close to dawn and easy enough to see her footprints in the sandy ground, so he followed the rambling trail through the bushes and came to a clearing bordering the area where tourists did hot air ballooning. In the distance, small clusters of people were being helped into baskets by guides. Burners glowed orange and balloons were swelling. Dozens and dozens of them. Quite beautiful, in fact. But there was no time to linger. He had to hurry. Soon all those balloons would fill the sky and many eyes would be looking down upon him.

He turned left and saw the farmhouse. Although he couldn't explain it, he felt certain Toni was in there. Call it what you will, gut instinct, divine guidance, whatever it was, he headed straight for it and found her huddled the barn. She had looked like a terrified child when he reached out to her.

"Don't be afraid," he had said.

"No, no," she'd said, batting his hand away.

It was pitiful, really. She was still so ill and vulnerable. Even so, she'd surprised him when he tried to pull her out and she bolted from his grasp. Rather than go after her, he stood watching, his heart aching at the sight of her desperate but futile attempts at running away. She only managed a few yards before her legs began to wobble and she collapsed on the ground.

As she lay there, he had looked around in the darkness and said a prayer of thanks for they were alone, in the middle of nowhere, and no one had seen a thing. By the time he marshaled her into the van, she had begun moaning in pain because her shot was well overdue.

"There, there. We'll soon have you right again, my love."

But when Daniel went to retrieve his medical kit from the driver's side pocket, it was gone. Then he spied something just outside the passenger window—his kit agape, contents spilled out everywhere. The pouch where he kept the medication was rolled open and all the vials were smashed and needles bent. When he realized what she'd done, a cold shot of fury hit him and he had shaken her.

"You stupid girl!" he had shouted. "You stupid, stupid girl! That was for you! To take the pain away! Why would you do that?"

So he did the only thing he could—bound her hands and feet and gagged her. She had started crying, but he was unmoved.

"You've only got yourself to blame."

So here he is now, outside the hospital, trying to fix her mistake. He's been here all day, watching the comings and goings of the clinic personnel. The lone doctor on duty smoking out the back. The nurses checking their phones. The orderlies tossing rubbish into the disposal bins to the left.

The sun is going down and the time will soon be right. Soon there will be a changeover of shift and people will be distracted and less likely to notice a stranger in their midst. And because small clinics like this one usually have poor safeguards on their medication cabinets, it is likely that Daniel will be able to walk right in and simply take what he needs. Still, there is a risk. And he would have preferred not to be here. But he had to have supplies, to subdue Toni for their journey. Then he will be able to hit the road, and in less than sixteen hours they will be at the Iraq border. In less than sixteen hours they will be free.

Daniel bends over the back seat to check Toni's bindings. Satisfied she isn't going anywhere, he returns to the front. He pulls his baseball cap down low, takes a breath, and opens the door.

74

Julia looks out into the fading light across the dusty expanse. The sun is dipping on the horizon and the arid, stony landscape has turned an exquisite shade of gold. She has come up here to the rooftop of the Cappadocia First Hotel to be alone. To gather her thoughts. To try and think things through.

They are stuck here overnight since regulations do not permit flying in the dark due to the dangers of navigating through the rock formations. Julia hadn't exactly been thrilled at the prospect, although in some ways she feels closer to Toni knowing that just down the road to the left, Toni had been huddled in Lucinda's kiln.

"I had a feeling I would find you up here."

She looks over her shoulder to see Leo in the doorway. He approaches holding out a plate of food. "Eat something."

Julia turns away. "If I see another cube of feta, I think I'll scream."

"Fair enough," he says, putting the plate to one side.

He stares at the view. "It's incredible, isn't it? I never even knew that places like this existed."

Julia's eyes track the landscape. "Toni was right here and we missed her again."

Leo touches her shoulder. "We know she's alive. That's a good thing."

She sighs deeply. "Please don't tell me not to give up, Leo, that it's only a matter of time, et cetera, et cetera...it's nothing I haven't already said to myself. I'm trying very hard to believe it but I'm not sure I can anymore."

Leo leans forward, resting his forearms on the railings. "I never told you this," he says. "But after we broke up, I went to therapy. I wasn't coping well. I ended up in some truly dark places. I'm not sure you realize how much I hated myself for what I did. Being here with you, going through all this to find Toni, I realize how weak and immature I was back then. I was jealous of your success and I wanted to hurt you. But it wasn't your fault that I fell short. It wasn't your fault I felt so inadequate. No one was responsible for that except me. But I'm not that person anymore. I'm stronger and more capable, and I'm here for you one hundred percent and always will be."

She squeezes his hand. "Maybe we both let ourselves down."

Leo looks at her deeply. "When we get back, when all this is over, I hope we can be friends, Julia, proper friends."

Julia smiles. "I do, too, Leo."

The moment is broken when the door swings back on its hinges and Detective Muhtar rushes in.

"Bambury was at the Göreme Medical Center trying to steal medicine. They tried to catch him but he got away."

Julia's throat tightens. "When?"

"An hour ago."

Julia's heart sinks. "I don't believe it. We're too late again."

Detective Muhtar breaks into a smile. "Not this time. Local police have just seen his van."

75

"I have instructed them to stay well back. We do not want to panic him," explains Detective Muhtar as they race to Göreme township.

"Is he in the van? Is Toni with him?"

"They do not know."

Julia looks out the window, a bundle of nerves. Please God, let this be the end of it.

"This is good, really good," says Leo, animated.

"I hope so, Leo, because I'm not sure how much more of this I can take."

They turn right into the Göreme center. The area is tiny, no more than a main street really, with several smaller roads branching off. Most of the businesses are small eateries or cluttered, dusty souvenir shops.

"So what's the plan?" says Leo.

"We will first put police in place to ensure he has no escape route, then we will talk to him. With no way out, he's likely to surrender."

"But how can you be certain he will?" says Julia, frowning.

Detective Muhtar pauses. "You are correct, Dr. Norris. We cannot be sure. But it is our best option."

Julia falls quiet. Detective Muhtar is right; apart from storming the van, talking Daniel out is probably the best they could do.

"How far away is it?" she says.

Detective Muhtar nods through the windshield. "Up there and round to the right. He's parked behind a Turkish bathhouse."

Detective Muhtar's phones rings. He answers. There's shouting on the other end.

"What is it?" says Julia, alarmed.

Suddenly a siren screams in the distance.

"Oh God."

Detective Muhtar yells into the phone in Turkish. Outside the siren grows louder.

"What's happening!" cries Julia, bobbing her head to look out the window.

Detective Muhtar tosses the phone aside. "They are coming our way. He saw the patrol car and fled."

Leo points out the window. "Look!"

On the opposite side of the road, barreling toward them, is the white van, police car in hot pursuit. The van shoots by and Julia glimpses Daniel at the wheel but no sign of Toni.

Detective Muhtar does a 180-degree turn and follows at speed.

"Seatbelts," he says.

Up ahead, there's a long stretch of empty road and the police car takes advantage of this, pulling out alongside the van in an attempt to get Daniel to pull over. But Daniel's obviously got different ideas and rams the police car instead. The police car swerves wildly but manages to correct itself and makes a second attempt to get Daniel to pull over. But he's not giving in and rams the police car again, this time much harder, and Julia watches in horror as police car skids off the road, collides with a concrete barrier, and somersaults into the air. Detective Muhtar peels away to the left, barely avoiding being crushed as the police car slams to the ground on its roof.

"Oh my God," says Julia, glancing out the back window at the carnage. "We should stop and help."

Detective Muhtar shakes his head. "We cannot risk losing him."

Daniel veers right and goes off road, heading toward the barren hills and canyons that Julia had observed when she flew in.

"Hold on," says Detective Muhtar, burning rubber to catch up to the van.

Julia's stomach lurches and she grabs the door handle to steady herself. Detective Muhtar follows Daniel at speed, fishtailing across the loose shingle. They drive along a ridge then dip into a valley before heading up a rise. Ahead of them, the van looks like it's struggling and Julia wonders how the heck the aging vehicle is managing to keep going in such harsh terrain.

The roadway, which isn't really a roadway at all, gets very narrow. Any idea that Detective Muhtar might have had for overtaking the van and heading it off is impossible now. Up and up they go, the strange stone pillars jutting into the sky around them.

Without warning, Detective Muhtar jams on his brakes, stopping inches from the bumper of the van, which has also come to a halt, millimeters shy from the precipice of a cliff.

Julia holds her breath, staring at the red brake lights in front of them.

"Back up," she says, hoarsely. "Detective, please back up."

She can hear loose rocks falling onto fixed rocks below. Detective Muhtar puts the car in reverse and carefully backs up, giving Daniel the space to turn around and escape if he wants to.

But the van waits there, its exhaust puffing smoke, brake lights constant.

"What's he doing?"

Suddenly the van roars to life and reverses at speed, nearly crashing into their car's hood. Then it screeches forward, tires spinning, and heads right off the cliff.

76

They watch the van fly through the air and then nosedive into the darkness below. There's a sickening boom as the van hits the rocks and Julia sits in the car paralyzed, unable to comprehend the horror of what's she's just witnessed. For some reason, she thinks of Toni's first day of elementary school, Toni's first date with John Leigh, Toni's high school prom when she got drunk and threw up all over herself. Suddenly, Julia snaps out of it, twists open the door handle, tumbles from the car, and races to the edge of the cliff.

"Toni!" screams Julia into the blackness.

She smells gasoline and crushed steel and wants to be sick. Leo calls to her and points to the right. Julia turns and sees the slow blink of an orange indicator light. She looks harder and can just make out the outline of the van, which is little more than a collapsed heap of metal in the bottom of the ravine.

Searching for a way down, she paces the length of the cliff then spies a slope that's barely a slope but better than nothing. Detective Muhtar and Leo yell for her not to go but she ignores them and scrambles downward, slipping and shimmying on her hip, clutching at vegetation and roots and anything she can grab hold of. The further down she goes, the more suffocating the stench of the crash becomes. She tries not to think about what terrible things she might find when she gets there.

She reaches the van and stands there in shock. It would be a miracle if anyone has survived. The van has come to rest on its side, the windshield smashed and half hanging out. The front end is twisted and crushed, like a tin can torn open, while the back half is relatively intact. It's there, at the back end, that the orange indicator flashes, back and forth, like a terrible parody of a journey gone wrong.

Julia tastes gasoline. The tank is leaking all over the rocks. She must hurry—there's no telling when the van might ignite. Julia yanks on the back doors but they refuse to open. She looks around for another way in but there isn't one, so she tries the back doors again, this time kicking them with as much force as she can. Finally, they give in and she clambers inside.

She finds Daniel draped over the broken driver's seat, still alive. Dazed, he blinks at her, blood dripping down his face. She turns away and looks for Toni. But there's so much debris strewn about that she has trouble telling a blanket from a human being.

"Toni, it's Julia! Where are you!"

Then it occurs to her that maybe Toni has been thrown clear of the wreckage. She races outside but can't see anything because it's so dark.

She cups her hands around her mouth and yells, "Toni! Toni!"

Julia waits and listens. Nothing. She yells again but is met with silence.

She smells something. Smoke. Horrified, she looks over her shoulder and sees the van on fire. Oh, dear God, what if she's wrong? What if Toni is in there after all? Without thinking, Julia clambers inside the van and grabs Daniel by the shirt.

"What have you done with my sister, you son of a bitch!"

Daniel struggles to say something but Julia can't hear him.

"Tell me!"

He garbles something again but this time the sound is lost in a sudden whoosh as the flames triple in size. The blistering heat is unbearable. She has to get out before the entire van is engulfed. Julia drags Daniel from the van until they are clear of the wreckage.

Breathing hard, Julia stands looking as the van is swallowed by flames.

She can't even cry.

77

They search all through the night and halfway into the next day. They search the valleys and ravines and canyons and hilltops and caves. They pick through the wreckage and turn over twisted metal and sift through charred debris and smashed-up trees felled when the van careened off the cliff. They look and look and then do it all over again but Toni isn't anywhere to be found.

By mid-afternoon the decision is made to call off the search. Julia has never felt so hopeless, and standing now at the cliff's edge and staring at the pitiful wreckage below, she wonders when this nightmare will ever end. Hours earlier a seriously injured Daniel had been winched to safety and taken to the hospital for emergency surgery. He had suffered multiple injuries including broken ribs, a skull fracture, and, most concerning, a tear in his spleen causing serious internal bleeding. Julia never thought she'd be praying so hard for Toni's captor to live. But they need him alive. He's the only one who can tell them where Toni is.

Leo appears at her shoulder. "We should go. You need that gash on your hand seen to."

She glances at her hand, temporarily bandaged by a medic earlier in the morning. She doesn't know how the laceration occurred but suspects she tore it open when she was dragging Daniel from the van. It's serious, a severed tendon between the thumb and forefinger on her dominant hand. Not great considering her career choice. Even so, it seems trivial given the circumstances.

"Anything from the hospital?"

Leo shakes his head. "He's still in surgery."

"He'd better make it, Leo, because we're all out of other options."

Leo looks out across the valley and exhales. "Yeah, I hear you."

"What about the other avenue of inquiry—where he went after he tried to steal the medication from the clinic?"

Leo glances at Detective Muhtar, who's standing near the car talking on his phone.

"They're still working on it. Göreme is not exactly rife with CCTV cameras. They're relying on witnesses who saw the van after Daniel fled the hospital. On the bright side, they can confirm the time gap between the hospital incident and when the police chase occurred was just under an hour."

"So where did he go in that time?"

"Wherever it was, it can't have been far."

Julia pauses. "What if after fleeing the hospital he hid Toni somewhere nearby? The incident would've shaken him, he needed to buy some time until things cooled off and gather his thoughts about what to do next. But for some reason, he left the hiding place and was spotted by police and the chase happened."

"That's what they're thinking, yeah."

Julia lifts her eyes to the sky, tracks a hawk across the valley. "What if we're too late, Leo? What if he panicked? What if he's not hiding her at all but killed Toni instead?"

"You can't think like that. It'll make you go crazy. A wise person once told me it's better to deal with facts than speculation and I think that's exactly what we should do."

Close to tears, Julia says, "I had so many things I wanted to tell her."

"And you will."

She nods and swallows. "God, I hope so."

78

Daniel opens his eyes. There's a searing pain along his left side. He turns his head and sees the IV drip connected to his arm. Confused, he struggles to put his jumbled thoughts together. Then he remembers. The chase, the crash, the fire. He'd been injured. A fuzzy memory of being wheeled into surgery comes to him, the words laceration to your spleen being uttered. Lord, how had things gotten so bad?

He tries lifting his hand to wipe his mouth but his wrist is shackled to the bed. Then he sees the armed guard in the doorway. Oh, this is not good. This is more than a spanner in the works. This is an absolute disaster.

He thinks of Toni. He must get to her. He'd intended to be away from her for only an hour at the most. But depending on how long he'd been unconscious for, it must be at least two nights since he first took her to the hiding place after almost getting caught stealing the medication. That's when things had unraveled so badly. Once he'd managed to give that hospital worker the slip, he'd been fortunate enough to find somewhere temporary to hole up until nightfall, when he and Toni would have a much better chance of slipping out of Cappadocia unseen. But then he'd made the fatal mistake of deciding to ditch the van to steal another vehicle. In hindsight, it had been a stupid, stupid mistake and resulted in him being recognized by local police, ending in that disastrous chase.

And now Toni has been without food and water and medication for an unacceptable amount of time. Daniel's heart aches at the thought of her being frightened and all alone. Hold on, Toni. I haven't left you. Please hold on, my love.

Daniel takes three deep breaths and tells himself to focus. He can do this. He can think of something. He will get out of this mess. That's when he sees movement outside his door. An old, thick-waisted nurse has come by and is talking to the guard.

Then Daniel gets an idea that might just work but he needs to act fast. He grabs the water jug on the nightstand and smashes it against the corner of the unit, quickly secreting away a chunk of glass beneath his blanket. Daniel waits a beat until the nurse's and guard's heads jerk around, then fakes a fit, contorting and flaying his body, mimicking a beastly full-on grand mal seizure. The pain is almost unbearable because of his wounds but he pushes through it, using the agony to heighten his performance. But the commotion does the trick and the guard and nurse come rushing in. When the nurse gets close enough, Daniel grabs her, hooking his arm around her neck, holding the piece of jagged glass to her throat.

"Don't move," he says.

The nurse gasps in broken English, "Please don't kill me."

He can smell her fear. She's ripe with it. It's the same smell as the mothers in the camps had, the ones with babies about to die.

The guard draws his gun. "Release her."

Daniel tightens his grip and the nurse begins to sputter.

"Put down the gun or she's dead," says Daniel.

The guard hesitates.

"Do you really want to be responsible for this?" says Daniel, pressing the glass to her throat.

The guard stares at him for a beat then places his gun on the floor and slowly backs up.

"Good man," says Daniel. He lifts his wrist and rattles his cuffs. "Unlock these too, please."

The guard removes the key from his side-belt and unlocks the cuffs.

Still holding the nurse, Daniel gets out of bed and retrieves the gun. "Move back."

The guard does as he's told and Daniel releases his grip on the nurse. He instructs them both to move to the left-hand corner of the room, furthest away from the door, and tells the nurse to lie flat on the floor with her hands on her head.

After that, he points the gun at the guard. "Take off your clothes," he says.

Then Daniel puts on the uniform and slips out the door.

79

"What do you mean he's gone?" cries Julia. "I thought he had an armed guard with him."

Detective Muhtar looks grim. "Daniel took a nurse hostage. He forced the guard to give him his gun."

Julia's hand flies to her chest. "Oh God, are they all right?"

Detective Muhtar nods. "Both are unharmed."

Julia lowers herself to the end of the bed. In the minutes prior to being woken by Detective Muhtar, she'd been dreaming of a flood. She can still taste the brackish water now.

"He stole a car," says Detective Muhtar.

"A car? In his condition? That's crazy. He's just had major surgery."

"All is not lost," says Detective Muhtar. "I have been doing some research about where he may have hidden Toni."

He pulls a piece of paper from his pocket and unfolds it. It's a printout of a map.

"I suspect he has taken her here, to the Derinkuyu underground city." He points to a section of hills to the left. "It is a thirty-minute drive from Göreme so it fits with the timeline."

Julia studies the map. "You really think there's a chance Toni could be there?"

Detective Muhtar nods. "I do. Derinkuyu was closed to the public two years ago after a partial collapse of a tunnel nearly killed a tourist. The area is quiet and isolated. The perfect hiding place."

Julia nods. "Yes, yes. This makes sense."

Leo appears in the doorway, hair mussed from a rough sleep. "What makes sense?"

Julia picks up her jacket. "We'll fill you in on the way."

80

The Derinkuyu underground city was discovered in 1963 during the renovation of a local man's house. A wall caved in and the man was astonished to find a tunnel that led to an entire subterranean city made up of thousands of rooms and corridors. Researchers later confirmed that the city had a depth of more than two hundred and fifty feet and eighteen distinct levels, with the capacity to house up to twenty thousand people. Each level contained kitchens, bedrooms, bathrooms, food storage rooms, oil and wine presses, wells, weapons storage areas, churches, schools, tombs, and domestic animal stables. Fifty ventilation shafts brought in air from above, while water was drawn from internal wells. For all intents and purposes, Derinkuyu was a completely functional and self-sufficient city.

"Across the centuries various persecuted groups such as the Christians and Greeks have taken shelter there," says Detective Muhtar. "Only the first eight levels were ever opened to the public. The other parts were never excavated because the government ran out of money."

Detective Muhtar turns off the main road and takes a dirt road to the left. A tiny village comes into view. No more than three shops and half a dozen houses. He continues on until they reach a small rundown prefab building with boarded-up windows. Out front, parked at an angle, the driver's door wide open, is a red car that does not look like it belongs there.

Julia's heart thuds. "That's got to be Daniel."

Detective Muhtar cuts the engine and they get out and inspect the car. There's blood on the seatbelt and more on the driver's seat.

"He's bleeding. He can't have gotten far." Julia lifts her eyes to the entrance. "Is that the only way in?"

Detective Muhtar nods.

"And no electricity, I take it?" ask Julia.

"Correct."

Detective Muhtar opens the trunk and hands Julia and Leo each a high-beam flashlight he'd commandeered from the Cappadocia First Hotel utility room. They head for the entrance and find the rusty steel grate door wide open, padlock broken in the dirt. Next to the opening is a giant, water-stained map fixed behind a badly worn piece of plastic sheeting. They study it. The scale and complexity of the place is overwhelming. Miles and miles of rooms and passageways and levels and stairwells. A labyrinth without end.

"They could be anywhere," says Julia.

"There's only one way to find out," says Leo, pulling open the steel grate door.

The three of them descend the stone steps into the darkness below.

81

At the base of the steps is a long dark passageway and Julia follows the beam of Detective Muhtar's flashlight projecting off the wall several feet ahead of her. It's cool down here, but not as cool as she had expected, and she imagines that with more bodies the temperature would probably rise to a pleasant level in which to live. Sandy grit crunches underfoot as she makes her way through the passageway, but apart from that, the place is serenely quiet, with no sound leaking in from the outside world at all.

She trains her flashlight on the ground, hoping for any sign of Daniel, a trail of blood, a few spots, but there's nothing. She reaches the end of the passageway and finds Detective Muhtar and Leo waiting for her.

"Any sign of them?" she says, letting her flashlight roam the walls and floors.

Detective Muhtar and Leo shake their heads. Julia looks around herself. She's standing in a large round space, enough to hold maybe a hundred people. Her heart sinks when she sees five different tunnels branching off from the area.

"Looks like we have a problem," she says.

"Yeah," says Leo, following her gaze. "There's no way to know which way he went. We're just going to have to try, maybe go in fifty feet and if we find nothing, we turn back around and try another passageway. A process of elimination."

Julia shakes her head. "That'll take too long. We have to split up."

Detective Muhtar looks at her. "That's out of the question, Dr. Norris."

Leo nods. "Detective Muhtar's right, Julia. We need to stick together. It would be too easy to get lost down here on your own."

Julia shakes her head, adamant. "It's the only way we'll be able to cover enough ground. There's no telling what mental state Daniel's in. He could be desperate enough to do something to Toni and himself, and we can't forget he's just had major surgery so there's a risk he could pass out and slip into unconsciousness. Then he and Toni would be trapped down here forever. There's just not enough time to search together. We each need to take a tunnel."

Leo pauses, thinking.

"What if we had some sort of system so we could find our way back?" he says.

"Such as?" says Detective Muhtar. "Cell phones will not operate down here."

Leo's face brightens. "I got it. What if we leave a trail in the sandy dirt? We can use sticks to mark our way, then use them to track our way back here to the entrance? I'll go up to the surface and get some tree branches for us."

Detective Muhtar rolls his lips together and nods. "That might just work."

82

Julia looks at her watch. They had agreed to meet back at the start in no more than thirty minutes. That means she has another ten minutes before she needs to turn around. She shudders despite herself. It's spooky down here all on her own. The air seems thicker than before, mushroomy, and the dark is the kind of dark she's never encountered before—blacker than black and frighteningly close. The only saving grace is her flashlight and the ventilation shafts beaming down shards of light every so often. She tries to keep herself in check and not let her thoughts run away on her—finding Daniel and Toni is the only priority.

It feels like she's gone in miles already. The twists and turns of the passageways are disorientating and the specter of getting lost is a very real possibility. She's careful to stick to Leo's tracking method, diligently marking a line in the dirt with the sharp point of the stick to help retrace her return.

She'd definitely underestimated the complexity of the place, with its myriad passageways leading to clusters of small cave-like rooms. At the other extreme end of things, there are enormous cavernous areas, most probably community gathering places or stables for livestock, although how they managed to fit animals through the narrow passageways is anyone's guess. Other times, the tunnels simply went nowhere. This was frustrating beyond belief, forcing Julia to turn around and go back the same way she came from, wasting precious time.

On and on she goes, checking around corners, sweeping her flashlight against the curves of the walls, looking down wells, getting on her hands and knees to crawl through low-lying passages. But there's no sign of Toni or Daniel anywhere.

She glances at her watch again. She can't put it off any longer; it is time to head back. Reluctantly, she turns to go when something catches her eye. A glistening smear near the tunnel entrance. At first, she thinks it's some sort of water leak from a crack in the stone. But when she takes a closer look, pressing her fingertips to the rock, she sees that it's blood.

Her heart thunders in her chest. She's not sure what to do. Go back and get the others or continue on by herself? She stands looking at the blood, thinking. Detective Muhtar and Leo would surely come looking for her if she didn't return on time, and Toni could be a mere few feet away—that's something Julia just can't ignore.

She decides to go on, stepping through the tunnel entrance, down the sloping incline, steadying her hand on the calloused surface of the wall as she goes. Her flashlight picks up more blood smudges here and there, along the walls and across the ground. She wants to call out for Toni but restrains herself. The situation is too unpredictable, especially given Daniel now has a gun.

Julia hurries forward, sweeping the flashlight backwards and forwards, following the traces of blood through the intricate network of tunnels and rooms. Suddenly the blood markings stop as abruptly as they began. She pivots, scanning this way and that, but there's no more blood as far as Julia can tell. She doubles back, thinking that maybe

Daniel may have branched off into a different tunnel, but there's no sign of him anywhere.

Julia stands there, unsure what to do. Then she glances down at the stick in her hand and her blood runs cold. She's forgotten to keep track of her path in the dirt. She looks over her shoulder at the tunnels, heart humping wildly. Which way had she come from? Left or right? She racks her brain but everything looks the same.

She takes a guess and chooses right, walks a few feet then stops. Nothing looks familiar. She goes back, looks around for any sign of the blood or the trail she had previously made in the dirt. But there's nothing. Oh, this isn't good, she thinks, this isn't good at all. With a shaking hand, she pulls out her cell phone and checks the signal. There isn't one, of course. She's takes a breath. Don't panic, she tells herself, you can do this.

She moves forward, rounding a corner into a room she hasn't seen before. Her flashlight dips, catching something to the left. A figure slumped against the wall. Daniel. He turns and looks into the light. Tears are streaming down his face.

"I can't find her."

Julia's shocked by the state of him and for a moment she can't speak.

"I promise you, I came back for her. We were going to start a new life together. We were going to be happy."

"What do you mean you can't find her?" says Julia, choking on her words.

"I've tried," he gasps. "I don't know where she is."

Julia grabs him by the shirt. "That's not good enough. You have to think. Where is she, Daniel?"

Blood is seeping from his bandage. His skin is gray and clammy.

"Oh God. Let me die. Just let me die." He begins to fade out.

Julia twists the fabric of his shirt until her knuckles are white. "Which way, Daniel? Which way did you take her?"

"Left," he says finally. "I think it was left."

83

Julia bolts from the room, her flashlight bobbing wildly against the pockmarked walls.

"Toni! Toni!"

Inside her head she prays to every God she can think of. Implores her dead mother for help. Strikes a foolhardy bargain with the devil. She searches frantically, checking caves and rooms, tunnels and passageways.

"Toni!"

She yells until her throat hurts. But there's no sign of Toni anywhere. Julia halts, breathing hard. The despair is so heavy, she almost sinks to her knees. It's impossible. There's no way she'll ever find her. Then she hears the voice.

"Julia."

At first, she thinks it's her mind playing tricks. Then she hears it again. The breathy, warm voice. The one she remembers from childhood, especially at nighttime when it wouldn't be quiet even though they were supposed to be sleeping.

"Toni?"

"Julia, is that really you?"

Julia sweeps the flashlight around and sees the opening in the wall, the precious form of her sister huddled on the ground.

"Oh my God, Toni," says Julia, darting forward.

Toni blinks sluggishly into the light. "You came. I knew you would."

Julia embraces her. She's just skin and bones. "Oh, Toni. It's so good to see you."

Leaning back, Julia brushes Toni's hair from her forehead and examines the head injury. The front right-hand side of the cranium is distended and purple, likely due to intracranial pressure, swelling on the brain. Julia feels a flash of anger. Toni should have been admitted to the hospital days ago.

"You hurt your head, huh?"

Toni nods, woozy. "I fell down the stairs."

"Look at me, Toni."

Toni blinks at her.

"We're going to go now."

Toni smiles. "Okay."

Julia threads Toni's arm around her neck and hoists her to her feet. "Hang on."

"Julia?"

"Yes?"

"I'm sorry."

Julia chokes back tears. "Me too, Toni."

Julia turns to face the darkness and wonders how on earth she's ever going to find her way out.

"Come on, Mom. We really need your help."

Then she hears Leo calling her name.

Epilogue

Julia hitches up her surgical mask and slices through the diseased aortic valve attached to Mr. García's fifty-five-year-old inert, unbeating heart. A few feet away, the machine keeping Mr. Garcia alive hums at a rhythmic pace as it pumps blood around his body. Two and a half hours earlier, Mr. Garcia's heart had been purposely stopped in order to connect him to the cardiopulmonary bypass machine, aka the heart-lung machine. Something necessary to carrying out the surgery. Monitoring this sophisticated piece of machinery is Billy Mathers, a technician known as a perfusionist who, with his flop of blond hair and tribal tattoos, looks more like a nightclub DJ than a medical professional.

Julia's eyes flick to the observation gallery above, where a small cluster of eight medical students watch her perform the surgery. To be more precise, six students are watching. The other two, both female, have their eyes trained on Billy Mathers, no doubt enamored by his good looks and cool hipster vibe.

Julia's pleased to see the med students each hold the briefing notes she had prepared earlier. Not all surgeons bother to do this. But she knows the notes will prove invaluable for their exams later on.

Today the students are doubly lucky because they have the benefit of Dr. Phillip Kincaid, teaching fellow at the UCSF School of Medicine, to talk them through the procedure. Not only is Dr. Kincaid one of the United

States' most respected cardiothoracic surgeons, he is also a very nice man with a gift for colorful commentary. With his snow-white Sigmund Freud goatee, satin waistcoats, and impressive collection of hand-carved pipes (which he never, in fact, smoked), he was a flamboyant figure. Julia can only imagine the graphic and eye-watering explanation he is imparting to the students as she carries out the operation.

Not that any additional gore is necessary. The surgery itself is brutal enough, beginning with a procedure called a sternotomy, in which Julia cut a ten-inch vertical incision along Mr. Garcia's chest, allowing access to the sternum, which she opened up with a reciprocating bone-cutter known as a sternal saw. Then of course there's the organ itself, the heart. Seeing it inside the patient's chest cavity is always a surreal experience. The heart is so central to everything. The Rosetta stone of the human body. The key symbol of humanity. Julia never tires of seeing it, and feels privileged to be entrusted with something so precious.

Julia turns her attention back to Mr. Garcia and begins suturing the new titanium valve into place. Hopefully, this will prevent any more cardiac arrests like the one Mr. Garcia experienced last Wednesday night, when he dropped to the floor in the middle of restaurant service of his family-owned pizzeria, and died for just over five minutes until paramedics managed to revive him with defibrators. A replacement valve combined with Mr. Garcia's relatively young age of fifty-five means the prognosis is good. With a loving wife, five daughters, eleven grandchildren, and two great grandchildren on the way, Mr. Garcia has a lot to look forward to, and if Julia has anything to do with it, he'll live to a grand old age to experience it all.

Julia finishes up and begins the delicate procedure of removing Mr. Garcia from the heart-lung machine. At precisely 2:05 p.m., Mr. Garcia's heart starts beating on its own. Julia shares a high five with Billy Mathers and then goes to inform Mrs. Garcia and her five daughters about the good news.

*

Forty-five minutes later, Julia emerges from the hospital and heads for the coffee cart over in Hansen Square, a pretty park with ginkgo trees and a man-made lake not too far from the hospital. When she gets there, she sees Toni in the distance chatting with a woman with a little shih tzu–Maltese cross. Typical Toni. Engaging a stranger in conversation.

Toni throws back her head and lets out a laugh. Julia smiles. It is good to see her sister happy after everything she's been through. It was actually astonishing that Toni had made such a fantastic recovery these past four months, especially given how close she came to losing her life. After the rescue, Toni had undergone a decompressive craniectomy, a procedure where a portion of her skull was removed to relieve pressure on the brain. Thankfully, Toni responded well and within ten days the swelling had ceased. Now, in less than two weeks, Toni was due to undergo a second surgery to reinstate the bone flap.

Toni spots Julia and waves. She gives the dog one final pat and heads Julia's way.

"Hey, sis," she says, brightly.

"How have you been?" says Julia. "Any headaches?"

Toni gives her a look. "Stop it. Sister. Surgeon. Two separate things, remember?"

Julia holds up her hands. "Sorry. Force of habit."

Toni smiles. "I'm doing swell."

"Very funny."

"I aim to please." Toni chins-nods toward the coffee cart. "Shall we? I'm dying here."

They get their coffee to go, short black for Julia, tall latte with a shot of caramel and vanilla for Toni.

It's a glorious, crisp autumn day so they decide to stroll through the park, taking the pathway bordering the lake.

Julia blows on her coffee as she walks. "Nervous about the surgery?"

Toni shakes her head. "It'll be a piece of cake."

"You're still going to stay with me the week after for your recovery, right?"

"If you're sure."

"Of course I'm sure."

Toni smiles. "Then I'd love to, sis. Thank you."

They reach a wooden park bench overlooking the lake and take a seat.

"It's nice here," says Toni, gazing out at the water. "Did I ever tell you about the first time I saw the Mekong? I was traveling from North Thailand to Laos so I decided to take the river border crossing instead of going overland. I always knew the Mekong was brown from photos, but in real life, it's really brown, and I mean really, really brown, like chocolate milk brown. And it has this pearly tone to it. It's strangely beautiful. By the way, that's when I knew the movie *Apocalypse Now* was a total joke because the river in that movie was not brown at all. I did some Googling and found out the entire movie was shot in the Philippines.

Did you know Laurence Fishburne was in it? He was just a kid, only twelve years old, I think. Now there's a useless piece of information for you. And apparently Marlon Brando was so fat that Francis Ford Coppola only ever wanted to film him at night, and even then, he only did close-ups of Brando's face." Toni laughs out loud. "That's pretty rough, isn't it? No wonder the guy had self-esteem issues. So the night before I'm due to go into Laos, I get to this hostel. At first, I think it isn't so bad, it looks right over Mekong, you can see locals fishing with nets, it has a cabana with a string of colored lights." Toni shrugs. "You get the picture. Then they show me to my room. It's a shared room with one other person. An old lady from Australia. She was actually pretty decent. She did Tai Chi every morning and was traveling around the world on her own after her husband passed away. Anyway, that's when I notice the smell. The room stinks of chemicals—I'm talking instant headache territory here, sis. They said it was for hygiene reasons but wouldn't elaborate. Needless to say, I wasn't crazy about it and asked if they could put me somewhere else, but they tell me nothing else is available—so I've got no choice, I've got to sleep in this place with this terrible smell and hope to God I don't die of chemical poisoning. Somehow I manage to fall asleep, but in the middle of the night, I wake up in shock when I feel something run over my chest. I leap out of bed, and the old lady's like, what's the matter with you? 'There's cockroaches running over me,' I tell her. 'It's just the malaria tablets,' she says. 'They make you hallucinate.'" Toni looks at Julia. "I'm telling you, sis, I wasn't imagining anything. I could feel those suckers running right over me. But the old woman didn't buy it and just went back to sleep, and somehow I manage to do the same. So get this—when I wake up in the morning and look out the bathroom window, I see the room is right next to an open sewer! There were goddamn roaches everywhere." She laughs. "That's what the chemical smell was about. They had doused the room with some God-knows-what-most-probably-banned-in-the-1980s pesticide to try and control the infestation."

Julia makes a face. "That's disgusting."

Toni chuckles. "Yeah, totally."

"I suppose you're already planning your next trip after your surgery."

Toni falls quiet. "I think I'm done with traveling for a while."

Julia looks at her. "Don't let what happened with Daniel stop you from living your life."

"I won't," says Toni. "I just think it's best that I stay put for now, process things properly, quit running away."

Julia nods. "Sounds grown-up."

"Yeah. I thought I'd give being an adult a whirl."

Julia exhales. "Well, at least you won't have to worry about Daniel anymore—twenty years is a good sentence. Let's hope he gets the help he needs."

Toni studies her hands. "I know what he did was bad, Julia, but I feel sorry for him. He just wanted someone to love him."

Julia's shocked. She's about to berate Toni for being a hopeless bleeding heart but stops herself.

Toni pauses. "I think I actually forgive him. Do you think that's stupid of me?"

Julia touches her arm. "I think that's one of the most compassionate things I've ever heard."

They lapse into silence and watch the geese glide through the pond weed.

Eventually, Toni says, "So. You and Leo."

"What about me and Leo?"

"Are you guys…?"

Julia feels herself color. "We're taking things slow."

"A wait and see approach?" says Toni, a twinkle in her eye.

"Something like that."

Toni nods. "Good. You two belong together."

Julia looks at her watch. She has to get back to work.

"I've got to go. I have consults this afternoon." Standing, she turns to Toni. "Would you like to come for dinner on Saturday? Leo can do his famous ribs."

Toni smiles. "It's a date."

Julia turns to go. "Walk me back?"

They take the pathway, the autumn sun on their shoulders, the breeze washing their faces as they go. They talk about nothing in particular.

THE END

More books you'll love from Deborah Rogers…

The Amelia Kellaway Series

Left for Dead

Coming for You

Speak for Me

Standalone novels

The Devil's Wire

Into Thin Air

About the Author

Deborah Rogers is a psychological thriller and suspense author. Her gripping debut psychological thriller, The Devil's Wire, received rave reviews as a 'dark and twisted page turner'. In addition to standalone novels like The Devil's Wire and Into Thin Air, Deborah writes the popular Amelia Kellaway series, a gritty suspense series based on New York Prosecutor, Amelia Kellaway.

Deborah has a Graduate Diploma in scriptwriting and graduated cum laude from the Hagley Writers' Institute. When she's not writing psychological thrillers and suspense books, she likes to take her chocolate lab, Rocky, for walks on the beach and make decadent desserts.

www.deborahrogersauthor.com

CPSIA information can be obtained
at www.ICGtesting.com
Printed in the USA
LVHW041502181020
669091LV00002B/213

9 780473 521462